Totally Bound Publishing books by Jaqueline Snowe

Out of the Park
Evening the Score
Sliding Home
Rounding the Bases

Classic Curves
Whiskey Surprises

Cleat Chasers
Challenge Accepted
The Game Changer
Best Player

I0524369

Cleat Chasers

BEST PLAYER

JAQUELINE SNOWE

Best Player
ISBN # 978-1-83943-756-4
©Copyright Jaqueline Snowe 2021
Cover Art by Erin Dameron-Hill ©Copyright November 2021
Interior text design by Claire Siemaszkiewicz
Totally Bound Publishing

BEST PLAYER

Dedication

To the hubs and that time you helped with my film class. Thanks for kinda, sorta helping me with all my homework. I'm still scarred from some of those movies.

To the one semester my brother and I went to the same college. It was awesome, awkward and we have some good memories. I could not imagine growing up without you and I'm glad I never have to.

To Tricia and Shiv — finding my tribe with you in Barcelona made all the difference in the world. I'll always cherish our friendship.

To my LLAK group — we have eleven years of memories that started at the VGD. Girls' trips, weddings, moves across the country and group chats, I'll always be thankful for you three.

As always, to Rebecca. Thank you for making me laugh while also making me grow as a writer. (Talking about my time in eyebrow jail.) Working with you is one of my favorite things to do.

Chapter One

Kenzie

Leaving the home I'd grown up in — the house packed with every memory I had — hurt more than I'd anticipated. My throat burned each time I held back emotion, but it wouldn't do any of us good to mention the overwhelming worry and sadness. We couldn't afford wasted sentiments when every second of every day we worried about our dad — fighting cancer wasn't a single person's battle. It took all our efforts.

"I can't believe our baby girl is going away to college," my dad said from the front seat of the old navy mini-van that smelled like used sports gear. He craned his neck and gave me a weak smile. I returned the gesture, hoping I hid the bubbling anxiety growing in my chest, and raised my fists in the air.

"Yay!"

He coughed, the sound better than it used to be, but I still tensed every time I heard it. Each breath he took was a struggle. "While I'm not thrilled you're going to be living with Aaron and two of his teammates for the summer, they seem to be decent young men. They're better now than they were his freshman year. Good lord, they were hellions. But he promised he'd take care of you for us."

"Dad," I mumbled. "Come on."

"I mean it. Your mom and I are going to be hours away trying out different treatment facilities. Someone needs to look out for you, K-Bug."

I will not cry. Nope. I will not. "I'll be fine. Really. I've been looking forward to college for years."

"But not everyone goes two months early…" My mom let the words hang and our eyes met in the rearview mirror. Hers were tired and gray. My heart hurt for her and how strong she'd been for all of us. She'd been our family rock forever and while the thought of being away from them was freeing, it also left a hole.

"It's better like this, I promise. It'll be a good way for me to get acclimated to the campus and I signed up for two classes already. Introduction to Film and Online Biology. Both sound awful, but it'll help me get ready for my hard schedule this fall."

"K-Bug, you've never had to worry about grades. You're our smart girl," my dad said, not hiding his pride. Another wave of gratitude went through me. Despite Aaron's insane athletic abilities, my parents had never once made me feel less important or talented. Not once. The world needed more of them and the gratitude switched to anger at the injustice of my dad getting sick.

It wasn't fair.

But showing my internal battle would do none of us any good on the already emotional day. I swallowed down the grief and worry, plastered a smile on my face and spoke with a practiced enthusiasm that I'd mastered with all the hospital visits. "I'm just excited for the newness. New friends, new experiences, new things to learn and new mistakes to make. I've always heard about how college is this life-changing experience of fun, embarrassing stories and the place where you meet lifelong friends. I want that. I'm ready for it."

"Then that's what you're going to do." My dad's voice held a finality to it and we all remained quiet for the rest of the drive. The campus was about two hours away from our childhood home—the house my parents had sold—and the moment we left the driveway that morning was the last time I'd set foot there. It was an odd combination to experience—utter excitement about what was next, and longing for what used to be. My constant battle was defining myself. I had always been Aaron's younger sister. The daughter. The girlfriend.

I wanted to be me.

College was my answer.

"Honey, we're going to stop and get some shakes. Would you like anything?" my mom inquired as she pulled into a fast-food place. My dad had a softness for milkshakes and we'd made an unspoken agreement that when he wanted one, he got one.

"Yeah, I'll get a coffee. Want me to run in and buy one?"

"That'd be great, K-Bug."

They handed me a twenty-dollar bill and I grabbed my phone before heading inside the diner. The humid air was hard to swallow, but it was a brief escape from the confines of the car. My dad got cold real fast, so we couldn't have the air on too high. I fanned myself, moving the end of my old jersey-shirt to get air on my midriff. Sweat dripped down my muscles and a cold milkshake sounded perfect. I ordered—my mom preferred chocolate, my dad mint-cookie and I always got banana.

My phone went off and I almost ignored it, since my ex-boyfriend had thought it a great time to reconcile after our disastrous prom weekend. *No thanks, Sean. That ship sailed.* But it wasn't him. It was Aaron, my ridiculous, awesome and obnoxious older brother.

Aaron: Yo, you almost here?

Kenzie: Stopped for milkshakes. Maybe fifteen minutes out.

Aaron: Coach just called and wants to meet me at the field — Tanner is here though. He'll help you unpack. That cool?

Kenzie: That's fine. Mom and Dad will be pissed if they don't see you though.

Aaron: I'll try and be back in an hour. Coach knows they're here but said this is important.

Kenzie: Okay, see you soon.

Aaron: No backing out now, kid. You absolutely sure about living here?

Kenzie: There's no home to go back to. Yeah, I'm sure.

I didn't expect a response from him, and the few minutes I had to wait for the shakes were spent thinking about my future roommates. Sure, it was only two months, but these guys had the personalities of celebrities.

Aaron — my brother who'd slept with countless ladies the past two years and suffered a sex scandal. Zade Willows — the all-star pitcher who had a fan club named after him. Tanner Johnson — the giant center fielder who could make girls faint with a wink. Yeah. It was going to be an adventure living with them until their fourth roommate, Jeff, got back from playing baseball overseas.

Me, the awkward kid without an ounce of athletic ability, was living in the baseball house in the center of Jockville. Life was funny sometimes.

"Order's up!"

I thanked the hostess and carried the drinks back to the car. Too soon, we were pulling into the chipped driveway of my new temporary digs. White house, large porch that had seen better days, overgrown trees in the front and backyard and the door wide open. I pulled my long dark-blonde hair into a high messy bun and took one final breath.

College.

Adventure.

New.

"What's up, Hill family?" Tanner's voice boomed from him. He leaned against the front railing, his height almost putting his head on the roof of the house. His hair was midnight black and it spilled from his head in messy curls, but his light brown eyes were killer. Yeah, I had a little bitty crush on him after having met him a couple times over the past three years, but it was hard not to. He was my kryptonite—long eyelashes, mischievous grin, the perfect dimples and real tall with broad shoulders. I gave him a little wave, hoping I didn't blush too much.

I was going to be living with him, so it didn't bode well for anyone to know about my crush. "Hey, TJ."

"Roomie, let me grab your stuff. Aaron had to head to the field, but he'll be back. Good to see you, Mr. and Mrs. Hill." He swaggered—it was the only way to describe it—to the car and gave both my parents a hug. It pleased me to see how good he was to my family. The warmth on the back of my neck had nothing to do with his fitted shirt and workout shorts that showcased how much time he spent in the gym.

"You're too kind, Tanner. Really," my mom gushed and I had to roll my eyes. Even she succumbed to his charm. She had to know how much he got around... I mean, he was one of two single guys who lived in the baseball house. I snorted into my fist and Tanner slid me a look.

"Laying it on thick there, TJ."

"What? I can't hug my second-favorite set of parents?" He dared to raise one beautiful dark eyebrow, challenging me to call him out. I did.

"They brought you all beer and homemade casserole for at least a week. You don't need to suck up."

His grin widened and, after patting my dad on the back, he walked to the trunk of the car to help get my five bags. It was sad that, moving into college, I only had five bags' worth of stuff. That was one lesson learned after seeing my dad go through his struggle—material things didn't matter all that much. Life was more about the experience.

He walked past me, smirking, and picked up two of the bags. "Come on, Kenny. Let me show you to your room."

He didn't lower his voice or do anything weird, but those words coming from his mouth sent a shiver down my body. I cleared my throat and picked up the final load. "After you, Johnson."

My parents took their time bringing food into the small kitchen while I followed Tanner into the house and up the stairs. I had been there before, but only for a small amount of time where they could hide their craziness. Now, they'd let it all hang out. The mess, the dirty bathroom, the pile of useless things stacked in the corner.

Why did they have a stack of empty boxes? And empty cups? They had a kitchen…why didn't they use it?

He led me down the upstairs hallway. There were two rooms on each side, two with their own bathrooms, but I wasn't that lucky. While Zade and Aaron across the hall had one each, Jeff and Tanner shared theirs. And Jeff's was the room I was using…meaning I had to share a bathroom with Tanner Johnson.

Two months was going to be a long time.

"Okay, Kenny. Here's Jeff's room." He opened the door and gave me a bemused look. "He's the neatest out of all of us. I saw you scowl on the way up. We're not total pigs."

"I'll just have to do some cleaning, that's all." *Thank God I brought supplies.*

He chuckled and dropped my large duffel bags on the beige carpet. I took a hesitant step inside the room and sniffed. Nothing smelled off and there weren't any weird stains on the carpet.

"Did you just *smell* the room?"

"Yes, I did." I jutted my chin out at him. "I've lived with Aaron. I know how smelly boys can be. It seems fine so far."

"God, this is going to be fun."

"I'm bursting with excitement," I deadpanned.

It earned me another grin, showcasing his impressive dimples, and I scanned the rest of the room. The walls had various baseball posters of the team and MLB teams. The sheets had been stripped from the queen-sized bed and the dresser drawers opened and emptied. I placed my bag on the desk and spun around. Tanner watched me with a curious expression and I did not look at his mouth when his lips quirked up on one side.

"We need to talk about some ground rules."

Shit. Butterflies formed in my gut and I felt foolish. I wasn't sure what I'd thought he was going to say, but it wasn't that. Crossing my arms, I scrunched my nose and asked, "About what?"

"Living here." He stepped farther into the room and with that small action, the walls seemed to close around us. He took up so much space and his warmth crowded me. "I know you're pretty chill from everything Hilly's told us, but I want to get it all out in the open, you know?"

I bit my lip to prevent myself from smiling. Was he going to give me the *talk*? *Holy shit.* I hoped he was because I wasn't going to make it easy for him. "Okay. I'm listening. Should I write this down?" I moved toward my backpack, but he shook his head.

"We share a wall and a bathroom. The foundation here isn't great and I don't plan on being a saint just because you're here." He winced and moved his hand to his neck, stress lines forming around his eyes. "I mean, I'll be more discreet about it. I won't...you don't have to see anything."

"Tanner, what are you talking about?" I asked, successfully keeping my face blank. He had to know what my life had been like with Aaron. Hell, everyone knew the baseball house was notorious for hooking up. I wasn't dumb or naïve. But watching him struggle through this was worth it. "What do you mean by *saint*?"

"Christ," he said, then rubbed his hand over his face. Gone was the playful expression — uneasiness replaced it. "I don't want you uncomfortable, but you might run into girls who...spend the night."

"Ohhh, you have a *girlfriend*?" I whistled, getting another worried look. "Do I get to meet her?"

"Kenzie." His cheeks turned just a little bit red and I pressed my lips together to prevent breaking character.

"You might hear...stuff. I don't want you to... *Shit*. I don't know how to do this. I didn't think it through."

"Okay, enough. I'll stop." I laughed and enjoyed the myriad expressions crossing his face. They ended in curiosity and I closed the distance between us so we stood a foot apart. "I know you'll have hook-ups. That's fine. All I ask is that she doesn't hog the bathroom the morning after and that you don't fuck *too* loud."

He blinked. It was slow and telling, and I bit my lip, but it did no good. I burst out laughing at how uncomfortable he was and I hit his shoulder without real force. "I was messing with you before, but I appreciate you trying to warn me."

"I thought—Aaron said... Never mind. I didn't want to shock or upset you."

His comment warmed me, but his use of my brother's name did not. "Whatever warning Aaron gave you, forget it, okay? I'm not this naïve, innocent kid."

"Okay."

"Your tone doesn't agree with your word." I pursed my lips and gave him my best leveling stare. "Mean it."

He gave me his signature crooked grin, narrowed those baby browns just a smidge and lowered his voice like a soccer coach. "*Okay.*"

We stood, not in a face-off or battle, but in a weird bubble of not really knowing the other person. He was the playboy with a bright future. I was the *innocent* younger sister of his best friend. Two months living with him, good or bad, would be an adventure, and my excitement for something new overshadowed the awkwardness. I held out my hand, grinning, and broke the tension that had formed in the last two minutes. "Thanks for letting me live here, roomie. I think we're going to have a hell of a time."

He placed his large hand against mine and shook, a slow smile forming on his too-handsome face. "I already regret agreeing to this."

Chapter Two

Tanner

I swear to god, if one more freshman whispers when I walk by, I'm gunna sock them in the face. A trio of them stopped stretching the second I stepped onto the baseball practice field, their panicked faces giving them away. I didn't need to ask what they were talking about. Everyone knew. It was difficult not to when my life — all our lives — were plastered on social media. There were no secrets about MLB-bound athletes, and that entailed the good and the bad.

The latest and greatest obsession trending around our campus — I'd declined an offer after being picked in the tenth round in the MLB draft. Yeah, fucking crazy. But I had my reasons and while I felt it was no one's business but my own, the world craved answers I wouldn't give. Coach understood and encouraged me to make my decision for me and my family, and that was what I'd done. If I was okay with it, then why couldn't anyone else be?

Life of the rich and famous, my ass.

"Yo, TJ. Let's go to the cages," Carter Bolt hollered at me. Yeah, he had a hell of a name for a ball player. The sophomore stood a couple inches shorter than me and had a killer arm for right field. It was his hitting that needed work and our hitting coach thought it would be good for us to pair up. Call it a stroke of ego, but I'd hit pretty damn good the year before—over three hundred—but it wasn't enough to satisfy my goals. *Tenth round isn't enough. The signing bonus isn't enough. Not for what my family needs.*

I shook off the tension as best I could, but it lingered. It remained in my shoulders and neck, straining when I threw. It always persisted until my mom called me with an update that she was okay. She'd called the night before, letting me know my younger brothers were doing fine and that she'd call again in three days. It was easy to busy myself with baseball, parties and women until the worry stopped, but it was getting old and the answer to all my problems was so close. I needed to play better, get picked sooner in the draft and get a better signing bonus. *That's all. No big deal.*

Carter gave me a look when I didn't respond, and I jogged toward him. He adjusted his cap, sending his shaggy red hair all over the place, and picked up a bucket of balls. "Party too much last night, eh?"

"Nah, just thinking about how to fuck with the new guys." I jutted my head toward the gossiping group stretching, their wide eyes still focused on me. "Know anything about them?"

"Peter is from an upscale prep school, but I don't know about the other two. Let 'em gossip. They won't get much playing time, so they need something to occupy themselves with," he replied, letting out a loud whistle at his own quip. It took a lot of effort not to roll my eyes.

"Nice one."

"I try. Oh, hey! Hilly!" Carter shouted and we both looked at my roommate and friend. I waved at him, but he flipped us off before sprinting onto the field for some defensive practice. When balls got through the infield, it meant I had more action, but lately, too many had been getting hit right up the middle where neither Aaron nor Blake, our second basemen, could stop them. Coach didn't like that and they were working on angles to prevent hits from getting through.

Aaron Hill had a new wave of determination this year — a lot of it because of his dad's condition, fighting cancer. But another part I would have put money on was his girlfriend, our once best friend, Greta. Like Zade and his girl, Callie, the guys seemed to play with more ferocity when they had a consistent woman in their lives.

I didn't get it. I really fucking didn't, and while the thought of having *something* with Greta had come and gone, the concept of committing to one person was just not sitting right with me. It often led to disappointment and my plate was full. I didn't have time for disappointment. Hell, my mom had had a revolving door of men who'd left her — and us — and no good had come from it. *Shit. Get outta your head, idiot.*

"I swear he gets bigger every time I see him," Carter said as he continued to watch Aaron with a star-struck expression. I smacked the back of his head, getting a loud cussword as an answer. "What the hell was that for?"

"Stop fangirling over him and worry about your own game."

"I'm not fangirling," he pouted, but we both knew he was. Hilly had a weird celebrity personality about him and with all the drama of his life the year before, people knew his entire story. I was just glad he was back on track and had stopped his self-destructive behavior. No one likes to see their friend in a downward spiral and he'd slowly brought himself up from the hole. Pride filled my chest when I studied him for a couple of seconds. He'd grown into the leader our team needed.

"Come on, Bolt. Let's get some swings in and maybe we'll invite you to the next party at the house. We're due for a beer pong tournament soon."

"Really?" he replied, his voice holding way too much hope.

"I said *maybe*. You gotta hit well, though."

* * * *

The last thing I wanted to do was start a bullshit summer class that fulfilled my Humanities and the Arts requirement, but that was what I had to do to get my degree. My mom's *'you're an injury away from being where I'm at. Get the degree, have a back-up plan, escape the life we had'* echoed in my head.

Being responsible sucked sometimes.

I walked into the house and went straight to the fridge to see if there was any chicken casserole left from the Hills, but backtracked when I found Kenzie sitting cross-legged on the couch with large black-rimmed glasses on her face. She had her hair piled on top of her head and wore a bright purple tank top paired with cut-off denim shorts. I couldn't stop my smile. "Hey, nerd."

She glanced up, pursing her pink lips, and made a face at me. "You."

"Why the attitude?"

"*Someone* ate the rest of the breakfast casserole my parents left for me and Aaron. That breakfast has been the reason I've gotten up all week. Literally, the only reason." She put her laptop down on the cushion next to her and pointed her little finger at me. "You are that someone."

"Yeah, I got the insinuation." Shrugging, I gave her a sheepish grin. "Sorry. Definitely thought they were a free commodity for all."

"They were, but that one was my favorite, though."

"Will you attack me if I warm up the chicken one? I'm famished from practice." I patted my belly and gave her my best puppy-dog look. She didn't take the bait.

"Just warm up a plate for me. I didn't realize it was dinner."

Fair enough. I continued on my path for food and got some for her. She'd surprised me since she moved in six days ago. She wasn't loud, messy, annoying or in the way. If anything, it was nice having someone else in the house as much as I was. Zade was with Callie when we didn't have games, and Aaron and Greta were attached at the hip. Jeff had been the last wingman in the house before he'd traveled abroad for the summer, leaving the position open. Kenzie smelled better than Jeff, didn't laugh like an idiot and didn't ask me questions I didn't want to answer. Yeah, I liked having her there.

"Here you go, Kenny." I set the plate next to her and laughed when her glasses fell down her nose. She had a tiny freckled nose that arched up just a bit at the end, so the glasses just slid right off. "You look like a dork."

"Perfect. That was what I was going for. Nailed it!" She made a fist in the air and cheered, the entire thing amusing me. Then she asked the question I dreaded. It was simple and meant no harm, but my reaction was immediate. "How was practice?"

I tensed because the next questions were usually about the draft, and people didn't understand my decision. *'Why would you say no? How could you say no? Do you really think you'll get a better offer next year? What if you get hurt and lose it all?'*

I replied with the most conversation ending word I could think of. "Fine."

She pushed the glasses up with her pointer finger and gave me a long look before nodding to herself. "Noted. Doesn't like to talk about practice. I'll file that away with 'likes to leave towels on the bathroom floor and plays weird music in the morning'."

It was her expression that broke the hold on my secrets. She didn't look at me with accusing eyes or pity. She looked at me like she genuinely cared about how I practiced. It was...nice. Not unlike when Zade, Aaron or Jeff asked me. "It's not—I just... Practice was great. I hit in the cages pretty damn good."

"Yeah? Thinking of beating your average from last year? Honestly, I think it'd be better to move you to hit second rather than fifth in the order. I know you got muscles and can hit homers, but getting you more at-bats would do well for your average *and* get you more opportunities."

What. The. Fuck. "Uh, I have so many questions now."

"Why?" She snorted and took a mouthful of the casserole. The action reminded me of the food in my lap—I never forgot about food—and I used the extra time to take a large bite. How did I respond to the fact she watched games and knew about my stats?

"You know a lot about, uh, baseball?"

"Don't insult me, TJ. I know where you sleep and I will cut you." She pointed her fork at me. "I swear it."

I fought a grin. "Okay." I changed my voice, mocking the tone she'd used earlier on me. "Noted, makes threats with silverware."

"Ha. Ha." She made a face and adjusted her position so she faced me on the couch. "I grew up going to baseball tournaments, going to Cubs games and entertaining myself when my parents hit Aaron grounders. Of course, I know a lot about baseball. Trust me, I wish I didn't."

"Did you ever play?"

"Nope. I know I'm super fit and all, but it seems Aaron stole every fucking athletic gene when he was born. My talents lie in sarcasm, the ability to drink an insane amount of Dr. Pepper, making to-do lists and knowing the lyrics to every country song made since two-thousand and four."

I chocked on my water, coughing and laughing into my fist. "Incredible."

"I know. Get in line with the rest of my fans."

God, she was refreshing. We shared a smile longer than I would've felt comfortable staring at my friend's sister, but she was like a breath of fresh air. I must've been quiet too long, because she took another bite, and soon enough, we were both chowing down on the rest of our food without saying a word. It was a comfortable silence and when I finished, she reached for my plate. "I'll clean up. Thanks for warming it up for me."

"Sure."

She got up, giving me a perfect opportunity to stare at her long legs. She had great legs, tan and smooth, toned and the perfect length to—no. As soon as the thought entered my mind, I shut it away. *She's Aaron's sister.*

Hell no. Like, never. He would actually kill me in my sleep. I ran my palms over my eyes and found her sitting back on the couch, next to me. I had to think of something, anything else. "What are you working on...on a Saturday afternoon?"

"Oh, this." She made an unhappy face at the direction of her laptop. "I signed up for two summer classes to get a head start on my undecided degree. They start Monday. Terrible idea."

"Yeah? I gotta class that sucks, too."

"Good. We can commiserate together. You don't by chance have an Online Biology textbook, do you? Or Intro to Film?"

Something like excitement formed in my gut. "Are you really taking Film 101?"

"Yes." She tilted her head just a bit to the side. "Why do you have crazy eyes?"

"I have to take that class too!" I shouted, causing her to back up a few inches. "Fuck. I was pissed thinking about doing all that work, but if you're doing it too—"

"If you think I'm going to do work for you just because you're some hot baseball dude, think again, Tanner Johnson. I don't work that way," she fired back with a little red tinging her cheeks.

"What? No. I meant—shit. I mean we can do the class *together*. I'm not a total asshole, but let's revisit that comment about me being hot."

"Let's not." She stared me down but, instead of looking tough, her glasses made her look cuter. I waited—more like refused to blink—until she cracked a smile. It worked.

"Have you always worn glasses?"

"Only when my contacts drive me crazy," she said and readjusted the frames. "Were you serious about doing the class together? It's, like, two movies a week. Do you have time?"

"Yeah, here and there. What's the first movie?"

"*Citizen Kane.*"

"That's a long one, too. Damn." I frowned, already thinking about practice and tournaments, and if I had to sacrifice a night out for this shit. "What's your night looking like?"

"I need to go rent or buy a book for my biology class, but after that, nothing. I don't know anyone besides you all in the house and Zade and Aaron's girlfriends. Who am I going to hang out with?"

She didn't say it for sympathy, or even have a look of sadness on her face. It was the truth. The simple truth. And a part of me wanted to be a friend for her, and not out of pity, but out of interest. "You're living with us all summer, Ken, you'll hang out with us."

"Going to ragers, doing keg stands and tits for days. God, sounds like my dream."

"You're a bit of a smartass."

"I'm not wrong, though, am I?" She made a face with a way-too-proud expression on it and I fought a laugh. "Your lack of response is my victory."

"First off, we do more than go to ragers. I'm past the point of doing keg stands. They're kinda gross if you think about it." I made a face and continued. "We have Taco Tuesdays and Brewsy Breakfasts. We support other sport teams and yeah, I'll admit, I see a lot of tits."

"Hm, while I could do without the tits, the rest of what you said didn't sound half-bad." She tapped her pointer finger against her lip for a second before shrugging. "Okay, yeah. It'd be good to go out sometime. I haven't left the house yet since getting here and it's suffocating."

I cringed. The thought of being stuck in a house without fresh air made my skin crawl. "Do you have plans tomorrow?"

"Again, no. Although, I do need textbooks." She frowned.

"I'll give you a tour of campus and see if we can find some used textbooks at the library. I'm meeting up with some of the guys tonight, but prepare yourself. I think we're having our annual summer-kick off next weekend. It'll be your first college party."

Chapter Three

Kenzie

Lists calmed me. They made me feel happy and as though I had some control in my life. The bright white pad of legal paper had four things on it and I tapped my favorite black pen against my teeth. It was only seven in the morning, early Sunday, and no one was up in the house. I had a steaming cup of hot coffee—French vanilla—and an odd sense of contentment hit me.

Yes, I hadn't made any new friends or had any crazy experiences that I'd been craving for the past three years, but I had a sense of independence. I could do what I wanted, when I wanted. I studied the list and was glad no one could see me smiling at it.

Schedule times to complete all school work.

Done.

Visit student union to get school ID.

I would do that after getting a tour from Tanner.

Hang out with Aaron's girlfriend.

I'd texted her the day before and she'd agreed we'd have a girls' night soon. And the best part of my list? The final item.

Have fun at my first college party and forget Sean.

It was stupid to get giddy over the prospect of a bunch of stupid people drinking, but I'd never gotten to do that in high school. I'd always been working, or at the hospital, helping my mom, or trying to hold on to a relationship with Sean that was never there. Kissing a random guy or meeting the perfect stranger for one night seemed like the best introduction to my new adventure. I underlined *fun* and was taking a long sip of coffee when the stairs creaked. Zade didn't get up early ever, and Aaron preferred sleeping until lunch. But Tanner liked mornings and I glanced up, expecting to see his handsome face, but instead, it was a beautiful, willowy woman wearing a tiny blue dress and holding her heels.

I covered my mouth with my hand. *She's doing a walk of shame. Oh my god. I'm witnessing a real walk of shame.* I almost clapped my hands with glee. *This is college!*

The girl froze when her gaze found me, so I did the only thing I could. I smiled. She returned it after a second and stopped at the bottom of the staircase. "Uh, hi."

"Hi yourself." I couldn't stop my snort from escaping. "I'm sorry. I'm not laughing at you. Would you like coffee before you go?"

"Sure?" She frowned and tried covering herself with her arms. "Um, who are you?"

"I guess that question makes sense. I'm living here this summer when Jeff is away. I'm Kenzie." I considered holding out my hand but second-guessed myself. As my giggles got the better of me, I tiptoed as fast as I could to the kitchen and found a to-go cup under the sink. *Ew, I need to talk to the guys about storing stuff there.* I filled it, leaving an inch at the top so it wouldn't spill, and handed it to her. She remained in the same spot, confusion and embarrassment oozing from her. "Here you go."

"Thanks. This has been…weird."

"I'm not sure the etiquette, but I knew living with Tanner would be an adventure."

"Do you know him well?" Her eyes widened at her question and my guard went up.

"Not really." I kept my tone short and moved toward the door to open it. "Hope the coffee tastes good."

She didn't move though. Her lips were a faded red from the night before and she sucked the bottom one into her mouth as she stared at the ceiling. It made her seem a little crazy and I cleared my throat. "You were on your way out, yes?"

Her attention snapped to me and I swore she grimaced. "Y-yes. I was. I'm sure I'll see you again, Kenzie."

With that, she strode out the door with a confidence I envied, and I made sure to lock it after she stepped over the threshold. It didn't shock me, Tanner's hook-up. Aaron had girls sneak out in high school all the time. Sometimes, I helped keep his secrets. But the vibe was different, especially with the news of the draft being so recent. I sighed and about screamed when Tanner peeked his head out from the railing with a stupid grin. "She's gone?"

"Yes, asshole." I clutched my hand over my racing heart and glared at him. "Were you waiting up there the entire time?"

"Yup. It's kind of my MO. Pretend to be asleep, wait for them to leave. It's easier that way." He shrugged and walked down the stairs. His bare chest and low-riding shorts shouldn't have affected me — hell, he'd just hooked up with another woman — but, oh baby, his chest was my new weakness. He had strong and broad shoulders that paired well with his defined pecs and toned abs. Trim, fit, dedicated. His body was his masterpiece and my mouth dried up.

He gave me a knowing smirk at my open perusal, but I just prayed he couldn't tell what my mind was saying. "You got a little blush going on, Kenny."

Kenny. The most unsexy nickname ever. That got my words going again and I shrugged. "Eh, you have an impressive upper body."

"I've got an even better lower body," he quipped and immediately blanched. "Shit, that just came out. I didn't mean — I wasn't — I can't turn it off sometimes."

"Settle down. It's fine. I've seen a lot of half-naked dudes. It's not that big of a deal. Yours just surprised me, that's all." I smoothed my extra-large shirt and tried to pull it down past my stupid short shorts I wore to bed. "So, Casanova, did you have a *happy* night?"

He snorted, breezed past me into the kitchen and returned with a mug of black coffee. He could've sat on any of the spots available in their living room, like the recliner, or the love seat. Instead, he sat on the cushion next to me and spread his legs so they almost touched mine. I ignored the swooping of my belly at how close his tan skin was, or how his bedhead and sleepy eyes made him dangerously attractive. He yawned, leaning back onto the cushion and gave me a lazy smile. "I did have a *happy* night. Thank you for asking."

"I'm friendly like that."

"You weren't friendly walking Mia out of the door." He glanced at me over the mug, laughter dancing in his eyes.

"Incorrect. I was the friendliest. I offered her coffee, to go, but I didn't like the way her eyes lit up when she asked me about you. It gave me the creeps, like she wanted to get dirt on you, and I was not about to help with that. No, sir." I pursed my lips, shaking my head with overdramatic flair. He chuckled, his entire body moving with the motion, and it took a lot of effort to not stare at his abs.

"You're like my mini bodyguard."

I held up my fists and kissed my left biceps, then my right. "I am tough."

He loved my response and threw his head back, cackling too loud for the early morning. When he finished, his stare got serious and he directed those warm brown eyes at mine. He reached over with his free hand and squeezed my shoulder. His warmth traveled down my arm to my fingertips. "Thank you."

His tone told me more than the words and a heavy feeling began my chest. Vulnerable. Tanner was someone who didn't show weakness and he'd let me be a part of just a sliver of it. "You're welcome. What are roomies for?"

I said the right thing to defuse whatever mood our unsaid words had built. He glanced from my face to the table a couple of times before he blessed me with his dimples. Leaning forward, he snatched the legal pad before I gathered what was happening. "Wait, no. No!"

He set his mug down, holding the paper out of my reach, and read my list out loud. "Schedule times for all school work. Get student ID. This is fucking adorable."

"Give me my list, asshole." I set my mug down in a hurry, the contents spilling over the sides, and jumped onto his lap, stretching to grip the edges of the paper, but I couldn't do it. "Damn it, Tanner. You weren't supposed to see that!"

"Hang out with Greta. My god, this is so nerdy." He laughed, a full belly laugh, and held me at bay easily with his other hand. "Have fun at first college party and forget Sean. Wait, who's Sean?" His tone got serious and he look me in the eyes with nothing but concern.

"My ex-boyfriend."

"What do you need to forget him?"

We both seemed to forget I was straddling him, my thighs placed over each one of his large ones, the heat from both our bodies combining into a dangerous shift of energy. He stilled, dropping the paper onto the couch and removing me from his lap in one swift motion. He swallowed hard, gritted his teeth and let go of me like I'd caught fire.

My heart beat in my throat. His hands on my hips made my knees weak. He had an innate strength I wanted to spend hours exploring, but it would never happen. Not with his future in the MLB in the way and mine just starting. Not with my lack of experience and his expertise. It couldn't be, but that didn't get rid of the want or the lust I had for him. Desire coursed through my blood at a disarming rate and it took more effort than I cared to admit to talk in a normal voice. "Don't steal my shit again."

For good measure, I picked up the pad and swatted him with it. He didn't react, just stared at the blank TV for a solid ten seconds before meeting my eyes. "Why do you need to forget about Sean?"

I fought not to scoff. "He was a shitty boyfriend."

"Did he hurt you?"

"What? No, not anything like that," I replied, the warmth of his protective tone pleasing me. "He said and did all the right things to get what he wanted, so he called it quits after prom. Said it wouldn't do any good to try something we'd know would fail once we went to college."

He pressed his lips together, to the point they turned white, and cracked the knuckles on his right hand. "He slept with you and left? What a fucking asshole."

My face burned red, and I was stuttering and hoping like hell I could figure out how to change the subject. "No-no, he didn't-it wasn't...you know, yeah. We fooled around for about a month and he got bored. Told me I worked too much, spent too much time at the hospital and lacked spirit in the bedroom. He was a fucking asshole but..."

I paused. Tanner breathed a little heavier and had a dangerous glint in his eyes. "It wasn't a big deal to me. I didn't cry. I didn't react. I just said whatever and walked away. I've always felt like my life would start in college and he was never going to be in it. I became a little numb after the diagnosis. It was the only way to deal with all the pitying looks and questions. Where Aaron exploded on the outside, I imploded."

I shrugged, alarmed at how easily the words flowed from me. My school counselors, my close acquaintances from class and even my fellow waiters at the restaurant had tried to get me to open up, but the words had never come...until now. I let out a nervous laugh that bordered on hysterics. "I don't know why I told you all that."

The intensity on his face disappeared in an instant and an almost tender expression replaced it. He gave me a proud smile. "Thanks for sharing it with me. I'll make sure to keep it and your list our little secret."

"Ugh." I held it tighter against my chest. "So, do I still get a tour today? I don't have get a tour on my list, but I'd like one anyway."

He didn't get a chance to respond when a massive bout of thunder shook the house. "If the rain clears up, then yeah. If not, we can go tomorrow, because you need the student union to be open to check that one off."

"Aw, you're being so considerate."

"I'm a man of the people." He stood, stretching his arms above his head and giving me the perfect, mouth-watering view of his hard body. I slammed my eyes closed, pretending to yawn so he couldn't see my reaction. "I'm going downstairs to play video games for four hours. Let me know if the rain stops."

He didn't look back before walking down the hall and opening the bright red door to the basement. I didn't close my eyes that time and let my gaze roam over his back muscles and the two dimples that hung right above his waistline.

I mentally added another item to my list. *Get a grip.*

Chapter Four

Tanner

Fuck me. I pressed my palms against my eyes and took a deep breath, reciting all the reasons it was inappropriate to think Aaron's younger sister was hot. But the list only had one reason, and it was who her brother was. "Shit."

I tossed the controller across the carpet and leaned back in the gaming chair Jeff had got last year for Christmas. It was pretty sweet how it rocked back and forth if needed, and it was almost a semi-circle shape so we could fit. My neck muscles throbbed with stiffness — which annoyed me more. The entire reason I'd brought Mia back was to help lose the tension. She had been great in bed, wild and willing to do anything, but instead of feeling relaxed and settled, I felt worse.

It had nothing to do with the draft and my future this time, and everything to do with how Kenzie felt on top of me, her hair hitting my bare shoulders and her legs spread over mine. The way her mouth had fallen open when she'd realized the position she was in and how sweet she'd smelled so close to me.

Baby Hill.

No.

Like, so much fucking no.

But the fucking list, that was what had my chest feeling tight. It had been so innocent, so sweet and for the life of me, I couldn't figure out why I wanted to be a part of that list. I groaned into my clenched hand. Sundays were supposed to be off days, where Coach wanted us to relax and not use our muscles, but the itch to release my pent-up energy had me jogging upstairs to grab a pullover and my headphones. I could do with a light run in the rain. Content with my decision, I'd taken two steps downstairs when my phone rang. It was my mom, and I sprinted back into my room and locked my door.

"Hey, Mom, how are you?" I always asked the same question, my nerves dancing until she responded.

"Hey, Tallen. I'm doing just fine, like always, and your brothers are doing good too." She chuckled, the sound sending a wave of relief over me, and I fell onto my bed. My middle name was Allen and my youngest brother had started calling me Tallen when he'd turned four, ten years ago, and the name had stuck. "I have a bone to pick with you. I got your care package. Son, what did I tell you about spending a dime on us?"

I scoffed. "I don't care. I had some extra spending money last month and wanted you and the boys to enjoy summer."

"You're too good to us. It should be the other way around, Tallen. It is my—"

"Mom. Stop. Must we do this every other week?" I hated how our guilt and worry seemed to compete. "We're so close to getting you, Marcus and Malcom out of there. One more year. If I get the signing bonus I'm hoping for, we can get the animal for Marcus sooner."

She sighed, emotion clogging her voice. "Honey, he's doing okay. Malcom looks after him. You should see how much older Malcom looks. I swear he grew four inches since school got out!"

"Yeah?" I grinned, picturing my punk little brother trying to act taller than me. "Is he up? Let me talk shit to him."

"He's a teenager. He'll sleep until noon." We both laughed at that and an alarm went off, signaling she had to go. "I'm off to my second shift for the day. I'll leave a note for Mal to call you. I love you, Tanner. You were my first real love, son, and I thank God every day for you. Call you in three days."

"You too, Mom," I replied, hating how helpless I felt being thousands of miles away. It would eat me alive if I let it, but if I shared even a hint of guilt, she'd say the right words to settle me down. *You're where you need to be. Focus on you.*

It still sucked, that I'd gotten a full-ride scholarship across the country, where I only got to see her and my brothers once or twice a year. I needed a bigger signing bonus. *Then I can buy Marcus the service animal he needs, let Malcom choose whatever college he wants and pay off my mom's mortgage so she doesn't need to work two jobs.*

It was easy to get lost in the sea of emotions, on what felt like a lonely island. The injustice of what my dad had done to her, to me and my brothers, was enough to light my blood on fire and was the fuel that kept me going. I took a deep breath, channeling the inner demons until I calmed my breathing. One more year. One more year of madness and all our lives could get better.

* * * *

Aaron and Greta suggested we all headed to her place of work, the Lion, for dinner since we'd run out of food, and it felt good to get out of the house. It had rained all day and the call from my mom had thrown me off my game. Some beer and wings would be a great start to feeling better.

Zade and Callie had plans with his sister, so that left Aaron and Greta on one side of the booth and Kenzie and I on the other. It did me no good to think about how our legs touched. *Nope.* I tried moving closer to the window, but it didn't help much. Greta sensed my discomfort and gave me her signature smirk. "What's up your ass, TJ? Have a bad hook-up?"

"No, she was pretty cute," Kenzie chimed in, and my mouth dropped open. She shrugged. "What? She was kinda hot."

"Oh, details! Did you bump into her in the hallway?" Greta had a crazy look on her face, her eyes dancing with mirth at Kenzie. "Did he pretend to sleep until she left?"

"Wait, does everyone know that?" I asked and Aaron narrowed his eyes at his girlfriend. If I wasn't feeling on blast, I'd enjoy his irritation.

"Uh, I guess?" I said, hating the tiny bit of shame that came with it. Kenzie had a line between her eyebrows when she frowned and that little groove made me feel like a total asshole. "I never lie to them. They know the deal, one night only, no phones allowed and there's no *morning after* bullshit."

"When do you present all this information to them? Do you have a pamphlet you hand out at parties that details your expectations?" Kenzie put her hand on her hip and Greta cackled into her hands while Aaron looked on with concern. I ignored him and focused on Kenzie.

"They just know," I said, again, the sinking feeling in my gut unfamiliar and unwelcome. "I'm not a monogamous type of person."

"Unbelievable," she said under her breath, and I swore she stiffened her shoulders. "You owe them an explanation up front and no one says that. Sure, you can be a pineapple on pizza or not type of person, but no one is just like, nope, I don't do committed relationships."

"No one likes pineapple on their pizza unless they're crazy." I'd said the wrong thing because Kenzie glared as though I'd told her Christmas was cancelled. "Great, you are, aren't you?"

"Guess what I'm ordering tonight, *player*?" She stuck her tongue out at me and looked so damn proud of herself that I didn't have the gall to make fun of her. I accepted defeat and took a long chug of the beer our waitress dropped off.

Greta chatted with Mallory—the gorgeous waitress who'd started working there six months ago—and I studied her for a second, but it was fruitless. I couldn't check her out without seeing Kenzie's profile and little nose. She wore a faded baseball hat with our team's logo—a home plate with a cleat—in bright blue and had let her hair hang around her face. She leaned forward and placed her elbows on the table, resting her chin on her hands as she chatted with Greta and Mallory. I had no issues watching them, but Aaron cleared his throat and glared at me. "What, man?"

"Letting your hook-ups hang around the house, huh?"

I let out a frustrated breath. "She left at seven, Hilly. It's not my fault Kenzie was up already and on the couch. She doesn't seem fazed by it."

"I thought we were cleaning up our act," he said through gritted teeth and tried to communicate something with his eyes. Yeah, I knew the scandal that had almost rocked his college scholarship the year before was still fresh on all our minds, but it didn't mean I, the only single dude in the house, had to give up sex. Because that wasn't on the table.

"I'm being careful, if you're worried about pictures or anything…"

"No, I'm worried about my sister."

"What about, exactly?" I didn't like the accusing tone in his voice any more than the way he kept looking back and forth between Kenzie and me. "Seriously, she grew up with you for a brother, dude. Ask her how many chicks she saw you sneak out."

"That's not here or — wait, how do you know that?"

"She told me."

Kenzie and Greta laughed real loud, and I turned to stone when Kenzie clamped her hand around my arm. "Guess what! I have a job!"

"Yeah?" I asked, eyeing Greta and Mallory's wide smiles. "I'm guessing here?"

"Yes! I turn nineteen in a week and can start then. Hell, yeah, go me!" Her smile stretched across her face, her joy radiating off her like rays of light. She leaned into me, doing an awkward combination of a shimmy and a dance, but her smile fell when she looked at her brother. "Why are you mad?"

"You're young. You shouldn't have to see TJ's flings in the morning or work in a bar."

"What would you have me do then, Aaron? Knit? Buy a coloring book and stay inside at all times, not enjoying life? Tell me." She crossed her arms and jutted her chin in defiance, and the air seemed to chill around us. It didn't help that I was stuck on the inside, unable to escape the sibling argument, and Greta's gaze met mine.

What do we do? she seemed to say. I shrugged. I wasn't sure why Aaron was being a dick to his sister, but the mention of his name had me remaining in my seat. Kenzie's green eyes glowed when she got angry, and it enhanced her sun-kissed skin. *Not now, asshole.*

"I don't want you having the college experience I did, tempted by the partying and drugs. I was severely against you living in the house but Mom and Dad guilted me to death to agree, making me promise to watch out for you, and if you work in a bar—"

"Forgive me for speaking candidly, brother, but you were a walking STD when you were my age. Why would I be anything like you were when I saw you fall apart? You are not my parent and I don't need you embarrassing me like this in front of the few people I know." She stood and I couldn't find a single trace of the joy that had been there just moments ago on her face. "I'll try and find a new place for the summer if it means we can't have a friendship anymore, Aaron. But think about how *my* life was growing up with someone like you." Then she got up.

The urge to berate Aaron came and went. Greta's face spoke the same thing I felt and she gave him a scathing look before saying, "You fucking dumbass."

He tensed his jaw, rubbing his hands through his hair, and let out a deep sigh. "I should walk her back."

"Actually, I'll make sure she gets home okay. You should let her cool off." I moved to get out of the booth, but Aaron laughed without humor. "You think it's funny? You were a dick to her."

"Why would *you* make sure she gets home okay?"

"Because while you've spent zero time with her, I have. She hasn't left the house once her first week here. I'm her only friend, Aaron. So yeah, I'm going to make sure she gets home okay."

I didn't worry about his response and took off after her. It didn't take long. She had her phone out, the light showcasing her frown and tight jaw. She wore her emotions on her sleeve and I hated the hurt in her pinched expression and slumped shoulders. "Hey, I'll walk you back."

"I didn't get pizza," she mumbled, and I couldn't be sure I heard her right.

"Come again?"

"Pineapple and ham pizza. My stomach's been growling since lunch and I don't regret leaving, but I need food and I don't know where anything is so I've been Google Mapping it."

It was hard not to laugh at her determination. "I know just the place."

She exhaled, relief evident on her face, and I didn't think twice before putting my arm around her shoulder for just a second. I hoped the half-hug was the appropriate way to show her I supported her and I didn't think about the loss of heat when I released her. "Zaza's is a new pizza joint that's open twenty-four hours. They have dollar slices and I can't guarantee they'll have pineapple and ham, but I'll bet my life you'll like it."

"Any place named Zaza's has my attention." She grinned, the gesture a shadow of the one I knew she could do, and I hated the mask she put on. We talked two blocks in silence before she spoke. "Did he make you come after me?"

"No. He wanted to about ten seconds after you left and I stopped him."

She froze, bringing her gaze to mine. "Why?"

"Because you needed a friend, not your brother."

"Are we friends, Tanner Johnson?" She had a playful curve to her lips, as if she held a secret, and it charmed me.

"Yes. So, if you want to talk about what happened, I'm here. If you want to eat pizza and talk about lists, we can do that too." I shrugged, desperate to say the right things to comfort her. "Whatever you need."

"Thank you." She wrapped her fingers around my arm and squeezed. "I can now add *make a friend* to my list and immediately cross it off."

"Ten points to you. Tomorrow, we can knock out two more. But you should probably put *talk to your obnoxious twat brother* on there, too."

Chapter Five

Kenzie

Monday morning was not off to a fantastic start. I deleted two texts from Sean asking me how I was doing. *No thanks, Sean. Goodbye.* My biology class posted the syllabus and it was a shit ton of work for just an eight-week summer course and my mom sent a quick update that Dad was battling a terrible fever, *again*. It also didn't help that I'd tossed and turned the entire night, replaying the argument with Aaron.

Why is he mad at me?

What triggered it?

Do I have to find a new place?

I went without contacts for the day, putting on my thick-framed glasses, and chose an old tie-dye shirt and black cut-off shorts. The rain from the day before had barely cooled the temperatures and instead made the humidity seem worse, as if my hands would stick to my skin if I touched it. *Gross.* The weather was disgusting and I fought a groan when I grabbed my laptop and headed downstairs to make coffee and eat some food. I was still hungry despite the two slices of pizza I'd gotten with Tanner the night before, and my chest felt lighter. *Tanner.*

My first friend.

I fought a smile, my already warm skin becoming a degree hotter, and narrowly avoided Zade on the stairs. "Oh, hey. Morning."

"Morning, Kenzie," he replied in a deep, sleepy voice. He wore plaid pajama pants and that was it. "You making coffee?"

"Yup."

"Thank god." He yawned, stretching and showcasing his hard-earned muscles, but his body was different from Tanner's. His was leaner, more toned to fit a pitcher's needs rather than for power to hit the ball out of the park. It didn't prevent my face getting red or my slight flustering. "Pour me a mug, would ya?"

"Uh-huh." I scurried down the steps, hating my reaction to him, and came to an abrupt stop when Aaron sat on the couch with an expression I could only gauge as concern. My anger from the night before returned and the sight of his stupid face had my jaw clenching. Unless he said the words *I'm sorry*, I had no reason to speak to him. My heart raced and I put one hand on my hip, waiting. It didn't take long. He pointed to a large steaming mug of coffee on the table.

"That's for you."

"Thanks?" I chose to sit in the recliner and tucked my feet under myself before grabbing the cup in my hands and facing him. We were close enough now that I saw his stress, the strain around his eyes and the worry lines on his forehead. My first thought surprised me. *He needs rest for baseball. He can't play if he's stressed.* "Aaron—"

"No, let me go first." He cleared his throat and leaned forward so his elbows were on his knees, putting all his attention on me. "I'm fucking sorry."

My throat tightened and I nodded. "Good start."

He laughed, the sound only lasting a couple seconds. "You're too good to go through all the things I did. You're so smart, Kenz, funny, and…innocent."

"I'm not—"

"I don't mean innocent in a bad way, not like you're thinking." He gulped and his knee bounced up and down, shaking the mug on the coffee table with his strength. "College is a lot to handle and I didn't know how. I partied too hard, made a lot of mistakes…ones that almost cost me my entire future."

"You still make mistakes. Take last night, for example."

He winced and ran a hand down his face. "Dad called me yesterday and asked how you were doing and read me the riot act. *Don't let her drink, don't let her follow your crazy path, Aaron. I need to know my baby girl is safe in college. You might be the force of the family, but she's the light.*"

My eyes stung when he changed his voice to match our dad's, the impression uncanny with the rasp and timbre. "And being an asshole to Greta, Tanner and me was the move you chose?"

"I wasn't…hell, I guess I was to them, too." He sighed and leaned back into the cushion as if the weight of the world was on his shoulders. "I just want you to have anything in the world you want. Dad scared me. He might not be around in…a couple months." His voice broke just enough for me to reach out and place my hand on his arm. "Who'll be there for you once he's…gone?"

"Is that what you're worried about?" I let out an incredulous laugh. "You're my brother, Aaron. I consider you one of my best friends, but I can't have you trying to replace Dad, especially when he's still here. If you do that, you'll ruin our relationship and if I'm honest, I love what we have. We bicker, we support each other and we don't have secrets. I mean, come on, I helped sneak Frannie out of the house when you were a junior. Why would you think me seeing Tanner's hook-up would be something new?"

"Christ." He released something between a groan and sigh and smiled. It was the first sign things were almost back to normal. "I'm such a dick."

"No, you *act* like one, but you aren't one."

"Is it hard, being my sister?" he asked in a small voice, so unlike the boisterous, larger-than-life personality the world was used to. "Tanner said something that kinda fucked me up after you left the bar and I can't get it out of my head."

Is it hard being my sister? I thought of a million different ways to answer that question, but the horror on his face stopped me. He was actually worried about my answer. I moved from my chair to sit next to him and put my arm around his shoulders. It didn't reach, so I looked like a kid next to a giant, but he leaned into me for a quick second. "I love being part of your tribe, Aaron. It has challenges and if you ever talk to me again like you did last night, I'll kick your ass."

He chuckled at my lie, and he reached over to ruffle my hair. "It's been three years since we lived together, huh? I've forgotten how to be a brother."

"You just needed a little reminder. I'm here to find happiness, have adventure and figure out life for me. Let me, even if that means I make a mistake. Just, be there as my brother and friend. Bring me tissues if I cry or beat up some guy if he fucked me over. Don't insult the only friend I have, either."

"*Tanner.*" He said the word with a growl, but I pointed my finger at his chest and poked. "What was that for?"

"He's been kind to me, more than you can say." I stood and felt so much better at our conversation. "I gotta ask…did Greta lay into you about the working at the bar comment?"

"Yes," he said into his hands. "That might be a reason I stayed here, alone, last night."

"It's so tough being you."

"Asshole," he quipped, and our banter was back to normal. "Do you want to hang out today? I'm free all afternoon. Maybe I can show you some of my favorite places on campus, the dorms, you know, whatever you want to see?"

I tried to hide my smile from him. "Sure, I guess."

"Cool. Be ready around four."

* * * *

Aaron showed me around the *entire* expansive campus. It all blurred together in my brain, the geology building, agriculture, education, art, blah blah blah. There was no way I'd remember all the buildings, but the three hours we spent walking around and talking were great. We had the same sense of humor and I realized he needed to get to know me without the shadow of Dad's sickness surrounding us. That was how he saw me, the girl holding herself together for her parents' sake, but that wasn't who I was anymore. We walked into the house around seven and found Tanner lounging on the couch in a cut-off shirt and red athletic shorts. God, he made my mouth water in an irrational way.

"Hey, Hilly one and two," he said without removing his eyes from the TV. The Cubs were playing the Sox and it was extra-innings from an afternoon game. I knew because Aaron had checked it on his phone every ten minutes on our tour. "You get your student ID, Kenny?"

Something like guilt clogged my thoughts for a second, which was stupid, before I nodded. "Yup. Check it out." I tossed it at him and he caught it, grinning when he saw my picture. "I know. My hair is..."

"Awful," he finished for me.

"I *know*. It was the humidity." I plopped on the couch and took the ID from his hand. "But I might claim to *lose* it so I can take another picture."

Aaron snorted and paused at the door. "I'm going to head to G's. I've been working on my groveling and I think it's time I try it."

"Good luck, Hilly. You'll need it," Tanner said, earning Aaron's middle finger.

But before he left, his face turned serious and he stared at me. "And we're okay." It wasn't a question.

"We are."

"Cool. Okay, bye." He left, leaving Tanner and me alone on the couch. It was silly how my neck got hot or how my pulse quickened when he shifted to look at me. His brown eyes were soft, almost golden, when he snorted at me.

"Are you just dying to check off your ID from your list?"

I punched his arm and let my smile stretch as far as it needed. I wasn't embarrassed by his question. If anything, I was proud. "You bet your ass I am."

"Go get it, then."

I ran upstairs and got my laptop, pad of paper and my favorite pen before rushing back down toward the living room. The game was still on in the background, but Tanner's gaze was on me and, if I wasn't mistaken, it lingered on my legs for a second too long and my stomach did the swoopy thing. "God, it gets me high when I cross something off."

"You're a nut."

"So be it. I got my ID, got a tour of campus and am still speaking to my brother. Today might've started off bad, but it's better now." Instead of setting the pad of paper onto the coffee table situated between us, I held it against my chest so he wouldn't be able to see all the items on my list.

"I thought I was going to give you a tour of campus today, hm?"

I winced and covered my face with the pad. "I knew I felt bad. Were you waiting around for me to come back? Please say no. I'd just feel awful if you were waiting on me."

"Nah, I stayed at the gym longer than I usually do once Aaron texted me what was up. I'm real glad you two chatted. I'm sure you know this, but your brother has an odd way of showing how he cares."

"Yeah, he does." I plopped down on the couch, both of us in what I considered our usual positions, and studied my second bullet point. "I planned on making a work schedule for biology, but not our film class. What's your schedule with baseball this week? Still want to watch movies together?"

"Absolutely." He pulled out his phone, frowning at whatever met him on the screen, but it was fleeting. He transformed his face, erasing the sadness from it and plastering on a fake smile. It was so close to the real one

I'd grown to know in the week I'd been there, and it bothered me that it wasn't real. He ran his tongue over his bottom lip a couple of times before he frowned. "Shit, it looks like tonight is the only night I have open. We're leaving tomorrow for a three-day tournament."

"All of you?" I hoped my voice didn't come out alarmed. It would make me look weak and pathetic, but Tanner didn't give any indication I did and I relaxed a bit.

"Yeah," he replied, giving me a coy smile. "We'll be back soon enough. You can do whatever you want for three days. Run around naked, watch girly movies—you name it."

I crossed my eyes at him, hoping he couldn't see the slight blush on my face. "You nailed it. That's exactly what I'm going to do."

"Good, take pictures."

"Pig," I said, without any heat. His real smile returned and with it, all his charm and energy that drew people to him. "I guess tonight it is? I checked my calendar and I can fit you in between…stalking Sam Hunt online and painting my toenails."

"What a busy night you have." He glanced at my toes and his smile grew. "I like the lime-green polish."

I wiggled my bare feet. "Yeah? Green is my favorite color. It's the color of summer."

"And also the color of the outfield." He stretched and motioned upstairs with his head. "I'll get it ready and you get popcorn?"

"We're watching it upstairs?"

"Yeah, you have a nice TV in your room. I'm assuming you can hook up a streaming service to it?"

"S-sure," I stumbled, suddenly nervous at the thought of watching a movie with Tanner in my room. "We could watch it down here?"

"It's Monday. Zade'll be back and he hogs the TV every Monday. He has his own set of shows and it's the one TV with cable. You don't get in the way of Zade and his shows."

Cool, cool, cool. I was about to sit on a bed, with Tanner Johnson, and watch a movie. I was totally chill.

Chapter Six

Tanner

It was challenging not to watch Kenzie's glasses slip down her cute nose every other minute, but I managed. I couldn't sit next to her for over two hours and not have a handle on what *Citizen Kane* was about—even though I was bored out of my mind. We were an hour in, watching an awful relationship, when I'd rather be at a party, losing myself in a video game or hooking up. But as soon as the thought entered my mind, Kenzie shifted on the bed and stretched her long legs out, her left foot hitting mine for just a second.

"Oops, sorry," she said in a tiny voice and jerked her foot back on her side. It wasn't really fair. She was tiny. I was large and I took up most of the bed. The wall pressed up against my entire left side, but I tried making more room for her.

"Here, you can scoot closer if you're falling off."

"Thanks." She gave me a sweet smile, pushed those glasses up and went back to the movie. She had her hair up in one of her ridiculous buns that had little curls escaping in every direction and it endeared her to me. She wasn't afraid to be messy, or herself, and a small part of me wanted to protect that about her. "Tanner, you're making me feel like I have something on my face."

"You don't. I was admiring your messiness."

"It *is* one of my redeeming qualities," she scoffed and gave me a hurt look. I laughed, nudging my shoulder with her. "I'll add it to my bio."

"I meant it as a compliment." I reached over, squeezed the ball of hair on top of her head and appreciated the way her body relaxed when I touched her. "I like this. It fits you. You can be put into this box of what you're supposed to be, like your hair, but the curls can't be contained."

"Hm," she replied, pursing her full lips at me. They curved up on the sides and goddamn, I wondered what they would feel like against mine. *Woah, what?*

"For someone who said they sucked at symbolism in movies, that wasn't too bad."

I wanted to reply to her, thank her — something — but I couldn't. Her lips distracted me and the unsettling feeling in my chest had me coughing into my fist and reaching for a bottle of water on her side table. She lowered her voice and asked with such a soft tone, "Are you okay, TJ?"

"Yeah, sorry." I wiped the leftover water from my mouth and told myself to get a fucking grip. People had nice lips all the time. Hers weren't anything special.

Liar, liar.

She stared at me for five seconds too long, as though she knew what I was thinking about doing to her, but then she leaned against the headboard and paused the film. "This sucks. I thought, I don't know, like, this movie would be life-changing. It's not."

"But it is a marvel." I quoted what it said in our syllabus. She smiled, my goal achieved, and I moved to grab my laptop. It caused me to reach over her, our bodies touching, our heat combining, and my throat got real dry. But I didn't linger, I picked up the sleek device and moved back to my nook pressed up against the wall. I was suddenly glad Aaron was at Greta's for the night. The two of us, in her bed, watching a movie in the dark, didn't look good.

My thoughts aren't good either.

"Okay," I said, forcing myself to finish the task. Once we wrote our papers, I could leave. "We need to write a two-page essay on the symbolism that Orson Welles used and how he helped shake the film world."

She made an exaggerated face of annoyance and eyed my laptop. "We have over an hour left of it. I'm not someone who can bullshit their way through assignments. If you want to stop, I don't blame you. I envy you, actually. But I think I'm going to have to force myself to finish every single second."

"Were you a nerd in high school? Wait, I already know. You were."

"Not how you imagine. I had to work hard to get decent grades and I learned how to retain information — by not cheating or half-assing anything. I didn't use SparkNotes on any book, I never copied someone else's math homework, and I never used Google Translate for Spanish. I'm one of those annoying people who should've gotten straight As, but worked hard for high Bs. So, I wasn't a straight A nerd." She shrugged at her self-deprecating statement, and it was the slight dimming of her eyes that gave away the shame in her story.

"You also had to balance more than most at a young age." I reached out and covered her hand with mine. It was instinct, and not something I did often, but it felt right and I made small circles on her palm as I finished my thought. "From what I knew of you from Aaron, and what I know now, you're so much more than any label anyone could give you. Don't let labels or preconceived notions deter you for one second. Fuck them. You're resilient and I wouldn't say that about a lot of people."

"Thanks, Tanner." She squeezed my hand and gave me the sweetest smile, as if I had told her the best compliment in the world. Then she released it and scrunched her nose. "With all those niceties out of the way, I still plan to watch the entire thing, and if I do, you will not copy my essay."

"You're no fun." I stuck my tongue out at her, and she returned the gesture. I immediately regretted my decision because hers sent me an entire wave of inappropriate images of her mouth. "You'll give me shit, too, if I skip out, huh?"

"No, I won't. Swear." She smiled before hitting Play and I slumped farther down onto the bed in defeat. "Sure, get comfortable. Stay awhile."

Her sarcasm wasn't lost on me, and my response was fluffing her pillow and moving onto my side. *Shit.* I now had the perfect view of her profile. Her small chin that led to a long neck that had a couple of freckles on it. She had a mole too, right underneath her collarbone, and I wondered if she had any more. Blood raced out of my head and rushed to the lower part of my body, my dick growing in length the more I stared at her.

Fuck. Focus on the film. Not on Aaron's sister.

I managed forty more minutes of watching the movie and not thinking about kissing the sliver of skin peeking out from her waist, before Kenzie let out the littlest sigh. She wiggled, causing her to move her legs so they hit mine. This time, she didn't move them. I waited, totally in uncharted waters, and glanced at her face. Her eyes were closed, her mouth slightly parted and those damn glasses falling off her face. It felt as if someone had stuck their hand into my chest and squeezed my heart — that was how good a picture she made lying there.

Shit, I couldn't wake her. I held my breath, carefully pushing myself up so I could step over her. She sighed deeper, the sound hitting me somewhere in around my gut, and I studied her. She had trim hips and breasts that strained the front of her shirt and made my mouth water.

I'm being fucking creepy. I shook my head, making the final push and landed on the hardwood floor with a soft thud. The movie kept playing, but I didn't want to pause it. There had been two nights where I'd heard the TV playing all throughout the night and I knew some people liked the sound of it as background noise. And with one more glance at my adorable housemate, I left her bedroom and went to mine. My libido pounded through me, a totally misplaced lust for my teammate's sister. I craved a drink or a wild night with a chick I wouldn't have to see again, but it was the night before a game and it didn't matter that it was just summer ball. I had a goal and my horny ass wasn't going to get distracted, no matter how much it hurt.

* * * *

My alarm woke me after a shitty night's sleep and I groaned at the raging morning wood that pounded through me. Instead of taking care of myself the night before, I'd watched old films of me hitting and made notes on how I could improve. It was probably a myth, but I tended to hit the shit out of the ball when I was pent-up. And I was beyond pent-up. I trudged from my bed to the bathroom, shuffling my feet on the gray carpet, and twisted the handle to open the door. It was unlocked, it was just past six in the morning, and I jumped back in surprise when Kenzie stood there in nothing more than a towel.

Holy fuck. "Uh—"

"Shit! I thought I locked it!" She clutched the little hot-pink towel to her chest, water dripping from her hair onto her neck, her shoulders and arms, creating a little puddle on the floor. That was what it felt like in my head—a puddle.

I couldn't form words. She dropped her gaze from my face to the tent in my shorts and the air stilled between us. Her mouth formed a small *O*, the color in her cheeks changing from freshly-showered pink to flaming red, and the sound of her swallowing was the only thing to break the silence. Then she darted into her room and shut the door. I didn't need to lock it. We both knew she wouldn't come back into our shared area and I took a minute to catch my breath.

How the fuck is she so attractive?

I gripped the edge of the counter, hating how it smelled like vanilla and *her*. God, it was as though I was experiencing lust for the first time. I yanked open the curtain and jumped into scalding-hot water, fisting my dick in my hands, and said 'fuck it' to my control. If I didn't get a release soon, I'd turn into the fucking hormone monster from *Big Mouth. And ain't nobody wanting that.*

I tried not to think about Kenzie's tight body when I pumped up and down, but the more I tried, the worse it got. Her wild hair, her free spirit, her little chuckle, the way her legs were everywhere all the time…yeah, I wanted to taste every part of her and *god yes*. The orgasm hit me hard, the ringing in my ears sounding like a goddamn alarm when I pumped three more times. I leaned against the shower wall, letting the water hit my face until it started to get cool, and the relief in my body was almost laughable.

Almost.

A part of me felt dirty. How could I think about my teammate's sister like that? There was an unspoken rule that sisters and exes were off-limits. Why would I even attempt to cross that line?

I packed my duffel bag, threw on workout clothes and found Zade leaving his room at the same time. He'd kill me if he knew what was going on in my head. "Hey, Z, how's the arm?"

"Ready to fucking rock. Let's do this!" He pumped his fist into the air and I chuckled. He had always been a bit of an idiot, but I appreciated the presence he brought to the mound. I forced myself not to see if Kenzie was in her room when we headed downstairs and ignored the twinge of guilt of not saying anything before leaving for three days.

It wasn't like I could text her…that would involve asking Aaron for her number and I'd rather strike out for a week straight than do that. Fuck, three days away from her was probably a good thing. I'd play baseball, hopefully celebrate some wins and come home to our summer bash party and get laid. It'd be perfect.

Chapter Seven

Kenzie

In three days, I had added two new items to my list. *Make friends to not die of boredom* and *make sure to never live alone*. Every sound the worn-down house made me jump out of bed and clutch a baseball bat. It didn't matter how many times I checked every door to make sure they were locked, or the windows to ensure they were shut, I didn't feel safe. It also didn't help I got suckered into watching a crime documentary on Netflix, scaring the shit out of myself to the point I called my parents with the excuse of checking in. Hell, I almost called Sean.

I decided I didn't like it when the guys weren't home. Their place was meant to be lived in, not to be vacated or left alone to a dork like me. They had one game Friday morning — making it six games for their tournament — and they would return home. It was two p.m. and they still weren't back and I wasn't a huge fan of checking my watch every ten minutes. I had a life without them, right?

Ha. Ha. I didn't, not yet.

My entire first week's assignments for both classes, my laundry and even a budget for the summer were done. Once I turned nineteen and could waitress at the Lion, I'd be able to save more money and contribute more to the house. There always seemed to be food and I couldn't say who exactly bought it. *Hm, a question for another day.*

I sat on what I deemed the welcome couch, my legs spread out on the cushions, and I was on my seventh BuzzFeed quiz about what type of cereal I was—I was Fruity Pebbles, by the way—when I heard their voices. My stomach felt filled with butterflies and when Tanner walked through the door, my breath caught in my throat.

He gave me a sexy head nod, still mid-laugh, and I couldn't picture anything more attractive in the world. "Hey, Kenz, you survived!"

"We had a bet going," Zade added, following TJ into the house. "Aaron said you hated being home alone growing up, so, how badly did you freak out?"

"You're all assholes. Trying to make a profit off my fear?" I set my laptop down and found the nearest cushion to throw at him. "And to think I ordered a Zwillows Pillows sweatshirt to support you."

That wiped the smirk off his face. Aaron entered behind Zade and all three guys dropped their shit right at the entrance and plopped onto the remaining seats in the living room. Zade and Tanner gave Aaron a long look, Tanner speaking first. "Dude, you're sure about this?"

"Yeah. It's been almost a year."

"We don't have to do it here," Zade added, and my concern went from zero to ten. "Seriously, it doesn't matter if we do it here or at one of the other houses."

"Guys, it's our senior year. Greta will be here and she would literally fight anyone trying to fuck with us. I'm

not in the same place I was then. We're having a party,"
my brother said, the reason for their serious talk making
sense. "Kenzie, are you okay with us having a party here?
It will be loud, messy and people will probably try to
have sex in your room."

Three pairs of eyes stared at me and a fit of giggles
came over me. It did nothing to show them how mature
I was. They rolled their eyes until I could contain myself.
"Sorry, that's just…gross. Sex in other people's beds is
wrong. But yeah, I'm fine with the party. Actually, I'm
excited."

"Yeah?" Aaron's eyes lit up, turning brighter blue.
"You always complained about not getting to party with
me in high school. Now's your chance, K-Bug."

"*Don't* use that nickname, buckwheat," I fired back
with the nickname our parents gave him…which he
despised. His left eye twitched for second before he gave
me a nod of appreciation.

"Fair enough. Let's see if our beer pong skills carry in
the family or not."

"They do, trust me."

"Ten dollars I beat you."

"Game on, bro. Game on." I gave him the most
confident look I could, laughing at Zade's whistle.
"Zade's on my team."

"TJ's on mine. Shake." He held out his hand and we
shook, both trying to get the other one to break, and he
won, with his strength. So I kicked him in the shin. "You
little shit."

"That's for letting your teammates bet on how much I
freaked out." I felt Tanner's stare and I met it, sensing his
amusement, and I knew he wouldn't lie to me. "Who had
more than ten times?"

"Your brother."

"Fuck, well, he wins. I started carrying the bat around after it got dark every night and I might've left every light on upstairs."

"We're back, and you're fine." Aaron gave me one last look before picking up his bag. "Let's get the house ready, boys, it's been a while since we gave her a good time."

* * * *

They weren't kidding—they had crazy parties. Music blared from the basement after Zade got the hook-up with some awesome speakers, and three large kegs of Bud Lite lined their back deck. It was just big enough to hold the massive barrels and there had to be at least twenty cups on the ground. It was nine p.m. and people were already getting silly. It had started an hour ago.

"Girl, you look incredible. Give me a hug." Greta Aske didn't wait for permission before throwing her arms around me, causing me to stumble into the kitchen wall. She wore a floral perfume and it tickled my nose, and I got a mouthful of her hair before she let go. "I love your skirt. Seriously, how do you Hills look good in everything?"

"He doesn't. It's just me," I replied, earning a huge grin from my brother's bubbly girlfriend. I eyed my high-waisted jean skirt that had buttons all down the middle. I'd paired it with my Chucks and a black crop top that didn't have sleeves. It showed two inches of my midriff and felt like the perfect balance of flirty and modest. "But thank you. I stressed over what to wear to one of these."

"Rookie mistake. It doesn't matter." She held a red cup up against her cheek and squinted toward the living room, where we'd removed all the valuables. Only the couches remained. "Shit, someone I know looks sloppy. I'm going to check on her. I wanted to tell you." She paused, waiting for me to meet her intense stare. "Your brother loves you. He needs you in his life and if you ever need help kicking his ass, you just ring. I got your number from him today and I'll text you mine. If I don't see you later, we're hanging out soon. That's a promise."

I didn't have time to smile before she took off. A girl I had never seen before slipped down the wall to the ground, unaware of how much she exposed to everyone, and Greta bent low to help her up. It didn't matter that she stepped in spilled beer or that it got on her awesome yellow dress. She helped people and I sent another prayer to whatever guardian angel that would hear me. I was so glad Aaron had her.

"Yo, Kenny, we're up on beer pong. I really hate losing to your ass-clown of a brother, so I hope you're good." Zade looked way too stressed for a party and I chuckled.

"I'll be fine."

"If we beat them, I'll buy you breakfast tomorrow. Anything you want."

"Incorrect. If we win, they will buy us both breakfast tomorrow, and I'm not talking about no IHOP. I want a buffet."

"It freaks me out how much I fear you and respect you. If that doesn't sum up how I feel about your brother, I don't know what does. Come on, Ken, let's do this."

He smiled and charmed his way through the small crowd of people and led me toward one of three beer pong tables in the backyard. My pulse raced at the thought of competition. It ran in our family and while I knew my strengths weren't athletics, I still wanted to win at everything. We approached the table to find my brother chatting with a red-haired kid who looked a little star-struck. When the kid saw me, his mouth dropped open.

"*Angel.*" He looked at me, then Aaron, and back to me. Aaron wasted no time before smacking the kid in the neck.

"You continue one second of your thoughts, I'll kill you, Carter. Death. Serious death."

"Is that your—"

"Yes, now leave."

The goofy kid mouthed *I love you* to me and I snorted. Zade gave me an incredulous look and shook his head. "That's Carter Bolt. It's a damn shame he has a name for fame, but the hair of a ging."

"Don't hate on gingers. Have you seen Prince Harry? Good lord, I can get on that train."

"Dude, no," Aaron yelled at me, causing another fit of giggles to escape me. His expression softened and his tone changed. He moved to our side of the table and blocked out the rest of the party so I could see him. "How are you doing so far? Are you okay?"

"I'm fine, Aaron." It was hard to be annoyed when he looked so worried. "I've had one drink and only seen two people making out. It's actually boring."

He pressed his lips together for a second before his playful smile returned. "You're such a dick."

"Nah, I'm sweet." I shoved him toward his side and froze when Tanner walked toward us with his arm around a girl. He wore jeans that showcased his strong legs and a black V-neck that left his glorious tan arm muscles for anyone to ogle. I couldn't control my physical reaction to him like that, hair styled and no stress around his eyes, but I could control my thoughts.

Who is she?

Does he like her?

Oh, Jesus. Of course he likes her, at least for tonight. He brought his face toward hers, nibbling on her ear for a second and causing her to giggle and lean farther into him. My gut tightened, the sight of them sending an irrational surge of jealousy through me. We were friends. Nothing more. He owed me nothing. Literally, nothing. But it didn't stop the feeling and I found every ounce of my inner badass to shove the feelings down. "Johnson, put your dick away for a second and come lose."

Zade barked out a laugh, Aaron gave me a look bordering on pride and confusion and Tanner lifted his mouth from the chick's neck and searched until he found me. When he did, my knees got a little weak and I leaned into the table for a second.

His eyes were on fire and he raised one eyebrow, pulling the girl with him to the table and making a show of patting her ass and gently pushing her away before he spoke. He looked directly at me and I swore I felt his words hit my exposed skin. "Our little freshman seems to be getting a bit *too* cocky. What do we do to the cocky players, Hilly?"

"Well, we tend to knock them on their ass." My idiot brother held out a fist and they bumped theirs together. If they meant to intimidate, they did the exact opposite. I shared a look with Zade and we both burst out laughing. It threw Aaron off his game, that was for sure, because he looked pissed.

"What's so goddamn funny?"

"You two." Zade wiped under his eye and handed me one of the ping-pong balls. "God, have they always been that douche-y?"

"Yup." I popped the p and flexed my muscles at them. "Say, Zade, what do we do to the douche-y players?"

"We beat them."

"Game on, fuckers," Tanner said, making the threat sound like it was just to me, and I had no idea why.

Twenty minutes later, we'd drawn a crowd. Greta pulled up a bar stool and sat right in the middle, claiming she had no sides, and that pissed Aaron off. She winked at me and looked all innocent. It was down to the final cup for both teams and it would be a lie if I said I wasn't feeling the beer. They made no exception to the half-cup rule, where they filled each of the ten cups halfway with beer, and that meant Zade and I had two beers each within that time frame. It might not have been a big deal to him, but it was for me.

Aaron threw the ball, everyone holding their breath when he missed the cup by a hair. "Fuck!" he groaned, stomping away from the table. That meant Tanner had a chance to win the game. He cleaned the ball I had just thrown in a cup of water, crooked his finger at the girl he would most definitely bring back to his room later and dropped a very loud kiss on her. The crowd cheered, but I refrained from reacting.

"I've never wanted to win more than this moment, with everyone watching." He kissed the ball and tossed it with a perfect angle. It landed into the cup, but no one cheered. It meant rebuttal. Zade and I each had one more throw to tie the game and if we both made it, we could steal the game from them.

Zade put his arm around my shoulder, turned me from the game and spoke low enough for just me to hear. "You know the rules, right?"

"Yes, this is it. Do or die."

"How are you under pressure?"

"Apparently better than my brother."

He laughed real hard at that, lifted his head over my shoulder and spoke to Aaron. "I love her. Can we trade you for her?"

"Fuck off, Willows."

Zade brought his attention back to me. "Want me to go first or second?"

"First," I said. The nerves dancing up my throat made me want to puke. I'd talked the talk all day, but if I didn't make this cup, my life would be hell. I would be known as that girl, the one who lost, and I wanted to be known as someone else. *The girl who kicked ass.* Yeah, I liked that title.

We faced our opponents and if Tanner thought his continuous flirting with the busty brunette would fluster me, it had the opposite effect. Zade tossed the ball into the air, sinking the shot with nothing more than a drop of a splash. The crowd cheered and the adrenaline in my body reached a new level.

It's just one shot.

Arch it, not too hard, not too soft.

Don't overthink it.

I got into position with my arm at a ninety-degree angle, and I released it. The ball soared. I froze. It landed in the cup.

Zade and I screamed.

Holy fucking shit.

"Kenzie! Oh my god!" Zade picked me up and spun me around in a victory hug, his expression wild. "You did it."

"Well, we told them. It's what happens to douche-y players. They lose."

The crowd of fifteen people roared with laughter and I was smart enough to admit that I was terrified of what I would see glancing at our opponents. Greta hugged me after Zade and I snuck a peek at Aaron and TJ. My mouth fell open at their reaction. I expected to see murder, embarrassment or even revenge on their faces, but instead, they raised their hands into the air and bowed.

I almost cried. It was stupid, just a game of beer pong, but I couldn't recall a memory in recent years where I had felt like this. *Weightless. Carefree. Happy.* I ran to my brother and threw my arms around him. "Thank you for not being an asshole. This is my favorite moment."

"It might be one of mine, too, Kenz." He held me tight against his chest for a long second and let out a huge sigh when I let go. "I'm happy for you, but I'm still furious and need to walk it off. Enjoy your night, champion."

He joined Greta, the two of them veering from the crowd, and that left Tanner. He ran his teeth over his bottom lip, his long lashes teasing me each time he blinked. "I can't believe you fucking did that."

I gave the most casual shrug I could, but it didn't fool him. He sucked in one of his cheeks and gave me a quick, one-armed hug. It didn't last nearly as long as I would've liked, and I didn't get to say as much as I wanted. The brunette cooed his name and he gave me a *what am I gunna do* look. It shouldn't have felt like a betrayal, him leaving me, but it did. How stupid of me. I looked around. Everyone I knew had dispersed and the high of winning that game left as quickly as it'd arrived. *Life is just a bunch of ups and downs.*

Chapter Eight

Tanner

Noelle had the body of a goddess with lips meant for pleasure and there was no fucking reason why I shouldn't enjoy feeling her tongue on my neck. She crawled onto my lap and moved my hands so they cupped her ass under her dress. She went without anything underneath and while my cock tingled with awareness, I couldn't wrap my head around my holdup. "You're so tense, TJ. Let me take care of that for you."

I am tense. I closed my eyes and caressed her smooth skin, wishing she interested me. I gave it another two minutes before accepting defeat. "Noelle, I'm sorry. I'm not feeling well."

"Tanner, is it the draft? I'd be stressin' about it, too. Come on, let me take your mind off it for a while in your room." She ran her tongue over her lips, her intentions glaringly clear, but just hearing her say the word *draft* was the out I needed. She batted her eyes at me but stopped when she saw my face. "Oh, you weren't kidding."

"No, perhaps another time." I picked her up and set her on the couch next to me in one swift motion. "It's not you, baby, trust me. You're a sight to take in, and if we meet again when I'm in a better headspace, you won't be able to walk home."

She flushed at my words, and any sign of disbelief left her face. I traced my fingers under her jaw and gave her my best fake smile before leaving her there. If I was honest with myself—which I really fucking didn't want to be—I kept thinking about Kenzie. God, the spitfire made my blood sing in every good and bad way, and three days away from her might've helped me forget about seeing her in the towel. But it hadn't helped my attraction. It was as though the time apart had made it worse.

I scanned the basement and struck out, so I moved upstairs and checked every room before coming up blank. She was probably playing beer pong again, the sneaky competitive girl, and I helped myself to a large beer. It was only my third one and the cool liquid calmed the storm inside me. Carter also walked into the kitchen, his cheeks a little red from drinking, and I laughed. "Dude, you look sloshed."

"I'm not. Swear." He refilled his glass and gave me a weird look, as if he was contemplating something. I waited no more than ten seconds before he said, "Dude, Hilly's sister is hot."

I didn't expect that. "Do you want to die?"

"No, that's why I'm telling you, not him." He made a stupid face, as though I was in the wrong, and put a hand over his heart. "She lives here, right?"

"Don't even finish your thought." I couldn't explain why I wanted to smash his face into the counter, or why I needed to find her that second. "I'll be back. Don't do anything idiotic."

The crowd had only grown since the beer pong game, but her crazy blonde hair wasn't anywhere in sight and a prickle of fear hit me. *The bedrooms.* But why would she— *fuck.* I set my cup down on the first surface I found and stormed up the stairs three at time. Zade's room was locked, Aaron's too. If she wasn't downstairs, would she be in her room?

I knocked on her door, impatiently waiting for an answer that didn't come. "What the fuck? Kenzie?"

Nothing. Questions raced through my mind.

Is she trying to forget Sean?

Is she drunk?

Is someone taking advantage of her?

She wouldn't leave with someone…right? *Fuck.* I sprinted down the stairs and asked the first person I saw. Ambar Henderson, a journalism student who'd written a story about Aaron the previous year. "Have you seen Kenzie Hill?"

"The girl who kicked your ass? I haven't since the game," she said, her expression changing to one of concern. "Is everything okay?"

"Can't find her."

She set her drink down and followed me through the crowded living room. I hadn't checked the front porch, but I couldn't see why she would be there. The cool night breeze greeted me but didn't calm my anxiety. "Kenzie!" I yelled on the off chance she heard me.

"What?"

Oh my god. I scanned the ten faces on the porch, searching for her. I knew I'd heard her annoyed voice.

People looked at me as if I'd lost my mind, but it didn't bother me. I hopped from the porch to the grass and scanned the few people walking up to the party. "Kenzie!"

"Tanner, what?"

Did her voice come – oh fuck. I went farther into the yard and craned my neck to see the roof. She sat with her knees pulled to her chest, her arms wrapped around those skinny legs and her head resting on those. My heart skipped a beat in relief. "You're on the roof."

"Keen observation."

I couldn't stop my smile. She was safe. She was there. I brushed past Ambar, stopping to thank her, but she waved her hand and was already distracted by something one of the juniors on the team was saying. *I'm an idiot.* I forgot about the roof access Jeff and Zade had in their rooms. It took less than a minute to unlock my bedroom door, rush through our shared bathroom and crawl through her window. She didn't give any indication she heard me and I moved to sit right next to her. Our shoulders touched, the red cup in her head swaying a little. "You shouldn't be on the roof if you're drinking. You could get hurt."

"It's water," she replied, something off in her voice. She sloshed the liquid and pointed it toward me. "You can smell it if you don't believe me."

"I do." I couldn't figure out what was wrong. She wasn't crying, or frowning. She was drinking water to sober herself up, but something didn't make sense to me. "Why are you up here?"

"It's peaceful." She still hadn't looked at me, just stared toward the direction of campus, and I placed my hand on her back, rubbing it up and down. She was cold.

"You're freezing."

"It feels good." She sighed, finished the rest of the cup and set it down. Only then did she face me. "Why were you screaming my name?"

"I couldn't find you."

Her only reaction was a slight curve of her lips. "I've been up here for about an hour."

"I thought something happened to you when I went to look for you. It...it scared me." There, I'd admitted it. It felt more terrifying than a bottom of the ninth, two out pitch, but her expression hardened.

"I don't need you *watching* after me."

"It wasn't like that. I remembered your list, and you were a little drunk from the game, and the thought of some asshole taking advantage of you..." I paused, taking a second to swallow down the lingering anger. "I'm glad you're okay."

"Thank you," she said, her voice losing some of the vinegar from earlier. "Head back into the party, TJ. You know I'm safe now."

"Will you come back with me?"

"I'll probably make for bed."

"It's ten-thirty. Don't be lame." I moved my hand from her back to her neck, placing it right above her collarbone. "Come on, if I can accept you beating me in front of all those people, you can return with me."

"I don't want to intrude on your night. What about that girl?"

Great question, but pass. I'm not answering. Instead, I studied her and realized why I felt drawn to her. We were more similar that she thought—both forced to remain strong for our families, both unable to show weakness because it meant inconveniencing those around us—but mostly, the way she carried the weight of the world on her shoulders was similar to mine.

"Tanner."

Shit, she said my name again and shifted under my hand, but I kept my touch on her. "I'd rather hang out with you."

That caught her attention. She spun, her green eyes dancing with amusement. "Is this some sort of revenge for beating you? Is someone recording this?"

"What? No. Don't be absurd." I didn't like how fast her mind went to a joke, as though I couldn't actually want to hang out with her. "Honestly, it's your first college party and I want to make sure you get the entire experience. You have beer pong and roof sitting down. There is so much more to be done."

"Is it like bingo?"

"Are you obsessed with winning? Seriously, you're sick."

She laughed, her normal fire coming back. "I might be."

"Well, make sure to add *get game rehab* to your list." I couldn't tear my gaze away from her lips when she smiled like that, as though I'd told her the best news in the world. It wasn't fair for her smile to have that much of an impact.

"I can officially check off *having fun* so I don't have to add anything I know I won't cross off." She scooted toward the window and, just before she slid through, stopped and gave me a warm look. "Thank you. I got into a weird cycle of thoughts and it overwhelmed me. I'm glad I have you on my team, TJ."

I most definitely am. But I just smiled and helped her through the window. My throat got a little tight at those words and the unsettled feeling I'd had all night disappeared. We rejoined the party and I dragged her back to the yard. "First up—flippy-cup."

Two hours later, I'd introduced Kenzie to five guys on the team, a handful of girls who I hadn't hooked up with and Greta had even joined us. It was past midnight, two kegs were out and things officially got sloppy.

"Hey." Aaron's voice carried over the yard and his tone worried me. "I need your help."

"What's up?"

"Gotta kick someone out. Need backup." I lowered my head and told Kenzie to stay there and I'd be right back. She nodded and stared up at me with the clearest green eyes and hopeful expression. It took every single muscle in my body to pull myself away from her. I hated drama, but it happened in a house filled with high-profile athletes. Aaron beckoned me to the basement where some kid I'd never seen before was yelling his head off about something incoherent.

"Shut the fuck up, Steven. You gotta go," Hilly said, the venom in his voice hard to miss. The kid argued and I did my part. I moved his arms behind his back and Aaron and I shoved him up the stairs and out of the door. He fell when we let go, but it wasn't our problem. I checked his pockets and took his car keys. He could *remember* where he'd left them the next day.

Aaron hissed and said, "Fuck, I forgot why we used to love this shit."

"Young, drunk and stupid," I replied.

"Man, my buzz is killed. Hey, is Kenzie having a good time?" His jaw tightened and a part of me was pissed. He'd left her alone, too.

"She is now. I don't think she appreciated us all leaving her after the game, but she's strong."

He stared at me with his unblinking intensity and I didn't flinch. Then he said, "I don't like your friendship with her."

"You don't have to." I shrugged, meaning every word. He could be as pissed as he wanted, but I hadn't crossed any line. "She's great to have around. Zade likes her. I'm allowed to, too."

He didn't have time to respond before Greta walked up and his attention went to her. She had that effect on him and, while it'd annoyed me at first, since I'd lost a little bit of both my best friends, they were perfectly created for each other. I left the two of them with their lovey-dovey expressions and went back outside to find Kenzie. She was leaning against the deck, her elbows on the ledge and two inches of her skin on display. I closed my eyes, took a deep breath and hoped I didn't look constipated.

I must've missed the dude next to her, the one leaning forward and running his nose down her neck. She giggled. I saw red. He brought his hand up to her bare skin and I clenched my fist, ready to knock him over the railing.

"Kenzie." I didn't mean to sound so pissed, but fuck it, I was. She blinked and looked back and forth between the soon-to-be-punched dude and me. She had the gall to look embarrassed and pushed him off her.

"Sorry, Keith. It was, uh, nice meeting you."

"I'll see you again, Mackenzie. That's for damn certain." He kissed her hand and gave me a look that said *she's mine*.

Nope. Nope. Nope. I took her hand with more force than I should and dragged her inside. "Why are you — Who is that?"

"Are you upset with me?" she asked in the smallest voice. It made my chest feel squishy, a feeling I had never had before and one I instantly hated. "I'm sorry. Was I embarrassing? I was, I know it." She hung her head so her chin rested against her chest, and I didn't think before picking her up.

It wasn't romantic. It was more caveman-like with how I carried her up the stairs and set her right outside her door. I tilted her chin up with my fingers and hated how sad she looked. "You didn't embarrass me. I promise. I shouldn't have made you feel that way."

"Why did you?"

"I didn't like seeing that fucking creep kissing you. Why did you let him?"

She leaned her head against her bedroom door and let out a small laugh. "I wanted to check off the other part of my list."

"What part?"

"The part about *forgetting Sean*. He was the last guy I kissed and I want to erase that." It was the way she said it. The words meant one thing, but the attitude and the subtle dare in the words were meant for me. I knew it. I could feel it in how she jutted her chin and wet her bottom lip.

I didn't think. I cupped her face in my hands and kissed her. Our mouths met with an explosion of lust, her taste my new personal favorite flavor. She moaned, the little sound sending something rivaling electricity through my blood, and I deepened the kiss with my tongue, the need to have her strong enough for me to forget how to breathe. I was helpless, lost in her sounds and the way she met every stroke with one more daring, with how she clutched my shirt in her hands in a quiet desperation and with how her mouth was made for mine. Seconds, minutes, hours slipped away, and it wasn't until a door slammed that I realized what I was doing. What *we* were doing, and where we were doing it. I pulled back, loving how swollen her lips were from me and how her wide eyes looked at me with the same longing I felt.

"Did you forget about Sean?"

She nodded, moving her fingers to touch her bottom lip.

"Good. Now, go inside your room and lock the door. Don't forget to check *forget Sean* off your list."

She nodded again and snuck inside. I waited for the lock to click before I went into my own room, wondering how the fuck that had happened and what it meant. Because if I learned anything that night, it was that I wasn't going to get only one taste of Kenzie Hill.

Chapter Nine

Kenzie

It was moments like these where I wished I had a girlfriend to confide in. *Tanner Johnson kissed me.* He'd kissed the hell out of me eight hours ago and my body hadn't stopped humming. Never in my life had anyone been able to completely disarm me to the point I forgot where I was, who I was or why it was happening. It didn't matter. I felt like one of the heroines in a romantic comedy, like the birds would start chirping in sync and rainbows would cover the sky.

Okay, that was a bit stupid, but it was the most passion I'd ever experienced and I'd never forget it. The way his soft lips pressed against mine, his strong hands gripping my chin like he never wanted to let go, and the way our tongues fought for control…that kiss destroyed me and I wasn't mad about it one bit.

My phone flashed the time at me. Nine a.m. I never slept in and a dull throb began in the back of my head when I sat up. I clutched my neck, groaning, and made my way to the bathroom. *My first hangover.*

I would've laughed if it hadn't caused the pain to increase, and I twisted the knob and gasped. Someone was already in there, and it wasn't Tanner. "Uh, hi?"

A thin girl wearing an oversized baseball shirt—presumably Tanner's—sat on the toilet and gave me a shy smile. Her makeup was crusted around her eyes, her long hair hanging in every direction, and her lips…swollen, as though she'd spent all night in his bed.

"I'm almost done. I'll hurry," she said, her mouth twisting into what I assumed was a smile. I should have responded, told her not to worry or something, but words became difficult.

He kissed me, but spent the night with her. Goodbye, birds and rainbows.

"Take your time," I said after an awkward thirty seconds of quiet. I backed out, shut the door, fell onto my bed face first and laughed. It made sense. Nothing was off brand to who Tanner was.

He had been nothing but helpful the two weeks I'd been here and maybe we'd had enough to drink where he thought he was doing me a favor so I could check it off my list.

Great. I got a pity kiss? I'd rather lick the bathroom floor than get a pity smooch. I rubbed my palms over my eyes, hating the shame and knowledge that our kiss didn't matter. I didn't regret it. Hell, life was too short to settle for mediocrity, whether it was with food, experiences or kissing. But I regretted the blissful feeling I'd had, thinking about him the second I woke up. Maybe I was a naïve, stupid girl who didn't know what college was like, hook-ups without feelings.

"Ugh." I covered my face with a pillow, the sadness of not having someone to talk about this hitting me a second time. I could talk to Aaron, who would punch him, or Greta, who would just end up telling my brother. That left...nada. *Okay, enough.*

I'd survived my dad fighting cancer. I would not let one single kiss fuck me up. I rose from the bed with a new resolve—nothing had changed between us. I'd try my damn hardest to act cool about it and not let him know a single thought. It worked on everyone back home—why wouldn't it be the same now?

A shower could do magic. Those three walls and shitty curtain somehow transformed my moment of self-doubt into a ten-minute, scalding-hot think session, where I found my inner badass. Dressed in shorts that flirted with an appropriate length and a black plaid shirt that hung off my shoulder, I left the privacy of my room and walked out to face what came next.

I hadn't expected to gag at the smell of leftover beer, sickly perfume and vomit. Covering my face with my sleeve, I tiptoed over trash and made my way downstairs. Aaron was already up and eating a bowl of cereal, sitting outside on the two-person swing, looking all sorts of grumpy. I got a bowl for myself and joined him. "Morning, bro."

He gave me a half-smile and scooted over so I could sit. "How you feeling, champ?"

"The shower helped. Plus, I switched to water for about an hour in the middle. I'm not a total newbie." I swallowed a spoonful of Lucky Charms and nudged his shoulder with mine. "Are you hungover?"

"More than I'd like to be. I don't drink more than a couple beers when I party. It's not worth it, but Greta was here and kept telling me it was fine... I don't get it."

I frowned, unsure what he meant. I was about to ask him, but he continued. "I loved parties my freshman year. They were my reason for existing and I lived for each weekend where I could lose myself. The anticipation of hooking—er, sorry. I meant—"

"I know what you meant, idiot. It's fine."

"I lost that excitement," he said, his voice quiet. "Did you have fun?"

"Yeah, I think I did." I took another couple of spoonfuls and let the meaning of his words sink in. "There was a moment, though. I was alone, watching the party like an outsider, and it was weird. You can be in a house of people but feel…lonely."

"What you said. That's it. That's why I was, you know, crazy for a couple of years. I needed to escape that lonely feeling more than breathing. I don't get it much anymore. My teammates and Greta help me with that, but I worry about you."

I sighed, hating the sadness in his voice but loving his honesty. This was a good step, for us to chat openly about how we dealt with the prospect of losing our father. "I'm learning how to escape that feeling. I make stupid lists, watch TV shows and spend a lot of time reading. Your friends are more like family and I want that, too."

"You'll find your people."

We shared a smile just as Zade walked out, wearing blue plaid pants and that was it. He held up a hand, high-fiving me. "Morning, champ. Hope you're hungry. Once TJ gets up, these bitches are taking us out to eat."

"It might be a while. Someone had a guest last night," I said, praying my voice remained even. Neither one of them gave me an odd look to suggest otherwise. "Is your house always this gross after a party?"

"Yup. Every time," Zade replied and leaned against the railing. "Our MO is food, then cleaning."

I finished my food when the girl I'd found in the bathroom opened the door to leave. She glanced at all three of us, her face turning bright red, then mumbled a goodbye before clutching her bag to her chest and running off. "Are you—do you guys drive the ladies home?"

"Ambar lives like five houses down," Aaron said, his mouth hardening as he watched her retreating form. "She was drunk last night. More than I've seen her."

"I know," Zade groaned, running his hands over his eyes. "I was too, shit. I need bacon to help this headache."

Aaron stood and walked back inside. "I'll change and wake TJ's ass up. We should be ready in five."

"Sounds good. I'll do the same." Zade joined Aaron inside and hollered for TJ to hurry up, which left me outside.

Who's Ambar? If she was drunk, Tanner wouldn't sleep with her. *What if he kissed her though? Or they did this morning? She was wearing his shirt…*

It doesn't matter. Nope. I finished the rest of the cereal and set the bowl in the sink. Then Tanner stepped outside, looking all sorts of tempting in an old pair of jeans and a freshly cleaned baseball tee. The air crackled between us in the morning haze. My breath caught in my throat and even the player appeared lost.

"Morning, TJ," I managed to say in an even voice. "You look ready for the day."

"How are you?" he asked, moving a couple of steps toward me so he was up in my face. It was hard not to stare at the stubble lining his jaw, the curve of his lips that I knew tasted like forbidden lust or the way those dark brown eyes clouded with uncertainty.

"Experiencing my first *real* hangover." I gave a weak smile, which he returned, and I ran my free hand through my hair. I'd left it down, the wild curls going in every direction, and made my move to get us back to normal. "I'm real glad you and Aaron owe us breakfast. This cereal did not do the trick."

"They say greasy food helps."

"You feel fine, don't you?" I pointed my finger at him, annoyed at his grin. Only he could be cocky about not being hungover. "Jerk."

"I didn't drink much. I wanted to make sure you had a good time."

Uh oh. My stomach did that swoopy thing again, but I shut down the thoughts that would surely follow. I swore his eyes heated when his gaze moved to my lips, but I was sure I'd imagined it. "I had a great time."

"Good."

Cool, we sounded like junior high kids trying to flirt. He was working on saying something, with the way he kept clearing his throat and glancing back at the kitchen and my face, but he didn't get the chance. Zade, Aaron and Greta burst through the door. "Let's go, assholes. If I'm buying breakfast, I don't want to wait any longer," Aaron barked.

That was our cue. I followed them to my brother's car and jumped into the back seat—Greta called shotgun so that meant I got the bitch seat between two large athletes, Zade to my left, Tanner my right. Their thighs touched mine, their body heat traveling straight up to my core, making me sweat.

Greta rambled on about something, making everyone laugh, but I couldn't focus. Tanner adjusted his position so his arm went around the back of the headrest behind me. That put his incredibly strong biceps centimeters from my face. I gulped. I swore he heard me, because he brought his fingers to my ear and ran them down my neck. *What the fuck?*

The car fell silent, and I feared that everyone knew about the kiss Tanner and I had shared. They knew and were going to laugh. But Tanner let out a deep chuckle that sent a warmth through my body, from my head to my toes. "I think Kenny is more hungover than she thought. She's not able to speak and looks a little sweaty."

"Girl, I tell your brother all the time, cereal is not the move the morning after." Greta spun around in the front seat with a pitying glance. "Hold tight. We'll be there soon."

Zade patted my arm and handed me a piece of gum. "This will help."

How cute. They all thought my struggle was from drinking too much. I snuck a glance at Tanner and regretted it. He damn well knew I wasn't hungover like they assumed. His eyes danced with humor, his lips were pursed and he had a ridiculous, smug expression that lit me up. *Okay, asshole. Game on.*

"Yeah, can we roll the windows down?" I made my voice shake and leaned all the way over Tanner, my entire upper body pressed against his. He turned into a fucking brick, unmoving and stiff. I wiggled against him, moving my hand to his chest so I could balance myself. *Mistake, abort mission.* His toned pecs tightened against my hand and my instinct was to lick him. *Not the right move. Get back in the game, Kenzie.* I collected myself and said, "I might — I could get sick."

"Fuck, come on, Kenzie. Don't do this in my car," Aaron said, more annoyed than concerned. He sped the car and rolled the window all the way down so the fresh air hit my face. I turned just enough for Tanner to make eye contact, and I winked.

His reaction was priceless. He tightened his jaw to the point I swore his teeth ground and he tightened his grip on me. We spoke unsaid dares with our eyes, his glowing with the challenge. It went on like that for a full minute before Aaron veered into a parking lot and stopped without warning. "Get out!"

I crawled over Tanner, making sure to touch him as much as I could, before opening the door and putting my hands on my knees. "Go ahead and get a table. I'll be inside in a bit."

Aaron patted my head once before following my order, but my plan backfired. Tanner put one of his large hands on my back and rubbed. "I supplied her with the beer. I'll make sure she's okay and come in with her."

"Thanks, man," my brother said, completely unaware of the sick game we'd started in the car. *No, it started last night when he kissed me.*

That left Tanner and me alone, in the parking lot of a rundown diner everyone insisted was the best place in our college town for hash browns. The bell of the door echoed as Zade slipped inside and it was then I stood, a smile on my face. "How noble of you, to make sure I'm okay when you damn well know I'm fine."

"My thoughts aren't noble right now, Kenzie. Trust me." He moved his hands from my back to my neck, taking his time caressing me there before tilting my chin up to him. I thought he might kiss me again and I admit I wanted him to. Ambar chick or not, his kisses could change the world. A wave of disappointment crashed through me when he used his lips for words instead. "We need to talk about that kiss."

Chapter Ten

Tanner

Since high school, every time I said the words *we need to talk*, the lady would gulp and say just about anything to please me. It was still the truth. Cleat chasers had started going after me when I'd made the news at fourteen after hitting two homeruns against a senior, and dealing with them and everything they entailed had become a game I'd learned to play. *Don't anger them, but don't make promises.* I was nicer than Aaron, with his disgruntled female fans who wanted to get revenge, and I couldn't recall a woman hating me after I'd ended the one-night, maybe two-night, relationship. Because that was what I did. My world was baseball, ensuring my mom and brothers' safety and whatever time I had left was for fun. But that kiss with Kenzie had snuck in and I wanted to clear more room for it.

I repeated the words, slower this time. "We need to talk."

She took a deep breath and exhaled mint. "No, I don't think we do."

Um, what? "Hm?"

"I don't think we need to talk about it."

"And why is that?"

Okay, this was new and I really didn't like the feeling of uncertainty going through me. I removed my hands from her skin because one, its softness drove me crazy and I wanted to run my tongue all over it, biting it and letting her know how much she'd been on my damn mind, but secondly, her eyes were no longer filled with the lust I'd seen the night before. She relaxed when I removed my touch.

"I know why you did it and I appreciate the gesture, but I don't think it's worth revisiting." She sucked her bottom lip into her mouth and shuffled her feet back and forth before she met my gaze again. "It was the best kiss I've ever had in my life, but I expected nothing less from the best player in the game."

"Tell me, why do you think I did it?" I asked, debating whether to feel amused or hurt at what she said. It was a compliment that reflected my own thoughts, but laced with words that were meant to deter me. They didn't.

"Because you felt sorry for me. It's okay, really. I will never think about Sean again after experiencing the force of you, but don't worry about me or any crazy notions you must think I have." She laughed, the humor not evident in her eyes — the most expressive thing about her — and I wanted to erase the insane words that she'd just said. They were false, so fucking false, but I didn't have time to respond. She patted my face, giving me a playful, almost flirty smile, and said, "Thank you. I wanted an adventure this summer and that kiss was adventurous enough for me."

Then she went inside. *Fucking hell.* I crackled every knuckle, twice, and followed her through the door and to the table, where the only two spots were right across from each other. *Awesome.*

How had our little game in the car moved into her turning me down...before I'd had the chance to explain my thoughts? Had this ever happened to me before? No. It didn't make me feel better about the situation. If anything, it hurt worse because everything she'd said about it being the best kiss of her life...was true.

"You did a good thing last night, TJ," Aaron said, passing the large pot of coffee that sat at our table. I forced a smile on my face, severely unsure what the fuck he was referring to. My mind had Kenzie's name in bright neon lights running across it, but there was no way Aaron knew about that, or his fist would connect with my teeth.

Fake it.

"I do a lot of good things all the time, Hilly. Be more specific." I ignored the mocking noises from my table mates but found Kenzie watching me with an unusual expression on her face. I tried to reassure her with a small wink, but her expression remained unchanged.

"Ambar. I didn't realize she got that drunk until it was...what, three?"

"Yeah, I needed water and found her puking. It didn't feel right leaving her on the couch with people still lingering." I cringed and took a sip of the drink, letting my attention slide to Kenzie. The coffee burned my throat and I choked when I saw her expression. She sat stock still, eyes as large as the plates in the middle of the table and her lips parted. It was a combination of shock and surprise, and I wiped up the mess I'd made and forced myself to look at Aaron. "She apologized about fifty times this morning. Poor girl slept on the floor of our bathroom."

"I take back my previous statement of you being a dick one hundred percent of the time. It's, like, ninety-five."

I laughed. "Did it hurt saying that?"

"A little," he joked, and the vibe shifted at the table. It was probably just me, but everyone seemed more relaxed. Our waitress came and everyone ordered the hangover special of bacon, eggs, toast and more bacon.

"Kenny, you feeling better?" Zade asked from my right side.

I waited for her response and stared at that goddamn beauty mark that was on full display with her shirt hanging off her shoulders. Her skin drove me crazy and I played with a straw wrapper to distract myself.

"Just being around the smell of bacon helped. Thanks," she said, adding a self-deprecating laugh. She did that a lot. In a weird way, it reminded me of my mom, who never took herself too seriously despite her situation. *My mom would like her.*

Okay, what the serious fuck? I didn't talk about my family to anyone. Ever. It wasn't worth it. *He* could find her if I shared too much about them, but the urge to even contemplate it freaked me out. *Shit, is it hot in here?* I pulled on the neckline of my shirt and found Greta staring at me with an amused look.

"Something on your mind, G?"

Her smirk grew but she shook her head. "Nope."

"Then why do you look high?"

"I was just thinking about something that made me smile. That's all."

No one paid attention to her quick glance between Kenzie and me, and I had a hard time sitting through the breakfast. Everyone joked, made fun of the fact Kenzie and Zade had won and rambled on about our plans for the Fourth of July. I chimed in when I had to, but I counted down the seconds until I could head to the gym or cages to get some swings in...or, get Kenzie alone to continue our conversation. It wasn't until hours later that my I found my opportunity.

* * * *

Aaron went with me to the cages to get a good hour or so of extra swings. The release of energy helped with the tension in my shoulders, but it did nothing about the state of my mind. I was with my best friend and teammates, thinking about his younger sister who was just starting college. Scum. I was fucking scum. I wiggled the bat in my hand, doing my normal routine of swinging four times in the direction of the pitcher. Aaron put the ball into the machine, and the ball shot to the outer corner. I swung, extending my forearms so the ball mirrored the direction and it blasted to the right side of the net.

"Nice one. Let's end on that."

"Sure." We picked up the extra balls that had escaped through various holes in the net protecting the cages and fell into a comfortable and familiar silence as we headed toward his car. He, too, had a fire burning inside him to make it to the Majors and was the only person just as obsessed as I was with getting better. The difference between us was that the world knew his story and no one knew mine. It was how I preferred it.

"Dude, you are fucking rocking the ball right now."

"I'm seeing it really clearly."

"I know. It's pissing me off," he said, laughing, and hit my shoulder before we put our gear in his trunk. "I can drop you off at the house if you want, but I'm heading to Greta's. Callie gets back from her trip and is cooking for Zade and us. You in?"

Impose on their double date and miss the chance to talk to Kenzie with him gone? No thanks. "Not tonight. I'm worn out from the party and cages."

"I feel you. I tend to hate off-days, but sometimes, like now, I can't wait to not break a sweat tomorrow. G wants to watch a season of *Game of Thrones*. I might not be back until Monday."

I laughed and slid into the front seat, desperate to change the subject. *Forty hours with no Aaron? Not good. Nope.* I asked the first thing that came to mind. "How's your dad doing?"

"Still going to chemo, still fighting."

"No news can be good news," I said, thinking about my own situation. "You know I'm here if you ever need to talk."

"I know, dude, thanks." He focused on the road and remained silent for the short drive to our house. "I appreciate it."

He dropped me off, giving me about thirty seconds to grab my shit out of the trunk, and flipped me off before driving away. The light in Kenzie's room was on and I made sure to stow away my equipment in our pseudo-garage/storage area before heading up there. I couldn't explain why my heart raced or why I had the same feeling in my chest as when I walked up to bat. The door remained open and I didn't ask before sticking my head into her room. She sat on her bed, legs crisscrossed, hair in two braids and those goddamn glasses falling off her nose as she read a large book. She wore the tiniest pajama shorts and oversized Cubs shirt that had my mouth watering. "Hey."

She looked up, smiled and set the huge text to the side. "Hey yourself. I wondered who got back first."

"They're all going to Greta and Callie's for her cooking. If you haven't had it, it's stupid good." I leaned against the door, loving the slight blush of her cheeks and the number of times she ran her teeth over her bottom lip. "Did you want to join them?"

"Ah, maybe another time."

"Got big plans tonight?" I motioned to the book. She pursed her plump lips and nodded with all the confidence in the world.

"I do. Thanks for asking. I'm assuming you're leaving...?" She let the words hang, sounding a little too hopeful for my liking. I pushed off the doorframe and took two large steps until I met her bed. "Sure, come in, please."

"Kenzie." The way I said her name caught her attention. She swallowed hard, blinking more and more the closer I moved toward her. "You're not drunk, are you?"

"What? No! Why would you think that?"

"I'm making sure because I want to tell you something I haven't been to get off my mind all fucking day." I scooted closer so our legs touched and took it as a good sign when she didn't push me away. "I didn't kiss you for any other reason then I wanted to know what your lips felt like against mine."

I had no idea how she reacted to that, because all she did was chew on her goddamn lip and stare at me. "And, Kenzie, they rocked my fucking world. I'm going to want to taste you again."

Yes. She sucked in a breath, her chest moving a lot faster than it had been seconds earlier. I moved to get closer to her, but she reached out and pushed against my chest. I froze, so goddamn confused at what had happened, but then she spoke.

"That girl. You helped her, that's all?"

I'm a fucking idiot. Pieces clicked together and I covered her hand with mine, trying hard not to laugh. *She thinks I hooked up with Ambar after kissing her.* "I helped her clean herself up, gave her a shirt and a glass of water. That's it."

"And our kiss was the best for you, too?"

"One hundred percent, yes," I said, carefully moving closer to her. "It would a disservice to kisses everywhere if we didn't indulge ourselves again, just to be sure."

She giggled and slid down the bed so she was completely underneath me. I propped myself up onto my elbows and stared at this beautiful, spunky girl, and time seemed to stop. "They're gone all night?"

"All night."

"Just us?"

"You and me, Kenzie." I pressed my lips against her jaw, moving along her skin until I got to the spot underneath her ear. She smelled like the shampoo I loved, a mixture of sweet and sweat, and my voice shook when I asked, "Can I kiss you again, before I lose my mind?"

"Hell, yeah, you can."

Chapter Eleven

Kenzie

Every reason why I shouldn't kiss Tanner again left my mind when he lowered himself so his weight was on me and, oh baby, he felt good. I explored those back muscles that drove me wild, dragging my hands through his hair that was always just tousled enough to look good and landed them on his firm and tight ass. *Good lord, so many muscles.* He bit down on my earlobe, dragging his warm tongue across the tender area, and moisture pooled between my legs. It took all my effort not to wrap myself around him and never let go.

"Ever since I saw you in that towel… Goddamn it, Kenzie," he murmured, dropping kisses from my neck to my collarbone. He moved his hands everywhere, caressing up and down my body and slipping underneath my Cubs shirt. My skin burned at his touch and I arched my back, the need to moan overtaking me. He froze at my sound, a sliver of doubt sneaking into my mind, but he erased that real quick when he attacked my mouth with his.

Our lips clashed together, fighting for control we didn't have, and he slipped his tongue into my mouth, sucking on it, and I felt it all the way to my toes. "God, yes," I said between breaths, every part of my body attuned to his. He smelled like soap and leather. The huskiness to his voice when he said my name and the way his callused hands touched me drove me wild. "Tanner…"

He groaned when I reached for the hem of his shirt and tugged it up over his head so I could ogle his chest. I licked my lips and moved so I could be on top of him. He let me gain a moment of control and gave me a devilishly wicked grin when I dropped my head to taste him. I bit down on the spot right above his nipple, feeling drunk on his reactions. He bucked when I moved farther along his body, spending a long down on his abdomen where a perfect trail of hair led to an area I really wanted to explore. I moved to pull his shorts off when he stopped me. "Nope, my turn."

"Your turn?" I asked, my need for him startling me. It pounded through me, my core pulsing with each heartbeat. He did that grin again, the one I felt was meant just for me, and picked me up and put me on my back. His brown eyes melted into something golden and he fingered the edge of my shirt. He waited, carefully tracing my exposed skin but not moving up or down until I nodded.

"I've been thinking for far too long about what you look like under here, Ken. I'm shaking with need right now," he said, officially turning me into a puddle of lust. He lifted my shirt over my exposed chest and head so I lay there with my boobs on full display. He sucked in a breath, his mouth going slack before he met my eyes. "Gorgeous."

He didn't seem to be in a hurry. He leaned forward, giving me a feather of a kiss, before he said, "Close your eyes."

I obeyed and gripped my sheets in my hands. The bed shifted and I didn't get to register where he was when something warm closed around my exposed nipple. "Oh my god."

He sucked the beaded tip, hard and soft, biting down and pulling just enough for me to buck against him. I saw stars when he repeated the action with my other breast, using his talented hands to touch every part of my upper body. My desire reached a point of desperation, and with his teeth biting down on the spot below my collarbone, I begged. "Tanner, please."

He paused, stilling his hand on my lower stomach. He hadn't reach inside my shorts yet and god, that was all I wanted. "Please, what?"

"I need…" I started but he inched his way into my waistband and I sucked in a breath, praying, wishing, hoping he'd go down four inches more. "Touch me."

"I am touching you." He moved his right hand another inch, teasing my bare skin with light grazes. "Every part of you feels amazing."

His words combined with the quick drop of his thumb, right onto my clit, and he swirled with the perfect amount of pressure. It was animalistic, how much I wanted him, and when he quickened the pace and slid two large digits inside me, I melted into him. "Tanner…oh…yes."

He swallowed my orgasm, our teeth clashing together as something like a growl came from his chest. "You're so fucking hot. *Jesus Christ.*"

My thighs shook from the aftermath, my head a combination of awe and euphoria, but Tanner didn't give me much time to recover before he bent down and took my nipple into his mouth. "I'm not done with you, baby. Not by a long shot. Stay here."

He jumped from the bed and his footsteps stomped between our two rooms, and I didn't even register that he'd left before he returned, holding a silver wrapper. "You are a fucking sight, lying there all perfect. You might be my weakness."

I chuckled, the sound muffled by my bliss, and eyed the wet spot on the front of his shorts. It sent a thrill through me. *Power.* I did that, to him, and the thought of bringing him to the brink of ecstasy had me crooking my finger at him. "Show me what's in those shorts, hotshot, and get over here."

He liked that. He dropped his shorts and my eyes almost bulged out of my sockets. It wasn't the size — which was exactly how I had pictured it from that morning — but rather how hard and turned on he was...for me. But he didn't move from standing in the middle of the room. "Tanner?"

"Are you sure?"

"About this? Uh, yeah." I pushed myself up onto my elbows and got another wave of attraction toward him at the concern on his face. "Do you need help with the condom, TJ?"

That snapped him out of the trance and he said in the sexiest voice I had ever heard in my life, "I want you to put it on me right now, Kenzie."

"Okay." I got up, loving how he had a hard time choosing where to look at me. He tried my face, then my tits, back to my face, only to land on my legs. "My body is trembling with the thought of feeling you inside me,"

I said, watching his throat move in long, strangled motions. His chest heaved when I took the wrapper, opened it and pushed it over the tip of his cock, sliding it all the way on. "You're going to slip right inside me."

He snapped. He gripped his hands around my waist and tossed me onto my bed, his massive, taut body right after me. We didn't say another word until he pushed inside me, letting me adjust to his size with an unexpected display of control. He said one word, but it lit me on fire. "Perfect."

He caged me in with his arms, alternating each thrust with a kiss, taking his time sliding in and out, torturing me in a way I didn't know existed. Our bodies sweated as we found a rhythm, the moisture between our bare chests thrilling me. He groaned into my hair, moving his hands to my ass, causing me to wrap my legs around him. The slight change in angle let him go deeper, and he said my name as he pumped, once, twice and three times and a slow burn began at the base of spine. The movement of his hips rolling against me put the perfect amount of pressure on my clit and I tightened my hold on him. The burn grew and he lifted my lower back, making the angle just right for me to feel every inch of him. The orgasm was slower than the first. Each time he stretched my walls, the pleasure increased and I screamed when it hit me full-force. The only thing I could do was ride it out.

"God, your sounds—Kenzie, I'm coming. *Fuck*." He held on to me even tighter, his impressive leg muscles tensing as he spilled inside me. His breathing slowed when he lowered his forehead to mine, and if I could have frozen any moment in my life, it would have been that one. He looked at me as though I rocked his world, his eyes swirling with warmth and tenderness, but I wasn't stupid enough to think it had nothing to do with the orgasm. He rolled and fell onto his back beside me. "Holy shit."

"My head is spinning right now."

"Same," he said. He was still panting, as though he'd sprinted a mile.

My body had turned into pudding and lost the ability to move. "Wow."

"Same."

"You at a loss for words, Tanner?" I meant it as a joke, so when he responded with a very firm yes, my body warmed. "I'll add this to my list."

"Add it, cross it off but add it about ten more times. *Have crazy hot sex with Tanner*," he replied, completely unaware of how his words affected me.

Ten more times?

He wants to do it again…ten more times?

"Kenzie?" He sat up and I felt his stare on me. "I'm going to clean up and be right back. Do you need anything?"

Do I need anything? Ha. Yes, a cool glass of water and a reality check.

"Kenzie?"

"Sorry, I was using one of your moves, pretending to sleep."

"So funny, smartass." He smacked my butt and went to the bathroom, giving me a couple of minutes to recover and collect myself. It would be easy to have regret creep into the blissful moment, and Tanner returned before I let my thoughts drift that way. He opted to wear just his shorts, leaving his chest on full display for me to ogle, and honestly, thank god for that simple gesture. "You haven't moved."

"I tried, but my limbs forgot how to work."

He chuckled and picked up my way-too-large shirt that oozed sexiness. "Want your shirt back?"

"Thanks." I quickly put it over my head so it covered my lady bits. Once I was covered, the mood seemed to shift between us. Tanner ruffled his hair with his hand, remaining right in the middle of my room and just out of reach. "So. That was…interesting."

He smiled, but not a genuine one. "I didn't come up here to do that, just so you know."

"What was your plan then? You came in here with those big brown eyes and batted your insanely long eyelashes at me."

He visibly relaxed at my words and rejoined me on the bed. He didn't lie down, choosing to lean against the wall and leave a foot between us. I moved my feet under my purple blanket, putting a thin barrier up. "I came here to remove that stupid idea that I kissed you out of pity."

"Well, when I saw Ambar in the bathroom in your shirt this morning… I rationalized why you would kiss me and sleep with someone else. Pity was the best answer I could come up with." I shrugged, unabashed at my admittance. He seemed to appreciate it too, because he nodded and playfully nudged my shoulder with his hand.

"Silly, silly girl. We can erase that notion out of your mind." His eyes twinkled at me, like a goddamn scene from a movie. "I'll trade you a truth for a truth, but I don't want to scare you."

"Scare me?" My pulse raced at whatever thing he could say to me. *He'll tell Aaron? Aaron knows already? What will scare me?*

He ran his hands over his face, a haunted, almost tortured look crossing it, before he said, "I tried to hook up with someone else, but couldn't, because I couldn't get you out of my mind."

Okay, not terrifying.

Just a little bit.

"Just what a lady loves to hear," I teased, regretting it when his face fell. "I'm guessing this is a first for you?"

"You think?" His eyes flared for a second, but I just kicked my foot out from under the blanket and poked him in the side. "What was that for?"

"Correct me if I'm wrong. You're mad…because you were thinking about me and couldn't get it up with another chick?"

"Dammit, Ken. No, what I'm saying," he started and moved back toward the headboard so our shoulders touched, "is that I've never been attracted to someone like this before and I'm really out of my element. You're my best friend's sister, my roommate for the summer, and there are at least twenty reasons why we shouldn't do this."

His voice got real low again, dangerously low, like I wanted to close my eyes and have him whisper dirty things to me low. He sucked in a breath, saying my name like a curse. "Don't look at me like that."

"Sorry?" I gave a cheesy smile. "I can't help it. Sex has *never* been like that for me. Now, when I hear your rough voice, I think about your mouth on me and I get a little hot."

"Christ, I knew this was a terrible idea."

I stiffened at his words, but he reached out and put his hand on my neck, stopping me from getting up.

"I meant, thinking I could not do this again."

Oh. *Oh.* I giggled. "I know what to do." I moved out of his grasp and found my to-do list on the small half-broken desk in the corner. "*Do it ten more times with TJ.*" I held it up, grinning at my quick thinking. "It's on my list, so it's official."

"Jesus, erase my name! What if Aaron sees that?" he asked, jumping from the bed and yanking it out of my hand. He took a blue pen and went to cross it out, but I stopped him.

"Woah, woah, woah, don't mix inks."

"I'm sorry, you spoke a different language. What?" He gave me an incredulous look, torn between laughing and disbelief. "Don't mix inks?"

"Yes, I only use black on that list. If you want me to cross out your name, I'll do it." I took my stuff back and let my touch linger just an extra second on his firm pec. "You're quite yummy, Tanner, but if you fuck with my list, I'll hurt you."

"Noted." He held up his hands in the air and jutted his chin at the paper. "What name are you going to put then? You can't just write *do it*."

"Oh, this could be fun. Hm," I said, moving back to the bed and leaving room for Tanner to join me if he wanted. He did. He looked over my shoulder when I flipped to another page and began writing names.

Chris.

Peter.

Joe.

Jude.

"You could be a Jude."

"No, fuck no." He took a deep breath and struggled to say something for about fifteen seconds. Then he said, "Put Tallen."

"Tallen?" I scrunched my nose and realized I had no idea where my glasses were. "Shit! Where are my —"

"These ole things?" He held them up and placed them on my face. "Those goddamn glasses. They started all of this."

"How's that?"

"You wore them, looking all sorts of cute and you kept pushing them up your nose." His smile had my legs feel wobbly again and it got worse when he reached out and pushed my frames up my nose. "These goddamn glasses."

It'd be easy to lose myself in his stare, and that wasn't something I wanted, so I used the only defense mechanism I had — awkward humor. "They say eyewear can be quite sexy. Are you an *eye* man, Tanner?"

"I'm an everything man."

I scoffed and pointed to the paper. "Now, why Tallen? I picture someone with that name as a lumberjack. Plaid, vest, beard that's two feet long."

"My family calls me that."

"Is your middle name Allen?"

"Good guess," he replied, shifting his position an inch away from me. "One of my brothers called me Tanner Allen and the other shortened it to Tallen. Even my mom calls me that."

"Tallen it is." I wrote *Tallen* on my list and showed him. *"Do it with Tallen ten times."*

"Better make it twenty, to be safe."

Chapter Twelve

Tanner

My plan was shot to hell once I kissed Kenzie good night and went to my room. It was only eight on a Saturday night and I had two missed calls from my sperm-donor father. *How dare he call me after what he's done?* I squeezed my phone in my hand, hoping it would someone break. But I knew I couldn't do it. My weekly Sunday call with my mom was the next morning. She'd be working her second job now, her best friend and neighbor checking in with the boys, and it did no good to worry her. We'd agreed that if *he* found me or reached out to me, it'd be okay. I lived thousands of miles away from them and he had no idea what their new last name was.

Seeing his name come up on the screen sent white-hot rage through me. I opened the voicemail and reluctantly hit Play.

'Hey, TJ, was in the area and thought we could grab a meal together. Been watching your stats, you've been playing real well, son.'

I cringed at the use of that word and continued listening.

'We haven't caught up in a while and, boy, I tell you, it was a real shocker you didn't accept the draft. I'm glad you didn't after I saw how much signing bonuses the others got. You deserve more. Give me a call.'

Fucking money. That was all he wanted. Every time he came back, he conned money out of my mom. He'd done it when I was six, had come back when I was eight, got my mom pregnant and bolted when he'd learned one of his sons was blind. Cleaned out my mom's bank accounts and took off. He'd been smart enough to always approach me in front of people the last seven times I'd seen him. The bastard deserved my fist to his face.

My phone rang again, the number I hated, and I picked up without thinking. "Leave me the fuck alone."

"Nice to talk with you too."

"We have nothing to talk about and I sure as hell am not meeting up with you. Nothing's changed since the last time you wanted to talk about money." I wished he was in the room so I could grip his arms in my hands and break them. "Stop calling me."

"You're my son."

"You left our family three times. I am not your son."

"Legally, I am."

Yes, the only retort he had in the argument we had every couple of months. "Sure, Roy, your claim to fame is the fact your stupid-ass name is on my birth certificate. That guarantees you nothing."

"I just need money for —"

I hung up.

Bastard. Fucking worthless. I chucked my phone across my room, the device hitting the small desk lamp and sending it to the ground with a loud crash. Kenzie dashed into my room, still wearing the Cubs shirt, and brought her hands to her mouth. "Tanner! Are you okay?"

"Yeah, fine," I barked at her and rifled through my drawers to find a pair of jeans. I stripped down, put them on and found an old shirt that didn't smell. I needed air. Beer. *Something, anything.* "I'm heading out."

"What happened?"

I hated the worry in her voice, as though she had any idea what Roy could do to my insides. An hour ago, I'd been so happy. This part of my life had to roar back and remind me I wouldn't be happy until I had money. "I'm heading out. Just leave me alone."

"Oh, you're heading out? Where are you going?" She crossed her arms, the little line between her eyebrows begging me to tell her everything. I wanted to share the burden with someone so fucking badly I tasted it. But I wouldn't do that to her. She had enough to worry about with her little list to find her place in college. She deserved better.

With a wave of disgust at myself, I said words that would surely get her to back off. "Just because we had sex doesn't mean I need to tell you where I'm going."

She recoiled, but dropped her gaze to the floor then back to my face. "That's fair. But just because I wrote twenty times doesn't mean I can't erase it."

God, I wanted to smile at her attitude. My lips quirked and the entire charade was almost over — a moment of weakness I wasn't equipped to deal with. *Sure, self-destruct the best thing that's happened to me in a while. Do it, idiot.* "We're not in a relationship, Kenzie. It's not great style to pine after a guy after a good fuck."

She sucked her bottom lip into her mouth, her knowing gaze studying me with a scrutiny that made me nervous. Then she laughed. "It was a *great* fuck and if you think for one minute that your stupid insults are going to get me to leave you alone, nice try."

It was an incredible fuck. I picked my phone off the floor and headed to the door to do god-knew-what, but I hadn't taken two steps out of the room before her body pressed against my back. "What are you — hey!"

She had her arms wrapped around my neck, almost choking me, and her legs crossed around my waist. "Go on about your business. Don't mind me."

"Get off me, seriously." I tried removing her, but my hand kept sliding off her smooth skin. *Does she use lotion? What kind?* "Kenzie. I'm not joking."

"I'm not either."

"Let go."

"Tell me what happened."

"Nothing happened. Christ." I walked down the stairs and opened the front door before a thought occurred. "Are you wearing anything underneath your shirt?"

"Nope."

"Fucking hell, Kenzie. You can't — get down. I'm going outside and you don't need to flash everyone your ass."

"I'll get down the second you tell me what happened, because I know we aren't in a relationship, dickhead, but we are in a *friendship*. Don't try and tell me you don't care, because you do. You sat with me on the roof when I was feeling sorry for myself and pulled me out of it. So yeah, insult me, push me away, but don't forget who I'm related to. You'll need to try a different move if you expect me to let it go."

"My dad called me."

"Are you close?"

"No," I said, letting the overwhelming emotions take over. "He left us numerous times. He only calls when he wants money." It was easy to talk when she couldn't see my face and I couldn't see hers. We stood there, her little body pressed against mine, right in front of the big wooden door. It was an unremarkable thing to look at when I was sharing something that felt remarkable to me. "I hate him."

She didn't respond with words. She pressed a kiss right next to my ear and squeezed me harder. It was so sweet it startled me. Then she said, "If I get down, will you give me like, sixty seconds to throw on pants and I'll come with you?"

"I don't know where I'm going."

"That's okay. I rarely do, either. But you shouldn't go alone."

Those words cracked through the ice-like hold I had on my past, and the idea of telling someone else about it, even a little bit, felt freeing. I patted her legs, signaling her to get down. "I'll wait for you."

"Forgive me, but I'm not one thousand percent certain you won't take off. So, up the stairs, cowboy. I'm not letting you out of my sight."

That got a smile out of me and I followed her crazy order. She made me sit on her bed before she got down and moved a rocky desk chair in front of the door. "I'm not going to bolt."

"You told me I was *pining* after you. Forgive me for being a little dramatic." She flipped me off and bent down for something, but all I saw was her bare ass in the air. It had only been a couple hours and fuck, it was stupid to think a distraction was needed beyond her. But she slid on red booty shorts — my weakness — and threw on her jeans. Damn, I liked the view. "Let me find a bra and I'll be good to go."

She removed the large shirt and had no issue letting me stare at her perfect pink nipples I'd had the pleasure of tasting over and over, and looking at her made my mouth water. They weren't large tits, not like the huge ones that I got flashed often, but they were the right size for me to cup in each hand. *And the way she moans when I lick them.* Yeah, I'd pick that over large ones any day.

It was over too quick and soon enough, she had a Sam Hunt shirt on and gray Chucks. With one final push of those glasses up her nose, she held out her hand. "Let's go. Lead the way and I'll follow."

We walked in silence for fifteen minutes with neither one of us trying to remove our hand from the other, and I couldn't decide what bothered me more. The rage that never went away despite the fact that Roy was so close to being removed from our lives, or how Kenzie's words repeated over and over in my mind, making each breath a little more difficult.

Lead the way and I'll follow.

We're in a friendship.

Try harder to push me away.

Sounds of laughter greeted us as we neared one of the busier areas of campus. Older students typically stayed on campus during the summer and the bars remained busy on weekends. Techno music blared from one of my favorites from junior year, but the urge to go in and get drunk wasn't there. Instead, a coffee truck caught my attention and I pulled her toward it. "Want a drink?"

"I could do a decaf, yeah."

I bought two small decafs and we continued our walk to nowhere. We passed Greek Row, the south quad and the campus cemetery before we circled back to the quad. There were benches surrounding its perimeter, but she didn't strike me as someone who preferred a bench. "Want to lie in the center of the quad?"

"Uh, hell yeah." She laughed and sped up until we reached the circle of grass dead center of the campus. "Look at the moon, damn. It's bright."

It was. It provided the right amount of light so I could see Kenzie's smile. We plopped down, her going to her usual crisscrossed position, and she sighed. It was a cute sound and I set my coffee down before putting my arm around her in a hug. "Thank you."

She gnawed on her lip, giving me an unsure glance. "For?"

"For seeing through my bullshit. I'm sorry for what I said. It was all meant for you to leave."

"Yeah, I know. That's why I didn't." She leaned into my shoulder, setting her head against my jaw, and I got a whiff of her lotion. *Vanilla.* "One thing I learned dealing with the fact my dad has a countdown of his life is how people deal with emotions. Some explode, like my brother, constantly searching for something to cure the madness. My dad battles through pain, not wanting to upset any of us anymore, and I swear he tries to pull away sometimes, as if it would make his passing easier. My mom loads herself with tasks, always keeping busy so she couldn't feel the pain. That's probably where I get my list-making from."

"And you?"

"I spent a lot of time in my head." She did the laugh again, making fun of herself, before she continued. "Everyone dealt with the diagnosis on their own, unsure how to move on, and that left me alone, floating, desperately trying to cling to something that made sense. I'm used to being alone and I'm content with it, but, Tanner, you don't have to be. Tell me, or don't, but if you need to talk about it all, I'm here."

My throat felt clogged, as if I'd swallowed cotton balls, but I didn't stop the words as they tumbled out of me with a desperation so strong I stuttered. "My f-father stole my mom's money every time he came back. H-he left when I was a kid, returned with the promise of ch-changing his ways, but once he got my mom pregnant and learned one of my brothers was blind, he bolted. My mom was smarter this time and didn't put his name on the birth certificate, so he can't use them unless he pays years of child support he missed. He's on mine though and when my talent made the news in high school, he came back, threatening my mom with a divorce that would wipe her out and leave her unable to care for the kids."

She reached out and laced her fingers with mine, not asking questions or commenting on my story, just listening. It was easy to keep going. "He wants a piece of my draft bonus once I sign and he's threatened to go after my brothers if I don't pay him. Before I left for school here, they went through a name change and move. Very few people know where they are, and I don't go back and visit. We're all waiting for the bonus so I can pay for their divorce, get my brother a seeing-eye dog when he turns sixteen, and into a school better suited for his needs and move them wherever they want to go."

"That's a lot for one person to handle."

"So is watching your family lose their patriarch. But we do it anyway, because what else can we do?' I asked, hating how my voice shook and my heart raced. I'd told her everything, things I hadn't told my teammates in the three years I'd known them. "Every time he crawls back into my life, I think about what he did to my mom, to my brothers, and I get so mad."

"Tell me about your brothers."

And I did. I told her about Malcom and Marcus, and how I loved them fiercely even though I wasn't around a lot. I showed her pictures of them and gushed about how strong they were, taking care of my mom despite being kids. The relief at telling someone about it was the same feeling I got when I hit a bomb out of the park. We sat there, our secrets and struggles escaping into the summer air, and I could've stayed there all night. But familiar voices carried over the quad. *Aaron. Greta. Zade. Callie.* The cute foursome.

"Shit." I removed my hand from hers and put some distance between us. I wasn't ready to explain why we were sitting on the grass, on a Saturday night, holding hands. Nope. No fucking way. "Your brother is going to see us."

"Wait, is he—"

"Kenzie? Why the hell are you out here with—" He stopped and practically growled my name. *"Tanner."*

I panicked. No reasons came to mind and as the four made their approach closer to us. Aaron and Zade eyed me with a well-earned suspicion, and I gripped my coffee cup so tightly that it broke. "How was dinner?"

"Why the fuck are you two out here?" Aaron asked, not hiding the accusatory tone. Greta slapped the finger he pointed at me, but he didn't stop his glare.

"Because, Aaron, I asked him to be. You were all hanging out and no one else was around, okay? I had a freak-out and needed air and knew enough to not walk alone," Kenzie said.

"You could've joined us."

"You didn't invite me."

His face blanched and Greta let out a curse. "You told me you asked her."

"I forgot, shit." He ran his hands through his hair and pulled on the ends. "Why did you have a freak-out? Are you okay now?"

"It was about dad, college…a lot of shit, but I'm fine now." She stood and put her hand on my shoulder, squeezing. To anyone else, it looked friendly, but it sure as hell didn't feel that way. She had fire in her eyes, to protect my secrets, and I had no idea how to process that.

"Do you want us to walk you back?" Zade asked, leaving both of his hands on Callie's shoulders. They always touched and it had never made sense, until right now. The way Kenzie kept her hand on my shoulder gave me more comfort than I deserved. I totally got it.

Kenzie smiled at him, gave me a squeeze and shook her head. "No, don't end your night because of me. Go on."

Callie looked unsure and gave her signature goofy smile that charmed us all. "Stay with us tonight. You need a night away from all this…testosterone."

"Cal, I haven't seen you in a week. You're kicking me out?" Zade asked, his voice going an octave too high.

"None of you know what it's like trying to fit into this tight group. It can be overwhelming and she's the official newbie, making me a vet, and I get it. You can still stay the night, Zade, but let her have a couple of hours with us."

He pouted, unashamed to do so in front of all of us. "Fine. But I'll be there soon."

I snorted into my fist and hated watching Kenzie walk away with Greta and Callie. That left Zade and Aaron, both unhappy, glaring at me. "Neither of you have any reason to be pissed at me. This is your doing, Hilly."

"Tell me why she's sad, please. I don't like how she's going to you instead of me. I'm her brother, not you."

Chapter Thirteen

Kenzie

My girls' night was not what I expected. Movies and TV shows painted a vastly different picture than seeing Callie and Greta sprawled out on their couches in baggy sweatpants, makeup free and their phones in their rooms. Greta spoke first, handing me a fancy IPA I had never tried before. "Can I speak freely, Ken?"

"Sure."

"Your brother makes me want to punch a wall sometimes. I love him—most times I think too much—but fuck. He's a hard person to love, because he has to make every mistake before he figures out the right thing."

"Ha, that's a good way to put it," I said, admiring her candor. "He is hard to love."

"Again, love the guy, but I'm so sorry he didn't invite you over for dinner. I thought he did and I feel bad because I want you to feel welcome and one of us, ya know?"

"G, bring it down a peg," Callie said, throwing a remote at her. She opened her mouth to say something, but someone pounded on the door and Callie rushed to get it. "Sorry, we all know Zade is pretty much one of the girls now."

Greta snorted, nodding. "He is."

Zade walked in, picking up Callie and carrying her to the couch. "Ladies, great to see you."

"You lasted, what...forty minutes? New record for you," Greta said, and I grinned behind my beer. Their friendship, ease with each other, trust...it was what I'd always wanted.

Zade gave a goofy grin and took the beer from Greta. "Stone IPA, one of my favs."

"Asshole, that's mine!"

Their bickering lasted another couple minutes before Zade narrowed his stealthy gaze at me. "You, Kenzie, lied."

"Uh, what?"

Shit. Shit. Tanner told them. That means Aaron is killing him right now.

"You were covering for Tanner."

Both Callie and Greta stared at me and I started sweating. I pushed my glasses up and shrugged. "Be more specific."

"That's all he said. You lied to help him out, and that he wasn't ready to tell us yet. He sent us on our merry way and ripped Aaron for being a shitty brother."

Tanner's standing up for me?

Why?

"So where's Aaron?" Greta asked the million-dollar question and my stomach filled with dread. This was too secretive, too sneaky. *What if they find out?*

Zade grimaced and tightened his hold on Callie. "To be frank, I admire the guy, but Hilly is a little dramatic and I wanted to spend time with my girl."

Greta rolled her eyes, but her smile was tight. She was worried. "I'm sure he's walking here now." She gave me a weak nod and got up to check her phone. "Kenzie, were you covering for Tanner?"

"I was being a friend to someone who needed one."

She made a face as though she was unhappy, but perked up when another set of heavy footsteps led to her door. She raced to the entrance, yanked it open and sighed when she saw my brother. She hugged him hard, and I understood Tanner's aversion to their coupledom. They were a lot to take.

Aaron set Greta on the ground and narrowed his gaze at me. "Tell me what's going on."

"Well, I'm at your girlfriend's place after we had an awkward showdown in front of everyone on the quad. That about sums it up."

Zade snorted, earning a smack from Callie, but I appreciated his unspoken support. Aaron *was* dramatic.

"No shit. Tanner told me you lied for him. Why?"

Maybe it was his tone, or the way that this was the second time in two weeks where he'd been an ass, but I snapped. "Because I know what it's like not to be able to open up about problems when everyone else around you has their own shit to deal with."

"Kenzie..." His voice trailed off as Tanner made an appearance at the door. Those brown eyes found me immediately and it took him less than a second to read the room.

"Leave her alone. I told you. She covered for me and when I'm ready to tell the rest of you, I will."

"Why can't you tell us, Tanner?" Greta asked, the hurt in her voice evident. Everyone waited, watching Tanner and the physical signs of his stress. He stared right at me, took a deep breath and spoke in a tone I imagined he used on the field — assertive, intense and leaving no room for bullshit.

"Because there was never room to bring my shit to the table when we were dealing with Zade's *and* Aaron's problems. I'm not lashing out, so don't act butt-hurt about it. You guys are my family, but you're giving *her* way too much shit for saying the right thing at the right time. My past is fucked up and I'll tell you when I'm ready."

An uncomfortable silence filled the room as they all digested Tanner's words. My heart hurt for him. He stood too straight and kept his fists at his sides, and I'd bet money he was counting the seconds until he could leave. Callie spoke first. "I'm glad you were able to talk to Kenzie about it, TJ."

"Dude, same. We'll be here when you're ready," Zade added.

Greta mumbled something similar and it was Aaron who broke the awkward tension with the question on everyone's minds. "But why did it have to be my sister?"

"Because she's the only person as stubborn as you and she didn't give me a choice. She physically forced it out of me."

They all turned their attention to me and I nodded. "When you chuck your phone into a lamp and smash it, no sane person would let you walk out without an explanation."

"I didn't smash my lamp."

"Yeah, you did. Pieces were all over your floor. I saw them when I ran in to rescue you from what I assumed to be a burglar."

His cheek twitched with annoyance and he tilted his head to the side. "Now that we've put on a fucking show for everyone, can I leave?"

"Yeah, Kenzie, you want to stay here?" Callie asked.

"Nah, maybe another night. All the couple-y shit is a bit much. Relationships aren't my jam." They all laughed, and I made my way toward Tanner. I stopped to ruffle Aaron's hair, like he always did to mine, and pulled a bit harder than necessary. "Buckwheat, do you want to have a movie marathon tomorrow? It could be an early birthday present?"

"It's your birthday?" Callie asked, a crazy ass smile taking over her face. "When?"

"Tuesday. I turn nineteen, yay!"

"Chocolate or vanilla? Ice cream or cookie?"

"Um, what?"

"What type of cake do you like? I'll bake you one!"

I gave her the stone-cold truth. "All. I like all cake."

* * * *

I wasn't sure if I was imagining it or if Aaron purposely spent more time around the house, asking me questions about nothing and inviting me to everything he did. No, I didn't want to go to the cages, or to IHOP, or to the sports store to look for new cleats...for him. I appreciated the effort, but it meant Tanner and I had a total of two hours of being alone. We couldn't do more than talk without Aaron finding a reason to come into one of our rooms. It was stupid, really, and when my birthday rolled around, he was gone when I woke up.

Tiptoeing to the bathroom, I about smacked into Tanner's bare chest. "Hey!"

"Shh," he said, picking me up and slamming my back into the door in a practiced move I had no complaints about. Our lips collided and the leftover taste from his peppermint mouthwash engulfed me, sending tingles to the back of my throat. It was better than I imagined. Even better than our last kiss, and I ground against him, pulling his hair. "He wouldn't fucking leave."

"How long do we have?"

"No idea. Don't care," he said, moving his hands up my little tank top and pinching my nipples. I bucked, causing him to laugh, and he replaced his hands with his teeth, biting the tips through my shirt. "Do you like nipple play, Kenzie?"

"More than I realized."

"Mm, I like that answer." He grinned, slid me down his body and turned me to face the mirror. He yanked my shirt off and pressed four kisses down my collarbone, trailing light touches over my chest and abdomen at a torturous pace. "Look at you, glowing when I touch you."

Our gazes met in the mirror and it was the most intimate moment I had ever experienced. He traced a circle around my nipples, pulling on them until I moaned. Then he lowered himself to his knees, taking an insanely long time sucking each peak. He made sure I watched in the mirror as he tongued my breasts.

"Are you wet for me?" he asked, moving his attention from my chest to the waistband of my shorts. He pulled them down, running his nose along my inner thigh and grazing my folds. I stood there, paralyzed, when he moved my legs apart with his arm. "Spread your legs wider."

He cupped my ass, dragging his tongue from my belly button to my clit, biting down on the nub desperate for release. "Can I taste more of you, Kenzie?"

I squeaked out a yes, and he picked me up in one motion and brought me to my bed. He didn't waste any time and kissed his way down my body, his hair tickling the sensitive skin around my pussy. He bit the inside of my left thigh, laughed when I sucked in air and moved his magical tongue to where I needed it most. He swirled, flicked, teased and probed, bringing me close to the edge and backing me away. "Tanner, please. I'm so close."

"I want your first birthday orgasm to be the best. Trust me."

Oh, I trusted him. He slid two fingers inside me, pumping me, combining the motion with his tongue and sending me into a whirl of sensations, each wave stronger than the one before. My legs shook, my body on fire, and I lost myself in that orgasm. It was dangerously slow and just as strong. I reached for anything to hold on to and pulled Tanner's hair, gripping it as I moaned his name. Time stopped as I came down from the high and when I opened my eyes, I found Tanner's warm and fiery ones staring at me. "Fuck, that was…"

"Part *one* of your birthday present." He grinned, licked his lips and leaned over to kiss me. "Taste yourself, Kenz. You just became my favorite flavor."

Those words. Good lord. They shouldn't be allowed to be spoken.

He took his time, letting me explore the evidence of my pleasure in his mouth and just as he pushed forward and ground his hard cock against me, the front door shut. He froze for one second before jumping off me. He threw the covers over me and darted into his room as the footsteps moved upstairs. It could've been Zade, or

Aaron, or Jeff coming back two months early...but I *knew* it was my brother. I didn't breathe, as though any sound I made would confess what we'd been doing, but it wasn't necessary. Whoever it was stopped outside my room and slid a card with my name on it under my door. It was Aaron's choppy handwriting, and I sighed in relief.

I wiped sweat from my brow, found the thin flowery robe I liked wearing when I got ready and chanced going to the bathroom. I'd brushed my teeth and washed my face before Tanner creaked the door open and gave me a dimpled smile that reminded me of just how good his mouth could be. I smiled and whispered, "Hi."

He lowered his heated gaze to my legs, groaned and shook his head to refocus himself. "One, that robe is fucking dangerous. Two, happy birthday. But third, and most importantly, don't you dare count that as one of the twenty. We don't count the ones that get interrupted."

"Really, now?" *Interesting.*

"Yes. Don't argue." He grabbed the front of my robe and pulled me to him so our noses touched. He bit my lower lip and pushed me away. "I have at least two more orgasms planned for you today, so be prepared. The second he's gone, you're mine."

He shut the door, leaving me in a puddle of anticipation, and I couldn't remember having a better birthday morning.

Chapter Fourteen

Tanner

I winced when I lowered myself into Greta's kitchen chair. Coach had put us through a brutal practice — a combination of conditioning and strength training that had every muscle in my body aching. Nothing sounded better than enjoying chocolate-marbled cake with my friends.

Callie had outdone herself and made three different kinds for Kenzie, putting an odd assortment of candles on each one. I smiled, enjoying everything about the moment, from how Kenzie dipped her head low to avoid the attention as we sang to her to the way Greta and Callie forced her out of her shell, and seeing everyone take care of one another. Zade joked about Aaron's stats, getting a punch to the arm in return, and laughter rang around Greta and Callie's small kitchen. The dust had settled from me not sharing my drama with them, and a bit of guilt wedged its way into my thoughts. *Should I tell them? What if they don't handle it like Kenzie?*

What if they think it's stupid?

"Okay, girl, make a wish." Greta moved around the table to light the candles, bringing me back from my derailing thoughts. The smell of burning wax filled the room and Kenzie met my gaze over the flicker of smoke. Those green eyes held a spark of amusement, as though we shared a secret, and I confirmed my original thought. *I only want her to know.*

She blew out the candles, making those plump lips purse into a gorgeous O shape that had me clearing my throat. *Not the time to think about her mouth. Nope.*

Everyone cheered and Aaron moved to hug his sister. She leaned into it, a bit awkward and messy, but he didn't let her shoo him away. I called that progress, because the Hills were emotionally challenged. It was understandable, but still painful to watch. Greta began cutting the cake and asked the age-old question, "What did you wish for?"

Kenzie made an *are you kidding me* face and grinned. "I'm not into wishes, but if I were, I sure as hell wouldn't tell any of you!"

Greta stuck her tongue out at her and soon enough, we all sat around the table laughing and shoving cake into our mouths. The sweetness hurt my tongue — the healthy food I normally ate did not have sugar — and I appreciated the calories. I was holding the fork inches away from my mouth for my fourth bite when Greta asked, "Now that you're nineteen, you can start working at the bar with me!"

Kenzie grinned, unaware of the little chocolate frosting on her face, and pushed her glasses up. "It's probably dorky to say it, but I'm legit excited for it. I like having a schedule and having money. I miss my routine.

There's so much free time and I don't know what to do with it, honestly."

"I know what you mean. It's a dope job, I won't lie," Greta assured her. "Damn...when I turned nineteen, I wasn't planning routines or trying to fill my time with responsibilities. I gotta hand it to you, girl. I was worrying about parties, hooking up with the hottest dudes and not even *thinking* about working."

"Greta, please." Aaron glared at her but she ignored him.

"Calm down. It's true." Greta gave him a pointed look before directing her attention back to Kenzie. "So, what's on your summer-before-college agenda? A boyfriend? A crazy fling? Flirting?"

"Wait, weren't you dating that dude?" Aaron asked.

"We broke up a month ago, Aaron." She huffed a little and I swore her cheeks turned pink before she flicked her gaze to me for one split second.

Greta swatted Aaron's arm, rested her chin on her hands and continued the questioning. It had me on edge, the words Kenzie would say. It mattered, but I couldn't explain why. "Okay, no boyfriend. Fling though, yeah? They say the best way to get over somebody is to get under someone new."

"Jesus, no. I don't want to hear about my *sister* having a fling, over or under anyone. She doesn't—she won't—just, stop." Aaron looked so goddamn uncomfortable we all laughed.

"Calm down. Act more like Ross and Monica. They were totally cool talking about this stuff," Greta said, referencing *Friends*. I shared a look with Zade, both of us grinning.

Aaron shook his head and took a huge bite, preventing him from talking. Kenzie had a look of amusement on her face and had no issues continuing the conversation. I liked a girl who didn't back down.

"Mom always told me to never start college with a boyfriend. Said it would prevent me from finding myself. I could do a fling though. That would be fun."

Aaron covered his ears with his hands and made obnoxious sounds as he left the kitchen. Kenzie's smile grew to cover her whole face. Her joy pleased me, but her words did more. *She could do a fling…*

"TJ, Carter was going on about trying to be your new wingman until Jeff gets back. You hitting up downtown tonight?" Zade asked me. Before I responded, I found Kenzie twirling her fork in her hands with a curious expression on her face. It wasn't accusatory or worried, just interested.

For fuck's sake. It irritated me.

I took another bite and responded with somewhat of the truth. "The workout kicked my ass today. I'm not really feeling it tonight."

"Dude, same. My quads hurt every time I breathe. Cal, can you massage me later?"

"Can you do all of us?" I asked, chuckling at the menacing glare I got from Zade. "It's only seven, Kenny. What were your plans for the rest of your birthday?"

I wish I could read her mind. She bit down on her lip and used her pointer finger to wipe away the chocolate — a totally innocent gesture, but it got my blood hot.

"I don't know. This has been perfect so far, hanging with all of you."

"You're so chill. I wanted to go out all night, no curfew, all that when I was your age, still living at home," Callie said, and I had to agree. When I'd been nineteen, I'd wanted to raise hell, fuck shit up, get laid. If she wanted any of those options, I'd gladly sign up. But I knew that wasn't her.

Kenzie shrugged, took the final piece of the cake and put it into her mouth with an inquisitive look. "If there's a place with games...not athletic ones, like dumb ones, I'd love that."

Callie and Greta cheered and jumped from the table. "Okay, we have options. Bowling, mini-golf, an escape room..." They continued naming different places to go that would all cost money. I studied Kenzie's reaction, trying to figure out why she carried a wave of sadness when she'd admitted the day had been perfect. I came up blank, but an idea struck me.

Growing up with little money, we would have card tournaments for hours when other kids went to the movies or the malls. Kemps, spoons, rummy, speed. They were fun, competitive and decks of cards were cheap. "I have an idea."

All five of them looked at me and I grinned. "Card games. We can each donate one thing for the prize. It can be anything you want, but winner takes all. We can go out and get some beer and play here? What do ya think, Kenz?"

Her face lit up. "Yes. I love that. Gives me and Zade another chance to kick your asses."

"Thatta girl. Keep it up and you're in line to be my fourth favorite lady. You know, behind my mom, sister and Callie."

"What the fuck, Zade?" Greta fired at him, but he just winked. Greta made an annoyed expression, but it soon turned into a crazy smile. "I love this card game idea," she said, already starting to clean up the kitchen. "Go get booze, boys, and we'll get the place ready."

"Done." Zade stood and pressed a quick kiss on Callie's head before grabbing his keys and heading to the door. "Hilly, TJ, let's go."

"I'm coming, hold on." Aaron pointed at his sister. "Any requests for beer?"

"Surprise me."

"That I can do."

We left the apartment and I chose to sit in the back of the car. That left Zade and Aaron able to talk in the front, ideally, so they wouldn't ask me too many questions. They had been respectful since knowing I had kept something from them, but they were aggressive, intrusive and persistent. It took two minutes for Aaron to spin around and stare at me with an odd expression. I tensed, waiting for the interrogation, but what he asked had nothing to do with what I thought.

"Has Kenzie talked to you about our parents at all? She's worrying me with how calm she is about everything. She's...acting way older than she is and it's freaking me out."

I'd thought the same thing, too. "Not any time I can think of. She seemed a little sad up there."

"Yeah. I know. I think it's my fault." He sighed, sounding mature beyond his age, and I imagined him and his sister had to be, for their parents. "Last year, I wasn't able to go home and that was right when our dad got really bad. Bad as in we didn't know if he'd make it through the summer. I called her, but she spent the entire day alone in that house plagued with sadness while they were at the hospital. Fuck. She's alone a lot."

Zade let out a low whistle and held up one hand, like he was a fucking student. I snorted. *His sister's a teacher, so it makes sense.*

"If I may, I have an observation."

"Why are you talking like a twat?" I asked.

He ignored my question, but Aaron's shoulders shook in a laugh. "She's clearly more mature than all of us combined—just let her figure shit out. She speaks her mind and if she didn't want to be here, with you and all our crazy asses, she wouldn't. I think it's that simple. From what I know from dealing with *my* sister, fretting and overdoing it will backfire. And you fret, Hilly."

"I annoy myself. Shit. Let's just stop this and get beer. That sounds better."

"Fine by me," I added and wished I had her number so I could text her. Greta and Callie made her nervous, I could tell. She was in good hands, but they were a lot to handle and despite Zade's insightful observation, I worried about her.

And not in a brotherly way. Not one bit.

Zade pulled in to the corner liquor store and we hopped out of his car, waving at two dudes. They smiled, gave us high-fives and the three of us shared a look. This was our life.

"I'm getting some Coors. It's easy to drink and won't fuck me up for tomorrow," I said, not adding that it was cheaper than the others. Not spending more money than the allowances I had was tricky without drawing attention to it. I hated to admit it, but people bought us drinks all the time and I reveled in the fact it wasn't my money.

One more year. Just one.

"I don't know how you drink that shit," Aaron scoffed, grabbing a shandy-type lager. Zade grabbed a twelve-pack of Sam Adams and we were heading to the cash register when Carter Bolt and Felix Ramirez walked in.

"My dudes!" Carter exclaimed. "Is this good timing or what?"

"Depends on if you're talking about us, or you," I said, getting the middle finger from him. I loved messing with the guy and he didn't care one bit. "You off to drink alone and watch chick-flicks?"

"Don't hate us because you ain't us, TJ. You're the old man on the team. I can run circles around you," he replied, Felix chuckling next to him. Felix was a walk-on this summer, a year younger than us and real quiet. He was the fastest kid on the summer team and would be a huge asset in right field. I gave him a nod and he returned it with the same focused face he often wore.

Carter pointed to our beer and looked at Zade. "Zwillows, you guys heading to a party?"

"Eh, not a party. Just a birthday thing for Aaron's sister."

"Dude, your sister..." He pretended to faint before hitting Felix's shoulder. "You should've seen her. She's an angel."

"Do you want to die?" Aaron asked.

"For her, yes."

I laughed, but only because he was so goofy and nonthreatening. But my laugh fell when Zade threw his arm around Carter's shoulders and invited them to join us for the games.

"It'll be fun, plus having eight players would be better," Zade added. Carter looked like he'd struck gold and Felix even smiled.

"Thanks, Z, I'd love to hang out and meet more people."

Zade's being the fucking captain our team needs. I hated how he was great at it, such a natural leader with his charisma and positive outlook. But the role fit him and my struggle was less than Aaron's. He gritted his teeth and nudged Zade's shoulder, giving Carter a warning I thought about giving myself. "Don't ogle my sister."

An hour later, Aaron's warning worked for Carter, but it did *not* work on Felix. The transfer chose to sit right next to our birthday girl and found every reason to talk to her. He talked more in that hour than I had heard the past three weeks. *Fuck.*

We were divided into two groups of four for rounds of speed, each person playing another for points, and the last change had me playing against Greta. Maybe it was my annoyance at Felix flirting with Kenzie, or the fact that Greta *used* to have a crush on me but had ended up with Aaron, or the sheer problem of my competitiveness. I loved winning and she was a *terrible* loser.

She narrowed her eyes at me, her brown irises turning darker, and whispered, "You're dead."

"Okay, G. We'll see."

She dealt the cards and we were off, finding the right numbers to place on each other. I was fast, but she was faster. We battled card for card, my forehead sweating when she had one more card in her hand, but the number seven appeared, the one I needed. I threw it onto the pile, ending the game and beating her. "Fuck, yeah!"

"Fuck you, Tanner Johnson!" She shoved the stack of cards at me and stormed off in a pout. I loved it, but my laugh caught in my throat when I saw Felix walking Kenzie to the kitchen, a smile playing on her lips.

"Dude, I haven't seen Greta this pissed in a while. It's hilarious," Aaron said, hitting me in the shoulder with a fist bump. He saw my line of sight and almost growled at Felix's retreating back. "If I cause a scene, Greta will yell at me and we leave for a tournament in two days. I can't get kicked out of her bedroom."

"It's your sister," I said through gritted teeth, hoping my voice didn't give me away.

"Fuck it. Felix's a good dude and she can do whatever the hell she wants. As long as I don't hear — no, you know what? I can't. Felix! Get over here. Let's talk about your defense today." Aaron walked into the kitchen and came back with Felix, an annoyed expression on both their faces. This was my cue. I went into the kitchen and smiled when Kenzie's ass met me. She was bent over into the fridge, her tight jeans showcasing curves that were perfect.

I leaned against the wall, the nook we were in completely cut off from the living room. An unknown feeling ran through me, almost like competition, like when a younger guy on the team made an incredible catch, causing me to make a better one. I closed the distance between us and waited for her to notice me.

I didn't like waiting.

"Kenzie."

"Oh, hey," she said, breathless, and spun around to face me. Her blush came back full force and she adjusted her glasses before meeting my eyes. "You want another beer?"

"No. I wanted to remind you I still have a couple presents for you, when we get back. You're owed orgasms."

"I haven't forgotten, but thank you for the reminder." She pursed her lips with a little smugness and moved so she could shut the fridge. I took another step, our chests less than an inch apart, and cupped her chin in my hand. "What are you — *oh*."

I bent lower, connecting our mouths with more aggression than I intended. She tasted like beer and lust and I sucked her tongue into my mouth. It was over too quickly, and my entire body was on fire from one kiss. She stared at me with her large green eyes filled with warmth and curiosity, all for me. It was...intense, for a stolen kiss fueled by jealousy.

That's what I feel, jealous. Jealous of Felix. What the fuck?

She looked at me with expectation on her face, as if she wanted me to say something, so I did. "You had something on your mouth. I was being a friend and helping you out."

Those sea-green eyes danced with amusement. "Oh, is that so? Thanks for being such a good pal." She ran her tongue over her lips, making a real show of it. My cock twitched in my pants, thoughts of her sucking me overtaking every ounce of common sense I had. "We've been in here too long. I'm going back out."

"Hungry to get back to your summer fling with Felix?" I didn't mean to say the words. I really didn't. But they slipped out without warning and my shoulders tightened with anxiety. *I'm a fucking idiot. I ruin everything.*

She didn't look angry. She didn't look upset or annoyed at all at my rude comment. She brought her fingers to my hair, ruffling it and running her nails through it. It sent goosebumps down my body and she leaned in closer, standing on her tiptoes so her mouth touched my ears. "I never agreed my birthday orgasms had to be given *only* by you." She patted my chest and left me in the kitchen, alone and with a semi-boner.

Fuck.

Chapter Fifteen

Kenzie

The assholes had lied to me. They'd told me they didn't do presents for birthdays, yet, when the card games wound down around midnight, they presented me with a college swag bag filled with T-shirts, a sweatshirt, fun socks, a notebook and a hat. Callie pulled me in for a hug, squeezing me harder than Greta did, and held on. "I'm glad you're here, Kenzie. This campus is wonderful. You'll have ups and downs, but you'll get to experience things you'll never forget for the rest of your life. Happy birthday."

"Thank you," I said into her hair. It was an oddly emotional thing, coming from her, but I appreciated it and patted her back. "This was so nice, guys."

"You haven't even seen the shirts." Zade picked up one and tossed it to me. "You got a different shirt for each of us. We expect you to rotate what you wear between games. It's only fair. You shouldn't have to wear your brother's dumb jersey all the time."

"Actually, there is something *better* in there she might want to wear," Callie said without hiding her amusement. "I got you an official shirt from the Zwillows Pillows group."

"Fuck off," Zade groaned, jumping from his chair into a fighting stance.

I laughed real hard at that and immediately put the shirt on. Zade's face flamed red and I twirled around, everyone else laughing. "This is incredible."

"Glad you like it. It was TJ's idea," Aaron said, clapping him on the back. "He makes a lot of stupid decisions, but this was a good one."

"The coolest part for me, coming here for school, was getting all the gear and feeling a part of something." Tanner shrugged but his eyes never left my face. "This campus is my home and I know you're looking for one too."

"Ugh, I just love our little family," Greta said, throwing her arms around me and Aaron in one gesture. Poor Felix and Carter looked on, half-smiling and half-drinking their beer with awkward expressions. We probably looked real weird.

"Thank you all. This was the best birthday in a long time. Maybe ever." I smiled at all of them, even the two newcomers, and yawned for the finale. "It's been great, but I need to sleep."

"Ha, yeah, we should head out. Thanks for letting us hang, guys. Callie, Greta, your place is awesome." Carter high-fived the guys and Greta and Callie. When he got to me, he gave me the biggest puppy-dog eyes I'd ever seen. He grabbed my hand and kissed the back of it. "Happy birthday to my future queen."

"Uh, thanks?"

"Ignore him. He's an idiot," Felix said, shoving him to the side. "It was nice meeting you, Kenzie. Hopefully I'll see you around sometime soon."

"For sure," I agreed, and didn't hate it when he went for a hug. He smelled nice and clean. "Thanks."

They took off, a prolonged silence filling the room until they closed the door, and all five of them stared at me with crazy expressions. "What?"

"Oh my god, he can be your fling!" Callie said, jumping up and down. "He's super cute and—"

"Right? He'd be perfect for a little fun," Greta added. "He checks all the boxes—nice to look at, polite, strong arms. What's the issue?"

Aaron and Zade stood straighter and I found my excuse to leave. "I'll let the four of you deal with this fun situation. I'm heading back. Tanner, are you going back to the house too?" I hoped I didn't sound desperate when I asked, because I wasn't. I was more curious…that was all. "I don't want to walk back alone, so if you're going out, I'll get an Uber or something."

He took a while to answer, those gorgeous eyes a little hooded. His gaze moved from my shirt to my face and he nodded. "I'm heading back. No need to call a service."

"Cool." I picked up the gift basket and gave my brother and his crazy crew the biggest smile I could. "All this, the food and presents…it's everything. You're…thank you." My throat felt full, my voice mirroring the emotion. "Take care."

Tanner took the basket from my hands and led the way out through the door and down the stairs. The summer night had the perfect smell, like a storm was coming. The air was cooler than normal and the sounds of the cicadas seemed to match the lightning bugs floating in the air. Peaceful. Pleasant. Comforting. I swore the knot it my chest loosened. *Is this what it's like, being normal?*

And happy?

Yeah, I think it is.

"Tanner, you don't have to carry that all the way back." I skipped up to him after I'd let myself enjoy the summer night for a full minute. "I can do it."

"It's either I keep my hands busy with this, or touching you. Your choice," he said, flashing his white teeth at me in a menacing smile. "Unless you have something else arranged, I still plan on keeping my word."

"Oh, the orgasms thing? Right. Forgot about that," I probed, enjoying how easy it was to rile him. He huffed, quickening his pace to the point I had to jog. "It's past midnight, so you actually didn't keep your word. My birthday is over."

"You're such a shit."

"Romancing me with such sweet words." I caught up to him and laughed when he gave me the poutiest look I had ever seen. "You're en route for a solo homerun, ya feel?"

He scoffed, but it caused me to laugh harder. I poked his ribs. "Like, you get yank your own chain with your hand?"

"Yeah, I get it, smartass."

"You seem a bit cranky. Did you not enjoy the card games? You won the most points *and* the first ever card champion, king of numbers award. You should be proud of yourself. I mean, sure, some guys get drafted into the Majors, but not everyone wins the pocket change, ChapStick and hair ties from their friends."

That snapped him out of his mood and his tight expression relaxed. "You're not wrong."

"I know. I rarely am." I blew him a kiss, the adrenaline from having such a good birthday leaking over into a weird sense of confidence and joy. He smiled at me and I swore, for one second, that smile meant something *more*. I didn't have time to reciprocate the gesture before we walked by a group of ladies hitting the town. *Cool, I'm in a Zwillows Pillows shirt.*

"Hey, Tanner!"

"My man, Tan!"

"Looking hot as fuck, TJ!"

They catcalled the centerfielder, running their fingernails through his hair and over his arms, as if he was a ride at a carnival. *Isn't he though, to them?*

Cleat chasers.

"Can't believe you turned down the draft, baby." One of the gorgeous girls stopped, letting her gal-pals continue walking so it was just us three standing there with my large basket in Tanner's hands. This chick wore black lipstick like it was her damn job. She'd paired it with an equally black outfit that caught Tanner's attention, but when she grabbed his chin in her hands, he pulled away.

"Felicia, we agreed. One time, that was it. I don't do more than once and I made that very clear. No time for relationships, ever."

"It was so good though." She said it with so much emotion I had no doubt it really had been *that good*. My chest felt tight, as if I'd suddenly come down with a cold, and I coughed a couple of times, hoping to relieve the tension. No luck, but it did draw their attention to me. The vixen grinned, her white teeth clashing with the black makeup, and I gave her an awkward wave that told her without a doubt I was a freshman.

"Your lipstick is fantastic," I blurted out. Her smile widened and she let out a little squeal. *Okay, that was weird.*

"Thank you! You're so sweet. Is she one of yours, Tanner?" Felicia gave me a curious glance, scanning my outfit before looking back at him. "She's not your usual type."

"Enough. She's Hilly's sister."

"Oh my god! Baby Hilly!" Her pitch went an octave too high and she opened her mouth to say more, but one of her friends hollered for her to join them and she gave us a sad smile. "I need to go. It's my best friend's birthday. It was nice meeting you, Baby Hilly, and, Tanner, we will enjoy a night together again."

His jaw tightened and he avoided my gaze until Felicia joined her friends. The pressure in my chest went away and I laughed. "Well, that was fun."

"We slept together once, a couple of months ago."

"Yeah, I gathered the evidence and reached the same conclusion. Did she wear the black lipstick then? I wanna know."

He rolled his eyes, a shadow of *something* crossing them, before they crinkled at the sides. "She did."

I burst out laughing and let go of the negative feeling that had rooted itself in my mind. "Did you mean what you said to her? You sleep with your ladies once and *bam*? Never again?"

He adjusted the basket in his grasp, switching it from his left side to the right, and ran his teeth over his top lip. "Typically. Maybe a handful of times. I think I did five hook-ups with a couple of girls."

Cool. Cool. Cool.

The pressure returned and I tried clearing my throat. "Does it get old?"

He exhaled loudly and made a face that did not look happy. "We don't need to talk about all this."

"Okay."

"Look, it's just—yeah. It does get old. But I don't have time for anything more with baseball. I've seen Aaron and Zade, the way their lives shifted to make room for another person. It works for them. They're stupid-happy. I think we both agree they're all a little annoying."

I snorted, agreeing. "Yup. Maybe even *a lot* annoying."

"I don't have room for more." He slid his knowing gaze to me, a hint of something deeper lacing his words, but we approached the street where the house stood and he lowered his voice to a dangerous tone. "I do have room for spending another night making you feel good."

Le sigh. "Homerun handy, remember?"

He chuckled hard at that and we quickly arrived at the house, Tanner rushing to open the door and setting my gift on the ground. I took two steps into the living room before he moved his arms around my middle, pulling me against his chest. Awareness shot through me. My nipples hardened when he bit down on my ear, his warm breath hitting the sensitive skin. I moaned, the sound echoing around the silence of the room, and he arched his hips into me, letting me feel all his hardness. "Tell me, Kenzie, do you still want my gifts, or do you want to go to bed alone?"

"I-I'd like my—" I stopped.

Tanner sucked my neck. His rubbed his rough jawline against me as his teeth grazed my flesh at an agonizing pace, like he had all the time in the world. I fisted the edge of his shirt behind his back, the intense desire to have him *now* startling me. "Upstairs," I breathed, earning a low growl from him.

He didn't waste another second. He lifted me over his shoulder in one swift motion and marched up the stairs, completing ignoring my protests. "Don't hurt yourself, Tanner!"

"I won't. Trust me. I needed you to move at my speed so this was my solution." He nudged my bedroom door open with his foot and dropped me to the floor. The air zinged every time our skin made contact, and it was no different when he reached out and traced my bottom lip with his thumb. My attraction to him flowed through my veins and I pounced. He made an *oomph* sound when my legs wrapped around him, but he reacted with the speed of an athlete. We moved to the bed, Tanner setting me on my back before devouring me with his mouth, tasting and claiming with each swift movement.

I didn't think about feelings or what ifs or sadness when he removed my clothes, kissing all over my body with precision. "Tanner, I want to feel you."

"I'm yours, baby." His voice was deeper in timbre and hearing it sent a thrill through me. I did that to him. He sucked one hardened nipple into his mouth, teasing my inner thighs with his fingers to the point I squirmed with need. "You're making an awful lot of sounds. Are you ready for me?"

"*God, yes*," I moaned, pulling his hair so his mouth connected with mine. "Please."

That was the magic word. He removed his pants, shirt and boxers within five seconds and sheathed himself with a condom from his disposed-of jeans. I licked my lips, loving how his muscles twisted with each one of his movements. "I'm not going to be gentle tonight, Kenzie."

"I don't want you to be."

He repositioned us so I was on my stomach. As I arched my hips, he guided himself into me from behind.

He went in slow, letting me adjust and pumping a couple of times. He gave the sexiest growl, lighting my body on fire with each thrust. Slow, then fast, Hard, then harder. He tightened his hold on my ass, squeezing the skin and fueling my desire.

"God, your body is perfect." He leaned forward and brought his fingers around to swirl my clit. He perfected the rhythm, matching his movements to his hips, and an orgasm built in my core, spreading through my veins and causing a slow explosion of pleasure. "That's right. Lose yourself with me, Kenzie."

Oh, I did.

I screamed his name as he quickened his pace, sweat pooling between my back and his chest. Our breathing came in pants and when he caged me in with his arms, the tingles began again, just out of reach. Tanner read my body, changing the angle so he went deeper. He pressed his lips against my neck, right where my back met my shoulder, and bit down. It was the added touch I craved, and I clutched the sheets in my hand when my third orgasm for the day overtook me. I panted, almost in tears at the strength of it, and Tanner's body tightened. "I-I'm—"

He gripped me tight, pumping into me four more times, an almost caveman sound coming from his mouth. "Kenzie, your pussy, *fuck*."

I lay there face down, unmoving as the high from my orgasms lingered and made words harder than normal. "Uh, wow."

He pressed his warm lips on my spine, then again, before he said, "Hold tight."

He got up and disappeared for a little, but I only managed to flip over and not much else before he returned. He stopped before entering my room, leaning on the bathroom doorway as if he had all the time in the world. He'd donned low-riding shorts and a grin that had me shivering. "Look at you."

"I lost feeling everywhere. Am I wearing anything? I don't remember." I grabbed my glasses from the side table and made a real scene out of looking down. "Oh, I guess I'm still naked."

He chuckled and made his way toward me, bending to pick up my clothes from the floor. "I'm not giving you Zade's shirt back."

"Um, it was a gift. Yes. I want it back."

"If you want a dude's shirt, I'll give you one."

"Don't get weird. I like it because it pisses Aaron and Zade off." I moved my feet from the bed to the floor, a wave of exhaustion hitting me. "I'll take it back, thank you."

He frowned but handed it to me. I put it on, forgoing panties and shorts, and enjoyed how his gaze didn't leave my legs. He ran a hand over his face and shook himself out of whatever funk he was in. "I don't think it would be too bold of me to say that you had a good birthday."

"I did." I grinned, yawning and hugging myself. "It was one of the best and you're one of those reasons. Thank you."

"You're welcome," he said, his voice getting low again. "I would ask to stay in here, but with Aaron…it'd probably be a terrible idea."

The tight feeling came back and I stretched my arms behind me, hoping it would relieve it, but it didn't. It just drew his attention to my boobs. "It would be awful. You'd pretend to sleep in the morning, letting me do the walk of shame, but it'd be my room and it would be horrible."

He laughed, but the light wasn't there in his eyes. "Good night, Kenzie."

"Night."

He wrapped his arms around me, pulling me in for a bone-crushing hug. It would be easy to lose myself in his muscles and safety, the way he cradled my head and understood me, so I broke the contact and pressed a kiss to his cheek. "I'll see you tomorrow."

He left, giving me one more look before leaving me alone in my room. I fell into my bed, ready for twelve hours of sleep. But it didn't come right away. A nagging, unsettling feeling kept taking root in my chest and I had no fucking idea what to do about it.

Why is Tanner breaking his rules with me?

Chapter Sixteen

Tanner

Off-days midweek were rare and while most guys were excited to have a day to do whatever the hell they wanted, the freedom bothered me. Coach wanted us to rest before leaving for a six-day road trip for summer ball. The thought of being on the road, staying in hotels and celebrating wins, was my shit. I loved it. It was a preview of what life in the Majors would be, but this time, a foreign sense of anxiety loomed over me. Maybe it was the phone call with my birth father, or worrying about my mom. Either way, it had me going to the gym for a light run to occupy my time.

"Yo, T!"

I glanced at Carter, fighting a laugh when I saw him and two other players also at the gym. *Glad we all have work-life balance.* "Hey, Carter."

"Why are you at the gym?"

"Dude, why are you?" I fired back, standing taller when Felix rounded the corner. He waved, unaware of my urge to punch his face. Carter hit my shoulder, like we were best buds, and called Felix to join our little chat.

"We don't own cars, really only know guys on the baseball team and this *punk* has the goddamn nerve to brag about getting Kenzie's number. I'd be furious if he wasn't my roommate."

"Wait—what the fuck did you say?"

"We don't own—"

"No. You have Kenzie Hill's number?" I asked, the desperate need to work out harder coursing through me. I cracked my knuckles and waited on edge for him to respond. When Felix nodded, I gritted my teeth. "Lose it."

"She offered it to me, man. Hilly can talk to me if he wants, but I'm not a bad guy." He gave me a bemused look and motioned to Carter. "I'm doing a quick rep on the machine and heading to the smoothie station."

"Cool, dude, see you soon." Carter gave me a weird look, a little too much comprehension on his face for my liking. But I didn't give him a chance to talk.

"I gotta head back. See your dumbass face on the bus tomorrow."

"We're friends, Tanner. You and I."

I ignored him, but I did have a slight smile on my face when I left the gym. The three-mile jog helped the boredom, but it did not help my anger at Felix or the new rush of adrenaline to my muscles. How did that kid have her number when he'd known her for five minutes?

Why don't I have it?

Because when I'm around her, I forget to ask. Well, that could be rectified, and sooner rather than later. I walked back to the house at a faster pace, showered and threw on jeans, a red shirt and my favorite hat. It would've been rude to barge into her room, so I knocked. Hell, I could be polite if I wanted.

No answer.

I knocked again, getting annoyed. It wasn't even noon, less than twelve hours from me being inside her — where would she be?

You could text her if you had her number, idiot.

Thanks for the helpful tip, brain.

"Hey, assface."

I spun and got a clear view into Hilly's bedroom. It was across the hall from Kenzie's and I hadn't even thought to check if he was home. *Not a good move for me.* Aaron had a stupidly happy expression on his face and I flipped him off as my greeting. He had a duffel bag on his bedroom floor and it reminded me I hadn't started packing for our trip. *Seriously, where is my head?*

"Where were you this morning? I wanted to see if you were down for watching the game this afternoon. Cubs versus Cardinals," he asked.

I eyed Kenzie's door and forced myself to act cool. "I went to the gym, but don't give me shit. Ran into a couple of the other guys there too."

"No judgment. I can't guarantee it, but I swear Zade snuck off to get some throws in." He smiled, the joyful, full-of-life dude I'd met three years ago flashing through. He always got that look when he talked about baseball. *We're a lot alike that way.*

And I'm banging his sister.

I suck.

I shoved the guilt down and nodded. "I'm down for the game. We watching it here?"

"Nah, the Lion. I think Zade invited some of the younger guys to come, to help us all bond and shit. Plus, G's training Kenz today. I'm hoping I can convince her to stay over here for a bit, or at least invite Kenz to stay there when we're gone."

That's where she is. Relief had me relaxing, but Aaron's face grew concerned and I needed to act quick. I nodded, a little too hard. "Good idea. I'm sure G and C would have her over."

"Why were you knocking at her door?"

Play it cool. "Found out she gave her number to Felix and wanted to ask about it."

Aaron blew out a breath and curled his lip before settling down. "Okay. Okay, yeah. See what she says."

I hated how guilty I felt, keeping something from him. There was no way telling him would amount to anything good. It didn't matter it was consensual, or incredible or perfect. I hit the railing and pointed to my room. "Wanna head there in thirty minutes?"

"You got it."

My normal routine consisted of packing my lucky socks, my favorite under-jersey shirts, and would end with the uniform. It had to go in a certain order. That way I could find my stuff as quickly as possible, and I preferred it that way. I had all my shit except toiletries packed when Aaron poked his head into my room, asking if I was ready to go.

We got about a block toward the bar before he asked, "How much was your signing bonus?"

Oh, okay then. We're going there. "Ten thousand. That was it."

"Fuck. Yeah, you're worth way more than that. Dude." He put his hand on my shoulder and squeezed. "Mine was even less."

"Wait, you were called?"

He nodded but didn't look happy about it. "It was underwhelming and in the midst of my parents moving.

Ever since I cut off all social media, people don't know shit about me and I like it that way. I haven't told anyone. Not my parents, Kenzie—hell, even Greta."

"Aaron. You should've—"

"Should've what? Told them? Get their hopes up? Nah, no thanks. I know I'll get more next year. You will too. I wanted to tell you…because, whatever it is you're going through, you're not alone." His tone got serious and it felt like a punch to the gut. "All I know is that you have some family stuff going on. I gathered that, but not much else. I'm not prying, just…what's the expression Coach always says? Extending the handshake?"

I laughed, hoping it hid the internal battle raging inside me. "Yup. Spot on. Thanks, man."

"I think it goes without saying this stays between us."

"Obviously." I gulped as we got closer to the Lion. It was so close, the truth about my family. It bubbled over, similar to how it had that night with Kenzie, but still different. This was my teammate, my brother on the field, and he'd shared *that* information with me… "I need the money to support my mom and my brothers. A service animal is fifty thousand dollars, for my brother who is blind, and my dad doesn't know where they are because he'll steal from them, so he comes after me. It's a fucking mess."

Aaron stopped walking, his laser-sharp eyes widening in shock. "Tanner."

"I know. *I know.* Let's not talk about it, okay? Making the Majors is *everything* for my family. That secret has been mine to keep the past three years. It was easy to act carefree and wild. I needed that escape."

"I get that."

"I know you do." I sighed and let the mixed feelings ravaging my mind settle. Something like relief and worry combined, making the ability to say the right words disappear. But Aaron took the lead, putting his hand on my shoulder.

"We'll keep pushing toward our goals. Anything you need, man, you just gotta say. Okay?"

"Yeah, for sure."

The same loyalty and brotherhood I felt on the field carried over into my personal drama and instead of feeling like a burden, it felt freeing. He didn't look at me with pity or worry...just friendship and trust.

Maybe I can tell the rest of the group.

He read the mood and we walked the rest of the way without saying another word. I appreciated the moment to myself and it wasn't until we walked into the bar and saw Greta's — and Kenzie's — boss, Clyde, that our banter was back. "This guy...he's something."

"I know." I laughed when Clyde walked up to Aaron and high-fived him. "Hey, Clyde."

"Behemoths. All of you. Well, find a seat. I'll tell Greta you're here."

We found a booth in the corner where a couple of our teammates filled the empty spots. My attention wondered until I found who I wanted and my mood lifted. No more thoughts of lying to Aaron, or hiding my past. Kenzie had a stupid grin on her face, those damn glasses falling down her nose and her hair up in that crazy bun. Greta was demonstrating something on the computer, and Kenzie seemed to be enjoying it.

She tilted her head and saw me watching her. It was stupid how my pulse quickened and visions of our last night together flashed through my mind. *She's fucking perfect.* I winked at her, getting her goofy, carefree smile as a response.

Everything felt right again.

More guys joined us at the table and I raised my glass to Greta when she brought another pitcher. "Thanks, G."

"Don't forget you guys have a game tomorrow. I know how rowdy you get and I will kick your asses out. It's only noon…on a Wednesday, fools." Her words didn't match the smile on her face or the way she teased some of the younger guys. They'd gotten used to her, she was around so much. In the best way, Greta redefined cleat chaser. Callie, too, but she'd interned with the team for so long that the guys knew her as well as they did our trainer.

At the thought of her, Callie entered with Zade and a small bout of applause exploded at an impressive play from the Cubs' third baseman. Since our town was in the center of Illinois, team loyalties were split between Chicago and St. Louis. It felt so fucking good to just hang with the team, drink beer and not worry about anything. *This*. This was what college was for me, the sense of belonging, the family, the trust, and I found myself scanning for Kenzie again. She had a place in this too.

It took a minute or two to find her, standing over a booth toward the entrance, her long legs on display in her black shorts. My fingers tightened around my glass. *Who's she smiling at like that?*

Fucking Felix. He had a dopey grin on his face and I thought of a million reasons why I, not him, could get her to smile. *Yup.* It was decided. I was going to talk to her about it. We had nineteen more chances to enjoy each other and sharing her didn't sit right with me. After that…hell, I'd think about it then, but I couldn't stand the thought of her hooking up with Felix. Or anyone.

Only hook up with Tallen. I'd write it on her dorky list. It'd be perfect because once it was written down, it was practically law.

But I never got the chance to talk to her — the game got heated after a fight broke out, the crowd jeering the TV and the beer flowing. It wasn't until two hours later that I escaped the booth with my teammates and caught her alone. She sat at a table, carefully placing silverware into napkins and rolling them up. She grinned when I sat opposite her and it didn't make sense how happy it made me to see that joy pointed at me, as if I'd caused it just by being there.

"Hey, Kenny, how's the first day?"

She leaned closer, her smile contagious. "Incredible!"

"Yeah? You look real happy." She did. Her face had lit up, her cheeks tinged a little red on the tops, like she'd worked out, and her lips were permanently curved upward on the sides. Happy. She was happy.

"There's just so much to do and I can get tips, which is awesome, so I don't have to worry about overspending my budget. It's so alive here. The people, the workers, even Clyde! He's so funny. But enough about that." She pushed the hair that escaped behind her ears and rested her chin on top of her hands, giving me an intense look. "How's the game? It seemed a little heated earlier."

"Oh, it's fine." I glanced back at the table of hooligans and ignored the way Zade stared at me with an accusatory expression. *Focus.* "Look, I want to talk to you about something."

"Okay?" Her smile fell a little and she blinked a couple of times.

"What time do you get off?"

"I think five? Before the dinner rush. Is this about…" She mouthed, *your mom*, and I shook my head.

"It's about your list."

"Oh, what about it?" I swore she tilted her head just a bit to the right at her question, and it charmed me. She wasn't assuming or ready to attack on what she thought I would say. She accepted it.

"There are a couple things to clarify. Specifically, with *Tallen*," I lowered my voice and watched the way she wet her bottom lip with her tongue. "I might need to make an addendum."

"Keep your talented hands off my list, Tanner Johnson," she fired back, leaning forward onto her elbows. Her face was only a foot away from mine, but it wasn't the time to get caught up in her.

"No promises."

"You wouldn't dare."

God, was it hot in here? I adjusted the neckline of my shirt and swore the electricity between us ebbed and flowed. *This is new.* "Enjoy the rest of your shift, Kenz. Find me when you get home."

"We'll see how I'm feeling," the tease responded, with an edge to her voice.

"*Find me*, Kenzie." I slid out of the booth and fought every urge to touch her. The little minx just winked at me in response and the anticipation of seeing her alone had my blood pumping.

No more fucking Felix. Just me.

Chapter Seventeen

Kenzie

We need to talk about your list. It wasn't worry or dread forming in my gut—it rivaled intrigue. What could he want to talk about? Adding more? Adding fewer times? *That could be it. Nineteen is a lot of hook-ups.*

Yeah, of course I edited the numbers each time we did it. I was an organized freak.

It stung, thinking about not getting to enjoy him again, but it made sense. He didn't have time for anything but baseball and I understood that. What I didn't understand was the fact we weren't talking about why we were continuing this. I didn't need affirmations from him, declarations that didn't matter, or promises. There were no expectations beyond hooking up nineteen more times, and that was the truth. I swept the foyer and let my gaze wander to the remaining players. They showed Dedication beyond anything most could comprehend outside of the sports world. I knew it—hell, I'd grown up with it.

Zade had his arm around Callie and toasted his beer to another kid on the team. Aaron looked on, the natural leadership in him making players flock to him with or without his permission. Tanner fitted in there too, with his silent style of leading and his intentionality of how he lived his life. He was intense, loyal, purposeful and, damn...I appreciated that about him. It showed in the bedroom and in all his friendships. *Tanner is a hell of a guy.*

"Looking a little flustered there, girl. Did Felix get the nerve to ask you out?" Greta knocked her hip into mine and spoke a little too loudly for my liking. She knew two volumes, excessive and obnoxious. Literally the only person to deal with my brother.

I laughed and shook her off. "Nope. Just sweeping and thinking. That's all."

"Your brother will fuck this up, but he wanted to talk to you about staying with us a couple of nights when they're gone for the week." She made a concerned face and I chose to understand her words as kindness, not as though I couldn't take care of myself.

"They're gone six days, huh? Long time."

"I know, it sucks. It's gunna be worse when they sign with a team next year, but..." Her voice trailed off and a deeply rooted sadness escaped. "No need to worry about it now."

I changed the subject, hoping to erase the look on her face. "I'm supposed to talk to Clyde about setting a schedule and, after I get mine, I'd love to hang with you gals for a couple of days."

Her expression shifted from sadness to joy really quickly and she pulled me into a half-hug. "I'm so glad. We like you, Kenz, for real. I know we're a lot to take but you're kinda sorta in our tribe and once you're in...you don't escape. We're like a friendship cult."

"I've always wanted a friendship cult!" I joked, getting a loud laugh from her. "Thank you for inviting me and getting me this job. It's been so wild and fun. I prefer to keep busy and, well, yeah, I love it."

"I knew it'd be a good fit. Fuck those idiot ballplayers. They don't know everything all the time." She gave me a coy smile before walking to greet the latest customers. It was still early afternoon and the crowd wasn't busy for a weekday. Clyde had told me that it could be packed at any given time during the school year, but the summer months were chill. *Fine by me.*

I finished sweeping and mopping the tiles and checked all the condiments at each booth. I was finishing up the final one when Aaron plowed into the empty bench across from me and I paused. "Yes, brother?"

"You'll be okay at the house alone? It's a big house."

"If I said no, would you stay home from your tournament?" I felt a little bolder and sat taller. "Forgive me, but, how many nights since I moved in have the three of you left me alone?"

"Shit. I'm doing it again, huh?"

"Being a bit of a twat? Yeah." I threw a packet of sugar at him and he caught it with ease. "Don't worry, Greta talked to me. I'll hang out with them a couple nights."

"Good. That makes me feel better. You don't have to be alone so much once you live in the dorms. You're fucking surrounded by people then and not left to fend for yourself in a massive empty house." He smiled, as if the thought of being alone was horrible. It didn't sit well with me.

"I don't mind being alone. Mom and Dad left me to watch the house for days at a time when all this started and I had a lot of time to deal with it. I'm not an extrovert like you, bro. Really, you don't need to worry. I like silence sometimes." I gave him a pointed look, daring him to contradict me, and he didn't. *Aaron can learn.*

"You'll let me know you're okay?"

"Yes. I'll send a carrier pigeon with a scroll detailing my safety."

"Such a fucking smartass." He rolled his eyes and got up from the table. "I'll be at Greta's tonight, but we'll do something fun when we get back."

"Sounds good."

He left and I continued my task. I'd barely finished when I was interrupted, again. Clyde poked his head over the booth ledge and gave me his typical blank look. "You're done. Want to talk about your schedule?"

I'd gotten used to it after one day, but even with Greta's warning, he was difficult to read. Like now, I didn't know if he thought I'd done a great job or a horrible one.

"Yeah," I replied, sliding out of the plastic booth and following him to his office. It stood in the back, beyond the U-shaped bar. He pointed to the blue plastic chair that had seen better days and chose the desk chair opposite me. A large burgundy binder that took up the entire desk held a calendar, and my god, my heart picked up pace at how organized it was. "Is that how you schedule staff?"

"Yes, why?"

"I love it." I leaned forward and admired his penmanship. Huh. Clyde was more my style than I'd thought. "You have great handwriting."

"Thank you." I swore he blushed a bit. "Now, you did good work today. Greta said you were focused and easy to work with and she didn't lie. I need help on weekends in the summer and, say, two weeknights. The school year will be busier, specifically during football season. The hours would increase then. You cannot serve behind the bar for another two years, but you can deliver to the tables, so I'll schedule you on the floor each time. Does that sound okay?"

"Yeah, that sounds great, Clyde! Thank you."

He gave me a semi-smile and pointed to the door. "I'll see you Friday and Saturday, three o'clock?"

"You got it."

"Welcome to the team, Kenzie Hill. You can leave for today."

I fought the urge to chuckle as I left his office. I was going to cross off *get a job* and *get my schedule* from my list the second I got back. With a huge smile, I waved to the remaining people in the bar and Felix held up a hand. He was sweet, almost innocent in how he flirted, and communicated in soft tones. I didn't get butterflies and my legs didn't press together when he was around, but I did enjoy chatting with him.

He was the complete opposite of Tanner, who was tall, hard, extreme and delicious. *Shit. Tanner is delicious.* The walk to their house was only about ten minutes and it was still light out so I headed there with more pep in my step than before. I could lie to myself and say it was because I loved my new job and schedule, but I knew it was Tanner. The heat in his eyes before he'd left...the almost predatory way he'd looked at me. Yup. We would have a fun night before he left. *And knock off another number from my literal someone-to-do list.*

I walked, a little breathless from my brisk pace, and found him relaxing on the couch in just a pair of loose shorts. His hair was messy in the perfect way, his jaw hinting at a day's beard and, *god*, I wanted to kiss him. He brought his gaze to my face and smiled so big I felt it in my toes. He spoke first, his deep voice like a siren, calling me to him. "A guy could get used to you coming home to him."

"Yeah?" I moved toward him, a moth to a flame, and stopped when the TV caught my attention. "Uh, what the hell?"

"Oh. This." He chuckled and curled his fingers around my belt loop, pulling me onto his lap. I straddled him, him bringing his hands straight to my ass and wasting no time exploring my thighs. He dragged his nose down my neck, my body betraying any resistance I had, and he nipped at my ear. "*Delicatessen.*"

"Huh?" Maybe it was the lethal combination of his lips and touches, but the word didn't make sense. "What?"

"I can't believe you didn't have this on your precious list, Ken. Our next film. *Delicatessen.* We have to write six paragraphs on how we felt about the visuals of it."

"Fuck." I leaned my forehead against his, grinding my hips against him before sliding down. "I forgot."

"When pigs fly. You forgot?"

"Shut up. I blame you." I arched up and grabbed his tousled hair, loving his throaty sounds of pleasure. "You're distracting."

"*You're* distracting."

We fought for control, kissing and tasting each other with a frenzy that didn't make sense. He'd left my bedroom less than twenty hours ago. We shouldn't be this crazed, but, fuck it. "Tanner," I breathed, biting down on his ear lobe. "I smell like fried food and beer. I'd like to shower. Dare I ask you to join me in five minutes?"

"Literally can't think of anything else I'd rather do." He held on to my hips and dug his fingers into my skin.

"God, thinking about your soapy body rubbing against mine… You might kill me, woman."

I giggled. Yup. I had a high-pitched giggle that sounded nothing like me. I hopped off him. "Five minutes."

"I'm counting down the seconds, Kenny. You better hustle."

I did hustle. I took the stairs two at a time, stripped out of my bar-scented clothes and threw them into the hamper in my room. I used mouthwash before turning the extremely hot water on, my body on fire with anticipation. *Will he lick every part of me, slowly?*

Yes, please.

I washed my hair, my face, and used my favorite floral body wash. I was still alone in the shower. *Where is he?* Worry took root and I second-guessed my invitation. Had I crossed a line, asking him to join me? Was that not part of our list game?

No. He wants me. I saw it.

Something must've happened. I'd felt how hard he was underneath me. It took me three minutes to put on shorts that flirted with an inappropriate length, a tight tank top that showcased my tits and throw my hair up into a wet messy bun. If something happened, I still wanted to drive him crazy.

My glasses were still fogged from the shower and I put them on as I stopped at the top of the stairs. Someone else was downstairs with him, talking. *My fucking brother.*

"This movie is about eating people?"

"Dude, I don't know. I'm not wanting to watch this shit," Tanner responded, his voice clearly showing how disgruntled he was. It made me bite my knuckle to not laugh.

"I can't believe you're taking the same class as Kenzie. You gunna watch all the movies together?"

"Obviously," Tanner said, and I knew I was the only one to hear the hitch in his voice. "She's heading downstairs now so we can get it over with before I leave."

"Kenzie loves weird movies... I do, too. Something fucked up about it, I know. Mind if I invite Greta over and watch it with you? This shit sounds interesting."

Tanner sighed. "Sure. We'll start it in ten minutes. I'm going to grab my laptop—make some popcorn, would you?"

"Hell, yeah."

Tanner's familiar footsteps approached the bottom of the steps. Our gazes met, his dark brown eyes warming at me sitting there. I put my finger to my lips and pointed to my room. He followed me, careful not to make any noise until I shut my bedroom door.

He ran his hands over my shoulders and down my sides until they rested on my lower back. He pulled me into his chest and closed the distance between our mouths. He growled, kissing me senseless for another minute before he pushed me away. "Fuck. I can't go down there with a boner."

"You left me alone, wet and soapy, in the shower. I think a boner is just fine." I traced his rigid cock from outside his shorts, enjoying how much I affected him. "I was so ready for you in there, wondering if you would eat me or—"

"Christ, yes. I would've." He got onto his knees and bit down around my hardened nipples, over my shirt and all. "Your goddamn brother."

"I know." I pulled him up by his hair and brought his mouth to mine. "One more kiss, please."

"You don't even have to ask, Kenzie."

His breathing hitched when our lips met. This one wasn't rushed or aggressive. It was tender, the way he cupped the back of my neck and kneaded his fingers into my shirt. He explored my mouth, knowing the perfect rhythm I craved. I melted into him and too soon, he stopped the kiss. "You're easy to get lost in. Put a sweatshirt on, head downstairs, and somehow we'll survive this fucking movie."

"Can't you kick him out?" I whined. I wasn't a whiner but by god, he made me one. "I can do it."

He chuckled, the sound magical, and pushed a lock of hair behind my ear. "I wish. We'll watch the movie and as soon as it's over, we'll head to bed separately. Keep your door unlocked, Ken. I'll sneak in so we can finish this."

And have our talk? I wanted to ask, but didn't. It was easier to go with the flow, not make promises, and he gave me one more fiery kiss, turning my thoughts into mush.

"See you downstairs and don't you dare sit by me. I won't be able to keep my hands off you."

"I don't know…it could be fun," I said, laughing at his horrified expression. He left my room, pointing his finger at me, and I planned how I could mess with him for the next two hours. Seeing him wild was my new favorite side of him.

Chapter Eighteen

Tanner

An hour into the movie, I deserved a fucking award. Kenzie thought it'd be a great idea for us to sit next to each other — thigh to thigh — on the smallest couch, so we could type our assignment together during the film.

"You just want to cross it off your goddamn list."

"Yeah, I like achieving everything I put on there," she replied, Aaron and Greta completely unaware how her eyes turned darker and how she moistened her lips every time she looked at me. Her double meaning wasn't lost on me, not one bit. That was why, sixty-five minutes later, I was almost dying.

She shifted her weight every couple of minutes, causing her warm body to touch mine, sending a straight shot of desire from my chest to my cock. She leaned closer to me and pushed those glasses up on her nose. I smelled her body wash — which got me hard when I used the shower we shared — and forced myself to not taste her skin just sitting there, inches from me. "What are you writing so far, TJ?"

I tilted my computer at her, the screen entirely out of view from Aaron and Greta, who sat on the couch ten feet away from us. An idea struck. It was either genius or stupid. I clicked out of the word document where I was typing our assignment and started a new one.

I can't stop thinking about putting my mouth on you. You smell so fucking good right now and I'm obsessed with that birthmark right under your collarbone. I'd start there, licking all the way down your sexy body, stopping on your perky nipples so desperate for attention, and moving to your clit, biting and teasing you until you scream my name.

She inhaled sharply, adjusted her computer in her lap so she could type. "Good idea. I think the colors of the scenes really shape the mood for viewers."

How the fuck could she think about the film right then? *Jesus.* All my blood went to my dick when I saw the faint outline of her nipples poking through her way-too-thin shirt. All I had to do was trace them and she'd go wild for me. If I brought my tongue to them, she'd buck under me and, god, I wanted it right then. *I'm a wreck.*

"TJ, you think my response works?" Her voice was so normal, unaffected by the turmoil ravaging through my body. It wasn't fair. She nudged me and tilted her screen to me.

Ah, fuck. My barely contained control threatened to break open, saying *fuck it* to keeping it secret. I gripped the edge of my computer harder, reading her sexy words.

I lose control when you use your teeth on me. It's a kink I didn't know I had. I wanted you all over me in the shower, spreading my thighs apart and eating me wild. It's a shame you couldn't make it up there…I almost had to take care of myself. You'd like that, wouldn't you? Watching me pleasure myself while you fisted your own dick?

All the air left my lungs. I choked, literally, and Aaron slid me a weird look. "You good, dude?"

"Uh, yeah. Water." I reached for the bottle on the floor and gulped it down. It was as if the words she typed grew and bolded in my mind, flashing like a billboard across my thoughts. *Pleasure myself. Watching me. Eating me wild.* When I calmed myself down enough to glance at her, she had the smuggest expression on her face. The only sign she felt anything was her pebbled nipples and that didn't bode well for me. *Nope.*

I wanted her to struggle through the next forty minutes, too, because I was a bastard. It took a lot of effort to join her again on the couch, and I positioned us so the blanket over our legs covered everything from her waist down. It was a challenge, balancing the laptop on one knee and sneaking my hand under the fleece. Aaron and Greta were curled into each other, their attention on the film, and Kenzie sat straight as a board when I grazed her knee with my fingers. I drew small circles on her heated skin, moving up her thigh to the edge of her dangerously short bottoms. Her chest moved faster now, the beaded points about to cut through the material. *Score. Now we're even.*

The light fabric moved out of the way with a slight flick of my thumb. I slipped inside the hem and found her completely bare, wet and ready for me. *Oh my god.* My body shook with need, every second I couldn't have her driving me insane. I tickled her folds, teasing her clit with my thumb just enough to have her clear her throat.

I paused at her sound, feigning interest in the fucking movie I gave no shits about. The other two still hadn't glanced our way and I went back to my plan. *What is my plan? I can't get her off with them here.* But I could get her primed and ready for the next thirty-seven minutes.

She sighed, leaning her head back on the back of couch and blinking way too much to be natural. I stilled my thumb, teasing two fingers inside her, in and out, slow and steady, the gestures not moving the blanket one bit. It was the hottest thing I had ever done in my entire life.

She sucked her bottom lip into her mouth when I swirled my thumb on her swollen clit, combining the motion with my thrusting fingers, and she reached out and gripped my shirt in her hands. The laptop shielded the motion from her brother, but my control was disappearing every fucking second.

I had to stop. Everything would be ruined if Aaron knew and I couldn't keep playing this sick game without blowing it, so I removed my hand from under the blanket and saw a bit of relief in her face. *Am I a bastard?* Maybe. But it was worth it. I brought my fingers that had been inside her to my mouth, closing my lips around them and tasting them. Her eyelashes fluttered, literally fluttered, and she let out the tiniest helpless moan that I felt deep in my chest.

We settled into our positions, her cheeks a little redder than before, and I counted the seconds until the movie would end. It physically caused me pain, watching her breathing and not being able to touch her. *This* type of craving was new.

Twenty minutes left... Kenzie chewed on her lip, keeping her gaze straight toward the TV. Fifteen, nothing had changed. I couldn't recall a single thing that had happened during the movie and it might be one of those times I bullshitted my way through an assignment, because every few minutes I studied her. The way her neck curved at a perfect angle, the dusting of freckles on the tip of her nose, and the innate confidence very few girls I met had. *What the fuck is this?*

I felt eighty years old when Aaron rose from his chair and grinned. "That was some movie. Damn, I don't know if I liked it or not."

"I know, I can't either. It's worth watching again, I think, but it left me feeling weird. Like, it was a love story but also insanely creepy. My mood is confused," Greta said.

I know the feeling.

Kenzie cleared her throat and clutched her laptop against her body. God, I liked looking at her. Her glasses slid down her nose and she pushed them up before addressing her brother. "I'm going to head upstairs to finish my paper before I forget. That way, I can ask you questions if I have any. Sound good, Tanner?"

"Uh huh."

"Cool." She smiled and wished Aaron luck for the tournament. "Play well and don't get hurt."

"Text me every day."

She blew out of the side of her mouth and made a dumb face at him. "Fine. I'll see you later, Greta."

That left me trying to figure out the perfect excuse to head upstairs. What would not be suspicious? A shower? Homework? No. Hilly knew me too well and I racked my brain, hoping for an answer that would work. Sweat formed down my back and I was a second away from telling him the truth when Greta asked him, "Want to go for a late dinner?"

"Hell, yeah. Want anything, TJ?"

"I'm good. Thanks though."

They took their sweet fucking time picking up their stuff, walking to the door and locking it. The fucking millisecond the lock clicked, I barged upstairs and into Kenzie's room. Only, she wasn't there. *What the hell?*

"Kenzie?" I searched the bed, her closet then the bathroom. She was nowhere. But then, I heard her whisper from *my* room. She lay there, under my covers on my bed with just her bare shoulders showing. "You're waiting for me in my bed."

"Yup."

"Naked?"

"Oh yeah."

Pounce. It was a goddamn miracle how I ripped off my clothes and joined her under my blue sheets. She was ready and needy for me, the perfect combination. I kissed her neck and removed her glasses to set them on the nightstand. Kissing wasn't enough—licking wasn't either—and I dug my fingers into her ass. "Fuck, you drive me crazy."

"Don't talk. Put your mouth on me."

My type of woman.

I obeyed and took those perky nipples into my mouth, sucking and teasing until they hardened. She moaned, pulling my hair and squirming the longer I did it. Her sounds fueled me and our passion almost became aggressive. She scratched her nails down my back when I moved to kiss her stomach, dragging my tongue across her sweat-covered skin until I got to her clit. "Tanner, yes."

I gave her what she wanted in record time. She screamed my name—my new favorite sound—and I ate up every ounce of her pleasure. My dick hurt at how much I wanted to be inside her, but I waited until she came down from her high and looked at me with her sexy, heated eyes. "I'm not going to last long."

"I don't need you to. Get on your back, Tanner."

Holy shit.

I did, and she found the condom I'd left on the table and opened it with her teeth. She made sure to not break eye contact when she slipped it on my dick, rolling it down with a patience I never had, and straddled me. "Jesus, you going to ride me, baby?"

"Absolutely."

She took her time letting me enter her, her walls tightening around me when I pushed farther. She clutched my pecs, her hair wild and all over the place, and I couldn't get enough. I held on to her hips and helped her figure out the pace—slow, then fast, hard, then soft. We found it and sweat formed between our smooth skin. "Give me your mouth."

She giggled and lowered her upper body so I could kiss the hell out of her. Her nipples tickled my chest and I used a free hand to pinch one, then the other, and she bucked against me. "Tanner, I-I…"

"Want do you need?"

"Touch me, down there."

I did and she cried out my name not long after, her hair falling in my face as the tingle of an orgasm started in the base of my spine. She arched her hips, giving me a better angle, and fuck, that did it. Four more thrusts, and I spilled into her, kissing her neck and palming her ass in my hands. Heaven.

She. Felt. Like. Heaven.

"Kenzie, wow. Just…" I couldn't finish. My body hummed with the lingering pleasure and I made sure to lift her off me carefully, setting her next to me. "I'm spent. One hundred percent spent."

"Samesies."

I chuckled and patted her leg before cleaning myself up. When I returned to my room, it startled me to see her lying there, in my bed, and I didn't have the urge to run her out. I always wanted hook-ups gone after it was over. There wasn't anything I cared to talk about with *them*, but Kenzie... I couldn't decide what to bring up first. The fact that I would miss her for the next week, that I didn't know what that meant, or the issue of making our...situation...exclusive.

She saw me staring at her and sat up. "Shit, you don't like it when they linger." She stood, covering her boobs with her hands, but before she'd taken three steps, I had my arms around her, carrying her back to the bed. "Uh, Tanner, whatcha doing?"

"I'd prefer if you stayed."

"I'd prefer that, too."

I couldn't explain the flutter in my chest when she said those words and I didn't need to. "I'd offer you a shirt, but I like you naked."

"Clothes waste time."

"God, you're incredible." I laughed and pushed back the covers so we could get under them. She did, and something about her kind and carefree expression pulled at my heartstrings. I continued to stare at her, when she twisted her mouth into a smirk. "What's that look for?"

"Just thinking I better add a check to my list and change it to eighteen."

"Uh, no." I turned onto my side, resting my head on my hand and dragging my fingers down her neck, collarbone, and ending on the curve of her breast. "Those times were specifically in *your* bedroom. Not mine."

"Really now?" she asked, scrunching her nose in the cutest fucking way. "I don't remember stating those rules."

"We did. You must've forgotten when I brought your clit to my mouth. Easy mistake. I'll forgive it this time."

"You're so kind," she mumbled, scooting closer to me so our faces were a breath apart. "We never got around to talking about my list—another easy mistake—but what did you want to talk about?"

Oh, right.

"I wanted to make sure—" Footsteps headed up the stairs, the heavy thud definitely not Greta's. "Shit. Just in case go—"

Knock. "TJ, you decent?" *Aaron.*

Kenzie had a look of horror on her face and I brought my finger up to her lips and mouthed, *go to the bathroom.* She nodded, her eyes larger than I had ever seen them, and trod carefully across the floor, her curvy ass distracting me for a second.

"TJ?"

"Uh, yeah. Hold on." I scrambled to find the nearest pair of shorts and threw them on. Kenzie got inside the bathroom, shutting the door to my side without making a sound, just as Aaron walked in. "Thanks for waiting. What if I was jerking one off?"

He barked out a laugh before saying, "Yeah, you never do before a game. Helps keep you focused. Wasn't that the bullshit you gave us last year?"

Oops—I forgot about my rule. "I play better pent-up. What did you need?"

"Right. My left shoulder has been giving me some trouble. I iced it with Nicole a couple of days but it's still pinching. Do you have that muscle relaxer from your pulled muscle last year?"

"Ah, yeah. I think it's in the bathroom."

"Sweet. I'll grab it."

"I can—" I froze when his fingers closed around the handle. I had no idea if Kenzie was in her room or had clothes on or was standing there, listening. *If we get caught...*

"Get the fuck out, Aaron!" Her voice came from the behind the door and Aaron jumped back, mortified.

"Hurry up. I need to get something from under the sink."

"I'm busy."

"Are you taking a shit or what?"

"I will *kill* you, Aaron. I swear to god."

Aaron laughed real hard and hit the doorframe before giving me his attention. "Can you grab it for me when she's...done in there?"

"You got it."

"I bet it's entertaining sharing a bathroom with her."

"You could say that." I kept my face passive, hoping he didn't suspect anything more than I was willing to share. Yeah, it was more than entertaining to have her in the room next to mine for the rest of the summer. It was torture, but yeah, I just nodded. *Keep it cool.* "I'm not bored."

He snorted and moved to my door. "Thanks for being so chill about letting my little sis live here. I appreciate it."

I'm the fucking worst. "Of course."

"See you tomorrow. I gotta get back to Greta." He walked into his room and left his door open. It felt weird to shut mine, as though he was baiting me. But that didn't make sense. Aaron would punch me in the face if he knew, I was sure. I waited five minutes before moving to the bathroom and grabbing the relaxer from under the sink. I poked my head into Kenzie's room, saw her with her goddamn list and winked at her.

She made an impatient face and crossed her arms. "I wasn't taking a shit."

"I know," I replied, hoping I kept my smile from breaking through. "Nice cover, by the way."

"Yeah, go give that stuff to my brother. I'm not done being embarrassed."

"You're so fucking cute."

I didn't mean to say it to her, but it came out and I had to own it. "Stay put, Kenzie. We still have to chat."

Chapter Nineteen

Kenzie

I eyed my list, adding more to it and crossing off the stuff I'd already done. *Getting a job, getting a schedule, hanging with Greta.* Those were all completed and the new addition to staying at Greta's place was written under the last one. *Finish biology homework.* I wasn't looking forward to having the guys away for a week, but I could use the time to get as much work as possible done for that class. It was brutal, tedious and not even a sliver of fun.

Ruled out majoring in science.

I tapped my favorite pen on the edge of the notebook and waited for Tanner to return. With Aaron and Greta staying here ruining our secret fling, I had no idea what to expect. We had been close to getting caught, the fear and adrenaline from that almost out of my system in the thirty minutes since my brother had asked if I was taking a shit. *God, I could wring his neck.*

How mortifying. *No. Just, ugh.* I shook out my hair and my glasses didn't fall off. *Shit. Oh my god.* I'd left them in Tanner's room when I'd snuck out. If Aaron had seen…

Tanner chose that moment to come through the shared bathroom with my glasses in his fingers. "Figured you were missing these."

"Mind reader." I stood from my bed and went to grab them, but he unfolded them and put them on my face. It was…sweet. "Thanks."

"Don't take this the wrong way, but I'm starting to hate your brother."

I snorted, my shoulders shaking at his exclamation. "Join the club." I nervously looked at my closed door and the bathroom and cringed. "Do you think we're good?"

"Yeah. I went to grab a snack, chatted with them for a bit about the Fourth of July tournament and made my way up here with the excuse I was tired." He jutted his chin toward the bed and grinned. "Ah, the list is already out. Excellent."

I jumped onto the bed. I held the list against my chest when he joined me a second later. We leaned against the headboard — like we'd done a handful of times before — and he reached for my pen. "You are not authorized to use my pen. We can discuss addendums, but you cannot change them yourself."

"Disagree." He was much stronger, bigger and faster than I was and he had the pen out of my hand in a heartbeat. "Now, let's see what I should change."

"Tanner, your handwriting isn't the same as mine. If you write, I'll have to redo it all. Trust me, my insane quirks know no bounds." I pleaded with my eyes, holding out my hand for him to return the pen. He did not. I blamed that for why I leaned closer to him, why he put his arm around my shoulders and why we sat cuddled together like a...couple. Because he took my pen.

"I see you added some stuff and shit, *there's* your reminder to watch *Delicatessen*. Safe to say neither of us watched that movie." He laughed, the deep sound vibrating in his chest, against my shoulder. He was so warm. "Ah, yes. This is what I wanted to discuss. This line."

He pointed the tip to the line, *do it with Tallen eighteen times*. "I'm adding, *in your bed*, to the list. So we know it's more specific."

"And if it's in the shower, or your room, in doesn't count?"

"Exactly. When those fuckers are gone, we have the whole house to explore." He winked and squeezed his arm around me, forcing me to snuggle closer. I didn't hate it. Nope. Not at all.

"Okay, *I* can add that part to it so the writing stays the same." He let me snatch it back, because we both knew he would overpower me. I added *in my bed* to it and sighed. "Now that we have that taken care of, anything else?"

"Yeah." He stilled, using his free hand to run through his messy dark locks. His muscles tensed, that action showcasing his delectable jawline. "I, uh, we both know this is a fling, right?"

"What we're doing? Yeah. I know." The pressure came back in my chest, and I made a mental note to drink some orange juice and buy vitamins to prevent any more sickness. "Why?"

"You're not seeing, uh, anyone else, right?"

"Tanner, why the hell are you nervous right now?" I would've laughed if he didn't look so uncomfortable.

"No, I'm not seeing anybody. I'm free as a bird, having all sorts of adventures before college."

"Can you add the word *only* to that bullet point?"

I frowned, thinking about what he meant when I stared at the line more. *Do it with Tallen eighteen times in my bed.*

Do it with only Tallen eighteen times in my bed.

"Ah, I get it." I added the word for him, not entirely sure why my heart hammered behind my ribcage to the point my throat hurt. It felt heavy, like this awkward conversation wasn't what I was prepared to do. "Noted. Just you."

"I hated seeing you flirt with Felix."

He said it in such a soft voice, I would've missed it if I hadn't been pressed right next to him. It wasn't jealousy, or a passive-aggressive comment meant to entice. It was how he felt. I remained quiet too long — or just the perfect amount — because he continued, "I have no right to ask this of you, so tell me to fuck off if you want, but while we complete your genius to-do list, I don't want to share you."

Damn.

"Do you tend to ask this of all your hook-ups?"

"No, that's the thing." He repositioned me so I stared straight into his gorgeous eyes. "I've broken a couple of rules with you, Ken."

"Are these rules like the speeding limit, where you're kinda allowed to go five miles over? Or like unforgivable curses? I need specifics." *Yes, use humor because I'm uncomfortable with my emotions. Real mature.*

"Such a dork. My rules have always been pretty simple. Don't hook up more than three times, don't have sex the day before a game and baseball is life."

"So you're saying your rules are your version of my list."

"Yeah. I guess, yeah. So how would you feel if your list went to hell?"

"Disorganized. But, Tanner, I'm still confused what all this means." I chewed on my bottom lip, hating the haunted look in his eyes. If he wanted to end this...thing, it'd hurt. More than I cared to admit.

But that doesn't make sense.

He exhaled, his breath hitting my face and a sliver of a smile popping out. "I don't know what this means, and I'm not able to try and figure it out. All I know is I enjoy spending time with you. It's selfish of me to ask you to not see other people, so I won't ask it outright. I will say, I don't plan to see anyone else while we're under your to-do list contract."

"I dig that." My entire face felt on fire and I held out my hand. "Let's shake on it. Just us, hanging out and not thinking about anything but having fun until we finish my list."

His grin grew, those goddamn dimples peeking out, and he took my hand. "Remember, those are only in your bed."

"Yes, Tanner, *that* is the most important thing of this discussion. Thank you," I replied, my sarcasm not lost on him. "This felt heavy, huh?"

"Yeah, I don't like heavy." He chuckled and released his grip on me. "Shit, it's late. We leave early tomorrow. I should get some sleep."

"Of course," I said, hating the slight break in my voice. "Good luck. You'll play well. You always do. Just, get on base more, would ya?"

It was the right thing to say. His eyes lit up with humor and he flipped us so he lay on top of me, our mouths aligned so he could easily drop his to mine. He kissed me, all playful and light, before moving to the floor. "Such a pistol. I'll see you in six days, then."

"See you in six days."

He stared at me a little longer, my cheeks heating at his attention, and shook his head before leaving my room. I had no idea what *that* look meant, but it made feel weightless. It took no time for me to set my list and glasses on the nightstand, close my eyes and fall asleep.

I was dreaming about thunderstorms and dancers — not related to my life at all — but it didn't matter. It startled me when the bathroom door opened. My room was still dark and I squinted at the figure entering. My pulse raced in my ears and fear shot adrenaline through my veins until I realized it was Tanner. "What are you doing?"

"Shh, go back to sleep. I was saying bye." He smelled freshly showered, a combination of soap and his aftershave tingling my nose, and I wanted to spray that smell on my pillow. He turned on the lamp next to my bed on and peered at me. "You look like an angel sleeping. A messy one."

"Oh god, what a line," I mumbled, covering my mouth with my hand. Morning breath was the worst.

"Not a line." He approached my bed, sat on the side and dropped down to kiss my lips. It was tender, totally out of the blue and it felt as though I was falling. "Where's your phone?"

"On my desk, I think."

"What's your password?"

"Seven-one-four-three."

"Great." He moved his fingers over the screen and gave me a huge smile. "I wanted you to have my number. Feel free to use it."

"You woke me up for that?"

"Sure did. Now go back to sleep, Kenny." He pushed my hair off my face and pressed his lips to mine for a kiss that was way too short. "We'll talk soon."

* * * *

I overestimated being cool about staying in the house alone. For one, I didn't take into account how boring it was not having sounds around me. Sure, watching the house when my parents went from appointment to appointment hadn't been fun, but I could entertain myself in my room with movies and favorite TV shows. This place wasn't mine, and even after spending five hours doing Biology homework, I was bored. I itched to do more.

Like text Tanner.

No. Chill.

It wouldn't hurt anyone for me to talk to myself, but that would cross a personal line of losing my mind. Instead, I made a nice pot of macaroni and attempted to watch *Delicatessen* again. Dressed in sweatpants, a ratty shirt that had seen better days and not an ounce of makeup on, I lounged on the couch. I got halfway through the movie, the unsettled feeling not sitting well with me. What did I need? It sure as hell wasn't orgasms. Nope. I'd had more than enough the past week.

Holy shit. Only a week?

I rubbed my eyes and hated the self-doubt consuming me. Did I text him, did I not? Why did I need to? *To see how he played, duh.*

Right.

I found my phone and typed the message three times before perfecting it.

Kenzie: I'm watching this weird movie again, wishing you were here. Let me know how you played today.

Three dots appeared right away and my stomach did a somersault.

TJ: Are you thinking about my hands on you?

Kenzie: Most of the time, yeah. It's not healthy.

TJ: Glad it's not just me then. I played well. Hit a triple and got two singles. We're back at the hotel now. I'm sharing a room with your brother.

Kenzie: Well, that scraps my idea of phone sex.

TJ: I just spit my drink out. Thanks for that.

Kenzie: Anytime. I'm glad you played well.

TJ: Missing me yet?

Kenzie: I barely notice you're gone.

TJ: Riiight. I'll try and call you later if I can. We're going to fuck with some of the younger players. I'll be the big man here and admit it. I miss your face.

That sent an unrecognizable thrill through me. No one had said that to me before, ever. It was stupid. It wasn't some compliment or declaration of love, but it made me feel…desirable. Liked. *I'm being a dumb girl with a crush.*

Kenzie: I do have a nice face.

TJ: And a nice ass…

Kenzie: You know how to make a girl blush, that's for sure.

TJ: I know you blushed when I licked my fingers after being inside you.

Kenzie: Jesus, TJ. You went from level one to ten real quick. How is it possible to be turned on, again?

TJ: Shit. This backfired. I wanted to tease you, not get you hot, because now I'm gunna have a fucking boner in front of the guys.

*Kenzie: **shrugs nonchalantly***

TJ: We're heading out. FYI – the guys think I'm hooking up with some chick named Mackenna.

Kenzie: Mackenna? Of all the names to come up with, you chose one that similar to my real name?

TJ: It's clever, I know. Okay, talk soon, babe.

Babe.
Babe.
I shouldn't read into it. It was a pet name for people who fucked. Yeah, I'd heard him use it on other girls before. It wasn't not a big deal. "Ugh, get a fucking grip." I tossed my phone onto the other couch, out of my reach, and forced myself to finish the movie and do my assignment. Shoving emotions down to where I didn't actively think about them was a talent I'd mastered living with my parents the past two years. This was no

different. I didn't think about Tanner or whatever feelings I had for him.

I certainly didn't think about the disappointment when he never called.

Chapter Twenty

Tanner

Life had a funny way of making me suffer. I hated distractions and refused to let something keep my mind away from baseball, yet here I was, in the dugout of our third game of the day, anxious as fuck for it to be over. I'd *never* counted down minutes until I could leave the field. Ever.

I could tell myself it was because I was worried my mom would try calling me and something could have happened—despite talking to her two days ago. I could blame my birth father's tactics, too. But if I was real with myself, it was because I somehow couldn't let Kenzie know my phone had gotten smashed the night before, after I'd told her I'd call her.

Fucking bad luck.

"Johnson! You're on deck. Get out there." Our bench coach spat out a bunch of sunflower seeds, like he always did, and narrowed his beady eyes at me. "Get your head out of your ass and focus. This pitcher is struggling to keep it in the zone. Knock it out of the park, TJ."

I nodded and grabbed my helmet and bat. It wasn't that I wasn't into the game—because I was—it was unsettling how I worried about how Kenzie was feeling. This was new for me. Letting a girl into my tightknit boundaries. *No, focus on the game.*

Stretching and shaking myself out of the funk, I did my practice routine in the on-deck circle, swinging three times and timing it with the pitcher. Aaron had batted before me and had already struck out twice. The pitcher had been nasty all game, but he was fading. *Sixth inning is when to strike.*

Aaron hit a soft liner just over the shortstop's head and the dugout broke out in cheers. We were down two runs, tired from playing all day and just needed a momentum changer. I could fit the role.

I walked up to the batter's box, eyeing the signal from my coach. He tapped his shoulder, forearm, wrist and shoulder again. *Hit and run.* That meant I had to make contact with the ball, because Aaron would be stealing second. I hit my helmet twice, assuring him I'd gotten the message, and got into my stance. The pitcher stared me down, but it was a futile attempt. He looked twelve. He did his wind-up, and fired a pitch on the outside corner. *My sweet spot.*

I cocked my arms and pulled back, twisting my hips and connecting the bat to ball with a loud pop. I knew. I knew it would be out of the park but I hustled to first until I heard the umpire yell, "Homerun!"

Our team hollered when I rounded third and stepped on home. This feeling was the best in the world. The high, the satisfaction of knowing I'd done it. *Nothing can replace this.* It helped. I didn't think of Kenzie at all for the rest of the game, or during the celebrations after getting first seed in our bracket.

This was my life. Baseball, celebrations, teammates. I was on my path, the right journey, and it felt perfect. Coach pointed to the scouts in the stands that game and told me two of them had asked for a schedule to see me play again. *Me.*

I'm making the draft next year, in the round I want.

Hours later, it was just after dinner and I was still without a phone. I couldn't recall a time I had gone this long without one. Elementary school? Junior high? Before my birth father had conned money out of us, I'd had an old flip phone that I'd used to call my mom for a ride after practice...but it didn't text. Yeah, that long, over twelve years, I hadn't gone twenty-four hours without my phone.

Yeah, I had a technology addition, but who didn't?

The coaches gave us a prep talk for the following day and Zade went into his room early to study the batter's patterns. Novatown – our opponent the next day – had heavy hitters and few weak spots, but Willows would study and get them. That left Aaron and me chilling in our room and I broached the subject I was desperate to open. "How's your sister handling the house?"

"Okay so far. She's at work now but I think Greta's having her over tonight after their shifts." He adjusted his position on the couch and switched the TV to a Cubs game. He whistled at a play where their shortstop dove four feet to backhand a grounder then jutted his chin at me. "You were on fire today, TJ. You're hitting the ball so fucking well. What's changed?"

"Desperation," I barked out an awkward laugh and tried to bring the topic back to *her*. The girl I shouldn't be thinking about so much. "I uh, am glad to hear Kenzie's doing well. I know you were concerned."

He gave me a grim nod and leaned back onto the couch with a loud sigh. He put his arms behind his head and studied me with haunted eyes. *Eyes the same shape as his sister's.* "Thank you for being a friend to her. I didn't realize she needed one, and I sure as hell wouldn't have picked you to be one, but I'm glad nonetheless."

I swallowed down my guilty thoughts and shrugged, hoping to look as nonchalant as possible. "I like her. It's not a hardship."

He relaxed his jaw at my comment, giving me a quick smile. "This is good for you."

"What is?"

"Being friends with a chick for once."

I'm going to hell. Fuck. I needed to think of something, anything to not give it away. One second, two seconds, three seconds went by and I hadn't answered. Then, by a small miracle, his phone went off and he mumbled *Greta* under his breath. He slid his fingers over the screen, no doubt texting her back, and I waited for him to look at me. "Not my first time being friends with a girl. Greta, remember? We never got together."

He did not like my reference to his girlfriend's minor crush on me the year before, one that we never talked about but one I loved to bring up. His eyes turned competitive and he muttered, "Fuck off."

"Just saying the truth. Sorry you can't handle it."

"That shit still drives me crazy. Like, I don't get it," he scoffed and chucked a hotel pillow at my face. It had the reverse effect he wanted. I caught it, laughed and tossed it back to him. "Okay, so yeah. Not your first time, but it's still good for your ego."

"Whatever, man." *Anything to move away from this conversation.* "Hey, it's not too late, I might go get another phone. I don't like being out of reach if my mom calls. Wanna tag along?"

"I might hang back here and stretch more. My arm has been killing me and it's pissing me off. Plus, it's the fifth inning and Cubs are down one run. I wanna finish the game. That cool?"

Even better. "For sure. See you in a bit."

I took off from the hotel after asking him to find me the nearest store. It was about half a mile away and I made the walk in good time. The anxiety from earlier came back and I hated it. *Will she be upset with me? Mad? Not believe me?*

Is she okay?

This was the bullshit I avoided. Fuck. *I don't do relationships.*

But this wasn't one. I relaxed at that notion and marched into the store. It cost fifty dollars with the insurance I'd paid for the phone — *thank god I could afford that* — and my phone was up and running after twenty minutes. My gut danced with nerves as I waited for it to power on, and when it did, I thought I'd have texts or calls. They could've been from my mom or Kenzie, but instead, they were from random chicks who had my number. Dissatisfaction flowed through me. *Why didn't she text me?*

I called Kenzie first, waiting for her to pick up, but Aaron's words replayed in my mind. *She's at work. Fuck.* I'd have to leave a voicemail.

"Hey, Kenzie, shit. I am so sorry I couldn't call or text. One of the freshmen ran into me and my phone shattered on the ground. We had games all day and I just now got a chance to get a new one. I know you're probably at work, but, let me know when you get home, okay?"

Click.

There, that would have to do. My phone buzzed, not five minutes later, on my walk back, from a text.

Kenzie: Sorry about the phone issue, thanks for telling me! At work now, taking a quick break for food.

Tanner: You're...you're not mad?

Kenzie: Well, are you lying?

Tanner: No! I swear. Ask your brother.

Kenzie: Then why would I be mad? It's not like you could ask Aaron to text me. Lol.

Tanner: I thought you'd be upset with me.

Kenzie: Sorry for trusting you? I can throw a fit if you want.

Kenzie: You lying scum. No more sex for you.

Kenzie: Is that better?

I laughed. She was a riot. My smile hurt my face and any ounce of anxiety I'd had moments earlier left. She wasn't mad at me. *How refreshing.*

Tanner: Save the fit until I get back. I want to watch you stomp around.

Kenzie: I bet you would, horn dog. Oh! Clyde needs me back. Good luck tomorrow! Aaron said you guys played really well.

Tanner: Thanks, Ken. Be safe getting back.

Kenzie: There goes my plan to run up and down alleys alone shouting 'I'm rich'.

Tanner: Smartass. Have you always been this way?

Kenzie: Yup. My tits distracted you though, so really, it's not your fault you didn't notice.

God, I laughed again and almost ran into a streetlight. *Shit. I shouldn't walk and text.* I waited to see if she sent anything else, but she didn't, so I assumed she'd gone back to work. That left me heading back to Aaron, her fucking brother, who I couldn't tell a single thing to. *Great.* My high from the games lessened and I accepted the fact I couldn't talk to her.

* * * *

Three days later, after seven more games, four strike outs and a pulled muscle in my leg, my mood plummeted. I played like shit, got hurt and wanted to punch anyone who disagreed with me. Scouts were there, at the fucking tournament, and they saw it. My teammates tried to pick me up or encourage me that I'd be fine, but they asked too much. They didn't get it—if I couldn't be one of the best, then my future was tarnished. *One injury could set me back for months, years even.*

I replayed the entire day in my mind, stretching, warming up, icing after the games. Nothing had been out of place in my routine, and yet, I'd felt a pull when I rounded third and had to be taken out of the game to *make sure I was fine.*

Not only had I not scored a run that would've tied it, but the backup centerfielder had made two errors. We lost. Yeah, it wasn't the regular season, but the loss felt heavy on my shoulders, mixing with my guilt and pressure to be the best.

Again, face punching sounded great.

"TJ, how's the leg?" Zade gave me a pitying look. He was carrying equipment from the dugout to the team bus — we were headed back early since the games had ended ahead of schedule. It was a four-hour trip back and already six p.m., and the thought of sitting in a cramped seat sounded like hell.

"It sucks," I said, hoping he'd leave me alone. Some people liked company when they were in pain. Others, like myself, preferred the solace of my attitude. "I'm the reason we didn't place in the tournament. I got on base three times? Fuck. That's shit."

"Nah, man, none of us've been finding gaps the past two days." He shook his head at me and laughed. "It's more important that you're healed and healthy for the spring. I know you're competitive and driven, but this'll only put you back a week or so. Use that time to rest."

"Chesterfield was here." One of the scouts from a west coast team. He'd nodded to me the day before and he could have approached and started a conversation, but he hadn't and my gut told me it was because I'd gotten hurt. *And played like shit. Who strikes out twice in one game…against a freshmen pitcher?*

I did. And for fuck's sake, I didn't know why.

"He's from NorCaL Cactus," I said, when Zade continued to look at me with an uneasy expression. "One of my top five teams to be drafted."

Zade sucked in a breath and that was response enough. But, being the perfect example of a team captain, he found a silver lining. "Injuries happen in the game. You might be pouting a bit now, but you handled yourself well when you got hurt. That matters, so don't get in your head and fuck it up. Okay?"

Shit. His words were like a slap to the face and shame consumed me. *I'm acting like a petulant child.* He watched me with an odd look and I mumbled, "Thanks, Z."

"Anytime. Now, you're not dying, so help carry stuff back to the bus."

He tossed me a large duffel back filled with hitting nets we secured to the ground for warm-up swings, and I hung it over my shoulder. *He's right. I can be a better leader.* The rest of the team scattered around the complex and Coach stood to the right of the concession stand, his hands on his hips as he spoke with Chesterfield. And they were both looking right at me.

My heart raced and I tried to act natural. *Be cool. Real cool. Walk to the undercarriage, drop the nets in there.* I stowed away the equipment with a ball of emotion in my throat. Would they come over here? Ask to talk to me?

Please, god.

They didn't. Coach shook his hand and moved on to talk to the hosting school's coach, not giving me a backward glance. It felt like a punch to the gut after a night of drinking. Bile threatened to come up at the strength of my disappointment.

I deserve it after playing like this.

I took a deep breath, grabbed my new phone, headphones and sweatshirt out of my bag and found a seat in the back of the bus. We hadn't played well and the guys didn't like to fuck around on the bus when they were in a shit mood, and I was glad. The last thing I wanted to do was listen to rap and do dumb dares. I put on some Black Keys, turned it up as loud as I could and got as comfortable as I could. My post-game routine was always the same—analyze every fucking detail to the point I understood how to improve the next time. This was no different and I started with game one that day, where I'd misread the line-drive, allowing the runner to advance a base.

It hadn't cost us the game, but I didn't misread plays. What was different?

My mind found nothing, and I went on to the next moment. Striking out. Sure, it'd happened in the game where an excellent batting average was three hundred, meaning getting a hit three out of ten times was incredible. But twice in a row, in summer ball, was *not* me. What had happened?

Coach gave me a fake sign and I signaled I understood. Something had caught my eye behind his left shoulder— blonde hair. *Kenzie.* I'd thought I saw her standing along the fence. *She* had been the reason I'd felt so distracted. She got into my head too much…the one thing that was non-negotiable. *Baseball, my family, draft.*

She didn't have a place there and I wasn't sure how she'd snuck in. *Fuck.*

Chapter Twenty-One

Kenzie

Something loud startled me. I clutched my chest and bolted up from my bed. *It came from downstairs. Oh my god. Someone's breaking in.* Adrenaline blasted through my veins, almost like ice going through them, and I tiptoed from my bed to the corner where Jeff kept a bat. I grabbed my glasses from the table and didn't make a sound when I twisted the doorknob and snuck out onto the top of the stairwell.

My watch read two-thirty a.m. *Who the fuck is here?* The guys weren't due back until that night and no one else had a key. *Burglars. Kidnappers.*

Okay, most likely not. If they were coming for money, the house wasn't nice. The most valuable things were our computers and I was not about to lose my life over a laptop. *Deep breath.* Gripping the bat like my life depended on it, I stepped down the stairs with the grace of a ninja. Not one sound gave away my descent, and I cocked my arms back to swing at the first sign of movement. Voices. There were people talking in the kitchen. I froze, hoping to place them, and almost laughed when I heard Aaron's.

"No fucking food. She didn't have the decency to buy *something*?"

"We stopped at the diner. Why do you need more?" *Zade.*

That meant…Tanner was back.

He must've texted me and I missed it. Speak of the devil. He rounded the corner to head upstairs, carrying bags over his shoulders, his face stern, and walking with a limp, if I wasn't mistaken. Seeing him, and how he made my body react all crazy, I was breathless. "Hi."

"Hey, mind getting out of the stairwell so I can head on up?"

Excuse me. Did he just… Yeah. He did. "Sure?" I still held the bat and moved to the side, letting him pass, and he didn't say a single word. Not a fucking one. "Tanner, are you okay?"

"Yes, Kenzie. I'm tired, I pulled a muscle, and want my own fucking bed." He spoke with an underlying tone of annoyance. As though I irritated him by talking to him. It was hard not to admire his back muscles straining against his shirt, but a bundle of dread formed in my chest.

"Uh, okay. Yeah, I'm sure you do. I didn't know you got hurt, what happened?" I moved up three steps, hoping to comfort him or see what else had happened. This version of him was so different from the one I'd chatted with before he left, or the one I'd exchanged texts with the entire time.

He sighed, dropped his bags outside his bedroom door and gave me a withering look, as though I was a groupie trying to get his attention. "I don't want to do this. Let me sleep."

The only thing I could do was nod. It felt like a slap to the face. "S-sure."

Then he went into his bedroom, shutting the door, and keeping me entirely in the dark about what just happened. I must've stared a little too long, because Zade walked up the stairs and burst out laughing.

"Dude, were you gunna try and fight us with a bat or what?"

"Yeah, I was!" I yelled, picking up the bat and pretending to swing at his handsome face. "None of you fuckers told me you were coming back tonight. I thought I was getting kidnapped or something."

Zade groaned and hollered over his shoulder. "You didn't text your sister? Aaron. Come on, man. We scared the shit out of her."

My brother joined us at our middle-of-the-night meeting and grimaced. "I'm so sorry, Kenzie. I didn't even think—thought you'd be able to sleep through it."

"I was until something crashed?"

"That was me," Zade said, shrugging. "I ran into the counter and knocked over all the dishes on it. Oops."

"Well, assholes, you scared the hell out of me for dumb reasons. You're getting me breakfast in the morning. I don't care who." I pointed at both their chests and stomped up the stairs. My pulse calmed down enough for me to get back into bed, but my mind was spinning. Sure, I'd expected my brother to give me a heads-up they got back early. He hadn't, so I was annoyed. But it didn't hurt, or feel like an intentional decision to keep me out of the loop.

Tanner's did though, and I didn't know why. I chewed on my lip, hating the uncertainty and how it played tricks on my mind. *Did I say something? Did he change his mind about me? Is our fling over?*

God, that pressure in my chest came back with thinking about ending our fling. It was always in my mind that our contract—my list—was solid, and we would abide by that for the rest of the summer. It would suck when it ended, but not *this* kind of suck. It would be an expected kind of awful, one I could prepare for mentally and emotionally. This, though... Something had to have happened for him to dismiss me.

I've hung out with him for three weeks. Why do I expect anything at all?

With negative and confusing thoughts, I drifted back into a shitty sleep in the hope of everything going back to normal the next day.

* * * *

Some people viewed being stubborn as a bad thing. I did not. It was something I was proud of and could remember all the way back to being a young kid where my parents wouldn't let me leave the kitchen table until I'd eaten all my vegetables. One time, the battle had gone on until ten p.m. and they'd given in. Again, I was proud of that. This same stubbornness plagued me as I bit into my chorizo burrito with extra hot sauce that Zade and Aaron had gone out to get me as an apology. Tanner hadn't acknowledged me, or anyone in the house, and I battled with what to do.

Confront him or ignore him?

Tease him or piss him off?

All the above, please.

"So, Kenzie, what did you do when we were gone?" Aaron asked, biting into his own breakfast burrito as we sat around the kitchen table. It was a small, not sturdy table, and Zade's large legs took up space from me, so I had to sit with both knees tucked to my chest.

"Worked three days, got all my homework done, hung out with Greta and Callie. They showed me the best dessert places and I met some of the football guys."

"The three of you went to hang with *football* guys?" Zade asked, suddenly alert for nine a.m. after getting home so late. "Like, a party?"

"Okay, first of all, calm down." I laughed at his crazy expression and waited a little longer than necessary to answer. They were rattled at the mere thought of their women talking to other dudes and that was dumb. I took another bite, a long sip of coffee and when Zade narrowed his eyes, I responded. "It was during my shift Saturday, you nutcase. They had a table in my section that was too large. Greta and I had to share it. They knew all about you guys. Seems they think they're cooler."

"Ugh, don't fucking start. I hate football," Aaron said, getting up after finishing his food. "Don't get involved with them."

"Because...?"

"They party hard."

"So do you."

"They...they're different."

"Again, so are you guys." I smiled at his flustering but stopped when Tanner walked into the kitchen wearing nothing but those goddamn loose workout shorts. My mouth literally watered seeing all his muscles move with each step. *No. We're mad at him.*

"You guys get any extra food?" he asked, his voice all sleepy and sexy. *Ugh.*

"Yeah, in the bag. Now, Kenz, back to this ridiculous notion of *football players*, after whats-his-face? You want to mess with that whole thing again?"

"Aaron." I rubbed my temples. "Sean was lame and it had nothing to do with the sport he played. Also, I'm just giving you shit. I'm not— I don't plan on dating anyone. With work, balancing classes and trying to figure out what to do with my life, I don't have time."

Did Tanner's back tense or no?

"Good. Good. Take some time and, uh, make good choices."

Zade and I snorted at his stupid answer. I gave myself a mental high-five when I hadn't looked at Tanner's face the entire time, even when he sat in the chair next to me. His body heat overwhelmed me and while my pulse skyrocketed at his nearness, my face remained a stone-cold bitch.

"Why the burritos?" Tanner asked. He took a bite— fitting half of one into his talented mouth—and I swallowed hard.

"We all get shitty housemate points. *Aaron* forgot to tell her we were heading back and we scared the shit out of her last night. Did you see her with the bat? Like, what were you gunna do with those little arms?" Zade reached over and picked up my right arm, laughing harder. "Can't do damage with these."

"Fuck off, and yes. I could. Want to test it out?" I fired back.

"Woah, woah. Simmer down, Ken." Zade held both hands in the air but kept the grin on his face. "I'm sorry we scared you."

"I survived." I pushed off the chair and threw the wrapper into the bin before sneaking a glance at Tanner. *Shit.* I shouldn't have. He was staring straight at me with his bedroom eyes. My entire body warmed at his perusal, but I shut that shit down. Without another look, I left them in the kitchen and made my way down to the basement. It was a sticky summer morning and nothing sounded better than a *Riverdale* marathon. I got the show up and loaded, perfectly content in my pajama shorts covered in cacti, and an old t-shirt that was frayed on the collar.

Relaxing was a new concept and I didn't like it. I'd gone from having my minutes planned for twenty hours at a time to nothing. No obligations besides working at the Lion and some homework. It had taken three weeks to get used to the idea and it was just starting to take root. *Let my brain not think.*

That was my intention watching the show and I got an episode in before someone headed downstairs with grunts and loud stomps. The tingles on the back of my neck warned me it was Tanner and I had two seconds to figure out what to say. A part of me wanted to reach out and call last night a fluke. He'd been rude, but if he was injured and hurting—well, everyone got grumpy sometimes. But he spoke first, derailing my plans.

"I'm going to need the basement today." He sucked in a breath when he walked toward the other shitty couch facing the TV. He plopped down, not covering his muscles at all, and faced me with the same intensity he did upstairs. I had gotten used to seeing a softness there, and this time, there wasn't one.

"Okay, what for?" I paused the show.

"For the TV."

"I've already gotten this set up for the next couple hours. You can use the one upstairs?"

"I'm injured."

Oh, right. That makes sense. My temper reared its ugly head and my voice rose. "Yeah, being hurt *and* a dick doesn't give you a right to demand an entire room. You walked down here. You can very well walk your grumpy ass back up and use that TV."

I hit Play and blasted the volume to drown him out, but it lasted about thirty seconds before I faced him again. He looked furious, an extreme emotion for a completely normal situation. My *crazy* smile came out. One that looked like joy, but was fueled with anger, and I'd been told it was terrifying. I swore he mumbled something, so I asked, "What did you say?"

He had the gall to look ashamed for a second, but he shoved that guilt away and fired back, "Sleeping with me doesn't give you special privileges."

"Well, fuck, that was the *only* reason I did it." I hated how my stomach knotted at his words and I thought of a million comebacks that would hurt him. But a flash of the night he'd shattered something in his room came back. *He lashes out when he's pissed.*

I sighed, waited for him to meet my gaze and said, "Look, Tanner. I'm sorry you're injured. I would ask about it, but you shut that shit down last night. Maybe you were tired and cranky. I would be too if I had to travel on a bus with an injury. But that doesn't give you the right to be a dick to *anyone.* It shouldn't matter we slept together. I don't expect anything from you besides respect and the truth. Something's bothering you, but I'm not gunna be your verbal punching bag."

Screw my original plans. I didn't wait for a response before marching my ass upstairs to my temporary room. I made sure to lock both doors—our shared bathroom and my bedroom door— and hang up signs ensuring *no one* would bother me in the house.

ON PERIOD—LEAVE ME ALONE.

Chapter Twenty-Two

Tanner

Aaron drove me to the stadium where I was expected to meet Nicole — our trainer and Callie's pseudo-boss — to get around noon the damage report on my leg. Eating and breathing were hard when my future was at stake and while part of me knew how I'd dealt with Kenzie was awful, I couldn't think about it. Not yet.

I needed the answers first.

"Call me when you're done. Don't be a dick to Nicole. She'll murder you," Aaron said, taking off the second I got out of the car. Her training room during our season was off to the side in a little office with glass windows. I hobbled down the cemented hallway, preparing myself for the worst. Each step caused pain in my lower back and I knew if I had a large tear in my hamstring, I could be out for six weeks.

That was just unacceptable. Something I couldn't afford to have happen. With a heavy hand, I knocked on her door and was met with a scowl. "Johnson, what did you do?"

"Not sure. Rounding third, I felt a pull, and it hasn't gotten any better."

She exhaled and led me to a table where she instructed me to lie on my back. I did, and winced when she lifted my leg and tried pushing my knee to my chest. I couldn't do it with the pain. "Lots of pain in your thigh when I do this?"

"Yes," I said through gritted teeth. "Iced it this morning, but it didn't help."

She did a couple more exercises, stretching and maneuvering my leg at different angles. Then she clicked her tongue. "Pulled hammie. Probably gunna be out for two weeks, minimum. See me in fourteen days and we can start light exercises."

I covered my eyes with the palms of my hands, pressing into them and digesting my reality. *Two weeks. Better than six, worse than none.* "Okay. I can do that."

"You don't have a choice. Ice, aspirin, stretches. You're an active guy, be smart about this. Short-term decisions won't help your endgame." She patted my knee twice and told me to hold still. She bagged some ice, twisted it off at the end and set it on my thigh. "Twenty minutes, then you can head out. I swear, Tanner, don't overdo it. You're not in season and this is more an annoyance than a setback."

"Yeah, I understand."

"Do you?" she asked, fire in her eyes that knew too much. She knew all of us really well, and I swore she could smell my bullshit. "I'll know. No playing until I clear you. I'm going to call your coach now and inform him."

"Yes, ma'am."

She left the training room without glancing back at me, and my swirling thoughts clashed with the silence of the room. *Nineteen more minutes.* That was a lot of time to think about my family, future and...how I'd treated Kenzie.

"Fuck." I groaned into my fist. I shouldn't have snapped at her when she'd asked what happened...and I sure as hell should've texted her we were getting back early. Being a dick wasn't my go-to for anyone, and I couldn't rationalize why I'd needed to act that way.

Because I blamed her for my playing.

Rationally, I knew that was absurd, but it didn't stop me. *She met football guys...*ugh. I pushed the thought away because it got my blood pumping with adrenaline. Overhearing her talking to her brother and Zade hadn't been the best way to wake up with feelings of shame and regret. I had major work to do when I got back and I wasn't sure how to go about it.

Am I such an asshole I never had to apologize before? God. Sometimes I hated myself. I knew why I rarely apologized. I never let myself care enough to feel bad about something, unless it was on the baseball field.

Not a pleasant pill to swallow.

My thoughts derailed when my phone rang, the familiar ringtone alerting me it was my mom. I scrambled it from my pocket and answered immediately. "Hey, Mom, is everything okay?"

"Yes, Tallen." She chuckled, the sound warm and *her*, and it had a calming effect on my spiked nerves. "I know we didn't talk yesterday since you had some games. How did you play?"

"Like shit. Scouts were there and had no interest in talking to me," I snapped, sounding like a pouting child. "I pulled a muscle so I'm out two weeks."

She sighed, letting a couple of seconds of silence go by before she spoke. "I'm not going to spend my time listening to you admiring the problem. Tell me the solutions instead."

A hard slap of truth. "I wasn't seeing the ball well at the plate and my head was distracted."

"Use your two weeks to clear your head. If it's worrying about me and your brothers…please don't. We're doing well. They're loving their summer camp and are part of a program at school to get free cellphones. They'll be so excited when they can start texting you. Be prepared."

"What? That's awesome!" My mood lifted. "Yeah, have them text me as soon as they get a device. Wow, how cool."

"I'm thankful. The service provides a phone easily adapted so Marcus can use it. It was a wonderful surprise. Now, about the scouts. You've spoken to a handful of them, but it doesn't guarantee anything. Focus on your goals. Getting on base, making plays in the outfield and silently leading your team."

"Thanks, Mom, I needed to hear this." I gripped the phone a little tighter in my hand, already forming a plan of attack. "This helped."

"It's what moms do. We help in whatever capacity we can."

"Love you. Tell hello to the boys for me."

"I love you, too, Tallen. I'll tell them and I don't want to hear any more complaints when we talk next week. Deal?"

"Yes," I mumbled, getting another chuckle from her. We hung up. Having a focus helped. *Clear my head, rest my leg, come back ready to play.*

Clearing my head meant one thing…talking to Kenzie.

* * * *

My plan didn't work out how I wanted it to — Kenzie was at the bar Monday night and she wasn't back yet. It was eleven, the familiar worrying feeling had returned and I couldn't distract myself. I tried video games, movies, social media and even reading a baseball book. I got only ten minutes into the activity before I'd check my phone, or the light in her room to see if she was back. *This is stupid.*

Tanner: Are you heading back home soon? We need to chat.

Kenzie: You might need to chat, I sure don't.

Tanner: Are you safe? Do you have a ride home?

Kenzie: Chill, I'm fine.

God, she was frustrating me, but I deserved the short answers.

Kenzie: Not being secretive. I met my future roommates and they are driving me back. I'm trying not to be a rude human and be on my phone with them.

I read the subtle dig at me in her text and adjusted my position in my bed so my leg could stretch fully. It tightened when I didn't move around enough or change angles, and with another thirty minutes of worrying, I finally heard her light footsteps coming up the stairs. Wincing, I moved from my bed and walked through our bathroom. She stopped at the door, staring at me with an unreadable expression.

God, I missed her.

She wore ripped black jeans, a tight black tank top and a cut-off jean jacket. Her hair was in a high ponytail and those cute glasses perched on top of her nose. My heart skipped a beat and I blamed it on my nerves. It wasn't often I apologized. "Hey."

Cool, I'm off to a great start.

"Can you let me know who I'm dealing with? Is this the guy I've spent the last three weeks laughing with or the one who is a total dick?" she replied, not stepping into her room or closing her door. Aaron could walk out from the other side of the hallway at any second, but she didn't seem to care.

I gulped. "I'm here to apologize."

"Then don't let me stop you." She sighed and entered the room, shutting the wooden door and leaving the two of us alone. She removed her jacket, putting her bare arms and neck on display, and the urge to kiss her had me stuttering. *She's so fucking pretty.*

"Could you look at me?"

She stopped removing her shoes and gave me her full attention, green eyes wide and patient, a smirk almost forming on her delicious lips.

I hobbled from my spot to her bed, sitting down two feet away from her. "I'm sorry for a couple of things. I should've texted you we were on our way back. It hit me today how scared you were last night and that's pretty shitty of me and Aaron."

"It was. I'm madder at my brother for that, but carry on."

I swallowed hard and ran my hand through my hair, hoping that would make this easier. It didn't. "I blamed you for me not playing well and getting hurt."

"Um, what?" Her eyebrows disappeared into her hairline and her chest heaved in what I could only assume was anger. "Explain how that would be my fault."

"No, I know it's not. I was looking for someone to blame and the only difference in my life is you, really. I worried about you when my phone broke, how you were doing at work, and it distracted me and my game. It wasn't fair to you and it was a shitty move." I stood, groaning at the pain in my thigh, and moved to put my hands on her neck—just over her collarbone and her sexy birthmark. "I'm sorry for my behavior. I'm out for two weeks and until I knew that, my brain was on high alert, like everything was ruined. I panicked and took it out on you."

She sucked one of her cheeks into her mouth and studied me for a minute before she spoke. "Thanks for being honest."

"Can you forgive me?" I moved my fingers up to her jaw, cupping it and pulling her closer to me. "I have two weeks where I can't do anything...fourteen days with you in this house. Think of all the things I can do to you...to help you forgive me."

Her eyes fluttered shut and I leaned in, not quite touching our lips together because I wanted her to make that decision. After some excruciating seconds, she closed the distance and let me taste her. It had been a long week, way too long, and I yanked her body against mine. I couldn't get her close enough—the sounds she made, the way her tongue danced against mine, the taste of gum still in her mouth. My dick sprang to life, desperate for a slice of our insane chemistry. I moved my fingers down her arms, over her sides, and landed on her ass. I moaned between kisses, "God, I missed your mouth."

She clutched my T-shirt, digging her nails into my abs, but too soon, she stopped. She pushed me a foot away and stared at me with her mouth parted, her lips red and swollen. "I'm not sure I'm ready to forgive you. Yes, our bodies are amazing together when naked, but you were hurtful on purpose. I don't condone that in any relationship — roommates, friends, lovers, colleagues. While I'd love to make you use your mouth in all my dirty places, you can't kiss your way to forgiveness."

Oh my god, is she ending this? Fuck. No. No! "Kenzie," I started, but my words jumped in my head because I wasn't sure what to say. "Tell me what I need to do."

"Let me sleep on it."

"Yeah, of course. Sure, I'll, uh, just go back into my room. Sleep on it." I blinked a lot, hoping she couldn't see right through me. The thought of not being with her again scared me, and I had no idea why. It wasn't something I had the emotional capability to analyze. I hobbled two steps toward the bathroom and paused, not wanting to end our conversation. We hadn't spoken in two weeks — being roomed with Aaron didn't help that — and I found I enjoyed her voice. It wasn't too high, or too low. Just perfect, and it became husky when she was turned on. "Work was good?"

"Yeah, I'm liking it so far." She gave me a small smile and began taking off her clothes.

Um, what? My mouth dried when she ripped off her shirt and stood there topless. Her perky nipples stood on end, begging to be sucked, the perfectly pink circles giving me a case of blue balls that sent pain to my core. She didn't stop there. She wiggled out of her jeans, standing in a lace thong that left *nothing* to my imagination. *Good god. Her body. This is torture.*

"Tanner? Did you hear me?"

"Hm?" I couldn't look away from her smooth skin — I knew how it felt against my palms and how it tasted when I kissed her. Her two dimples on her lower back drove me wild and I bit my knuckle to stop myself from panting for her. "What did you s-say?"

She gave me a coy smirk, stopping her movements and putting her hands on her naked hips. "I'm sorry. Is me being naked awkward?"

"N-no." I gulped again, loudly.

She traced her fingers along her chest, biting down on her lower lip, and tilted her head at me as she pulled on her taut nipples. "Oh, good. I was worried. But yeah, as I was saying, I've enjoyed working there. It's good money and I get to meet cool people."

She continued teasing with her small hands and without warning, she slid on an oversized shirt that barely covered her ass. It had an old-school logo on it. She gave me an expectant look and I had no idea how to respond, so I said, "That's c-cool."

"It is. My new roommates stopped in and I got to chat with them. I'm fucking pumped to live with them — one has a twin brother on the football team and the other is a golfer. How cool is that?"

"Yeah," I agreed, sounding dumb as shit. "Roommates can make or break your living situation."

"I know," she said, giving me a pointed stare. "It gave me a lot of hope for starting college. It sounds cheesy, but I'm ready to have what you guys all have — friends that are more like family."

Calm the fuck down and be a good friend. I forced my voice to remain even and gave her my best impression of a smile. "You're a part of our family, Kenz. But you'll get to create your own, too, and that's pretty damn special."

She gave me the widest grin and pushed her crazy hair behind her ears. "Thanks, TJ. See, this is how I view you. Someone who is kind, supportive and respectful. Sleeping together doesn't give you privileges to act any different."

"You're the first girl I've been with where we even had to have this conversation."

"Good night, TJ. I'll see you in the morning."

"Night, Kenzie." I couldn't stop myself. I placed a kiss on her forehead before heading into my room. It wasn't the night I'd planned to have—a raging boner without release—but it was one that made me happy in a totally different way. *Weird.*

Chapter Twenty-Three

Kenzie

With an empty house and a little bit of revenge planned for Tanner, I couldn't decide what to wear downstairs. Sure, my intentions were to drive him crazy for a bit before succumbing to our attraction. I would forgive him after his apology, but I didn't have to make it easy for him. Plus, maybe I was sick. I liked seeing him struggle around me. No guy had ever made me feel this sexy before, and forgive me for wanting to embrace it.

You're the first girl I've had to have this conversation with.

Butterflies. Those words made me feel all tingly and I wasn't sure it was for the right reason. He blamed *me* for playing poorly. That wasn't a good sign and I knew we weren't more than just two people hooking up — monogamous — for the summer. God, my head was spinning.

The easiest part of my whole array of jumbled thoughts was our attraction and how good we were together. After my awful experience with Sean, this seemed like an entirely different world. Our attraction was explosive, new and exciting…that was all. That was what I told myself when I chose a see-through bra that barely contained my tits and a tank that was so low in the front my nipples could almost pop out, and paired that with my favorite booty jean shorts.

I even put lotion on my arms and legs. Yeah. I wanted to have him panting for me and it felt empowering as hell. I went with contacts for the day and knew Tanner would be downstairs already. The rest of the guys had headed to the field for a two-day training camp for youths—a camp Tanner couldn't go to because he had been instructed to stay home and ice his leg. *That leaves us alone for ten hours.*

I'm having my cake and eating it, too.

Feeling bold, I walked downstairs and blushed when Tanner's mouth fell open and his warm chocolate gaze landed on me. *Flutters. I have flutters in my belly.* "How's the injury, TJ? You feeling better? Nothing *stiff* going on?"

His throat bobbed as his stare went all over my body, landing on my chest before he said, "Fine."

"Good. Good." I moved in front of the couch, right in front of the TV, and spun around. "I'm trying this outfit at work tonight. What do you think?"

He gulped, his face contorting into a variety of emotions, before he said, "Great. You look g-great."

"It's not too much?" I bent over, shimmying for him. "My nipples don't pop out?"

He squirmed on the couch and did nothing to hide the growing erection in my favorite shorts of his. He licked his lips and spoke in a real deep voice that sent shivers all down my body. "You look fucking insane, in the best way."

"Aw, thanks, TJ." I smiled at him and walked past the couch and into the kitchen. Not two seconds later, he followed me. *Perfect.* I spun around. "Oh, did you need something, Tanner?"

"Are you trying to *kill* me? Goddamn, woman," he groaned into his fist and eyed me up and down. "Did you sleep on it? Am I forgiven? Is this my punishment? It is, huh? Fuck. I need to know because I'm going to have to start stroking myself here."

"Do it."

Woah, what did I say?

His eyes flared and he gave me the sexiest look I had ever seen. He lowered himself onto the kitchen chair and reached into his shorts to wrap his fingers around his massive wood. He fisted himself, pumping up and down a couple of times, and letting out guttural sigh. "*Fuck.* Kenzie… just looking at you drives me wild."

"Yeah?" I moved closer to him, slowly removing my tank top and showcasing my one piece of sexy lingerie. His eyes turned to small saucers when he saw my bra. "Do you like this, Tanner?"

"Christ, yes." He bucked and his jaw became slack — but his gaze never strayed from me. "Forgive me and let me taste you."

"Ah, yes. Forgiveness." I straddled him and unbuttoned my shorts. "Tell me. Are you ever going to blame *me* for your actions on the field again?"

"No. No," he mumbled. So I sat on his lap, moving my chest closer to him.

"And are you going to lash out at me when you're hurt or angry?"

"Never again."

I smiled, giving him permission to touch me, and he attacked my breasts. He dug his fingers into them, squeezing, before he replaced his digits with his warm mouth. He sucked my nipples hard, through the material, and bit down with the right amount of pain that had me arching my back. He did it again with the other one, licking and teasing to the point of madness before he moved from my chest to my neck.

I couldn't recall ever having been this turned on before in my life. My pulse raced all over my body — between my legs, my ears, even my fingers. I gripped his hair and pulled so he brought his mouth to mine, and I lost myself in that kiss.

It was hurried but without rush. Aggressive, but without pain. We breathed in each other's moans, grinding against each other in a frenzy. "Naked. We need to be naked."

"Yes," he said, moving his hands to take off my shorts within three seconds. I stood for enough time to grab the condom I'd placed in my pocket and put it on his welcoming cock, ready and desperate for me. "Please, Kenzie, I'm craving you."

Wow.

I slid onto him, my walls stretching to fit him at our angle. We were in the middle of the kitchen, at nine in the morning, fucking on a chair. I was so wet and turned on. I arched my hips and moved against him at a rapid pace. He placed his hands on my waist, helping me find the right rhythm of up and down, fast and slow, and I couldn't contain my moans as pleasure grew and grew.

He held on to me, meshing our bodies together as he brought his fingers to my clit. He gave the right pressure and soon enough, I fell apart. He didn't last too long either. His face tightened and he crushed our mouths together before he spilled into me. Our breathing was heavy, our foreheads touching and sweat pooling between our chests. It was awesome.

He spoke first, rubbing my bare back with his calloused fingers, and his voice was almost unrecognizable with its tender tone. "I'd be happy to give you more orgasms if you'd like. My intention was not to have you ride me in the kitchen, but, holy fuck, this might be the hottest thing I've ever seen. You grinding against my dick like that."

"Yeah?" I grinned down at him, loving how relaxed and pleasured he looked. *I did that. I put that there.* "My plan of making you suffer backfired. I thought about you all night and had to stop myself from busting out my dildo."

"You…you have a dildo?"

"Oh yeah." I laughed, carefully hopping off him without hurting his leg. He painted a beautiful picture sitting there with his shorts at his ankles and a dumbass grin on his face. "Sometimes, I use it on myself. I'm scandalous."

"You'd think my dick would be satisfied, but nope. Already itching to be inside you again when you talk like that."

I pursed my lips and put on my clothes. He did the same and there was an awkward ten seconds of silence before I joined him on the other side of the table. He poured us cups of coffee and had a stupid handsome and relaxed look on his face when he said, "I take it I'm totally forgiven?"

"Eighty percent, yes. One thing worries me, though, the more I think about it."

He furrowed those dark eyebrows and leaned closer to me. "What is it?"

I placed my palms flat on the surface and thought about how to word it. It was crazy, how comfortable I felt with him, but also scary with how easy it would be to be upset when our time came to an end. "While we continue our countdown until our fling is over, I can't have you blame me for how you play. I am under no false pretenses about what we are. There are no secret plans to convince you to make this last longer. But you can't be that rude to me again. It'll affect our friendship and end our fuckfest."

His nostrils flared and a smile broke out. "First, you said fuckfest. That made me laugh. Secondly, you're right. I don't have room for any type of distractions — gorgeous blonde ones specifically — with baseball."

"I understand. I do." The pressure came back and took root, just behind my ribcage, and I coughed, hoping to get it to go away. "So. We enjoy each other as much as we can until you're cleared to go back to playing?"

He leaned back in his chair, resting his chin on his hands and giving me a thoughtful look. Then he slowly nodded, understanding dawning on his face. "Yeah. Yeah. That could work. I'm out at least two weeks, probably three."

"Yeah. That'll put us well into July…and I'll be moving out into the dorm first week in August anyway."

"Then it's settled. This has been great so far, so I can't wait for more with you," he said, giving me a playful smile. "I've been instructed to not do much for fourteen days. I have a lot of energy inside me that'll need a way out. Can you think of anything?"

"We'll manage, I'm sure."

He eyed me over his mug and I dared to ask the question that still hadn't been answered. "You played shitty. Describe that to me."

"Didn't make every play in the outfield, didn't get on base as much as I wanted."

"Vague statements. Are we talking straight errors in the field or base hits you couldn't cut off?"

He exhaled and tensed his jaw. "No errors in stats, but the scouts there saw me not read a ball well."

"Did a runner advance?"

"Yes, to third."

"Did they score and was that run the one that won the game?"

He snorted and the tension around his eyes lessened. "I forgot you actually know baseball."

"Hello...ball park rat. I wish I didn't know it. But I take it by your lack of response it didn't lose the game. I might be far off here, TJ, but there is a *slim* possibility you overreacted."

His broad shoulders relaxed and I knew I had him. He gave a goofy smile, something between regret and embarrassment. "Maybe."

"I knew it. Also, correct me if I'm wrong, summer ball is...not a big deal. Like, anyone can be on this team, right? Transfers, people in town...it's not legit. So if scouts didn't talk to you, why is it a big deal?"

"Because I want to be on their radar all the time."

"Fair enough." I thought about how to add to that, but he interrupted me and had a playful smile going on, one that sent those goddamn flutters in my stomach.

"Do you have plans today, Kenzie?"

"Hm, no. No work, no homework. Why?"

"Want to watch baseball movies all day? We can make popcorn, eat and watch them naked. If I only get to enjoy your body when I'm injured, I want to get as much as I can."

"Depends on the movie. *The Sandlot* better be on your list."

"Please," he scoffed and pushed himself up from his chair to grab ice from the freezer. "We can start with that movie."

Chapter Twenty-Four

Tanner

Four days later, the pain wasn't throbbing in my leg, but the limb still ached when I didn't stretch. It was almost torture not being on the field with the guys and the only thing keeping me sane was Kenzie. When Zade and Aaron were at home, she suggested we go to a café to write our papers for our film class. When they were gone, we were in bed, naked and starting a tally of orgasms.

It fucking rocked.

"Hey, you're smiling over there like a weirdo." She nudged my side at the coffee shop she'd found ten minutes from the house. They had incredible cold brew and the walk was good for me, even though it sucked. "You have this cute expression on your face and your eyebrows come together to form a little triangle right here." She pressed on my forehead and the gesture caused an odd flurry just below my ribs.

It felt as though the ground shifted under our table, but I ignored it. "I don't have *cute* expressions."

"Yes, you do." She smiled and pushed her glasses up. "Why are you so happy today?"

"I was thinking about what we did last night." I slid my hand under the table and squeezed her thigh. She blushed red and squirmed against me. It did not help my dick, because whenever she was around, I was ready to go.

"Last night was pretty incredible."

We shared a heated look before she winked and went back to her computer. I kept watching her movements, like how she chewed on her lip when she read, or how she adjusted her hair every couple of minutes, or the way she kind of hummed when she sighed. I liked her gestures and I had to force myself to stop staring at her. We finished our assignments for our class and submitted them, but Kenzie wanted to stick around for a bit to work on class selection for her freshman year.

She has her entire life ahead of her. New start.

But it didn't stop the fact I wished I could keep her as mine even after I went back to baseball. She fitted into my life so easily. It *could* happen. It was just the possibility of it not working that held me back. The situation when I'd gotten hurt, thinking I'd seen her in the crowd... I couldn't afford it and I shook my head to clear my thoughts. *Baseball first, always.* She was jotting something down in her notepad filled with lists when I saw a dude approaching our table.

He was shorter than me, a dark-haired kid decked out in our school's colors. I had no idea who the guy was but he was bold, walking right up to Kenzie and staring at her. It amused me that she didn't see him for a solid thirty seconds, until the guy said, "Kenzie."

She glanced up at me first. *Score.* But she followed the voice and her entire body stiffened when she eyed the stranger. "Uh, hey. What in the world? How are you here?"

He smiled, darting his gaze down her bare legs. I did not like that. "I'm having an informal tour with my mom. She wanted some coffee and we were literally right here. What are the chances?"

"No shit." Kenzie scanned the entryway but the dude moved closer so he could touch her if he wanted.

He lowered his voice in a practiced move and twitched his hand, as if he wanted to reach out to her. "How are you? I heard you moved here early and I saw your house is already sold to someone else. I've texted you a couple of times…I missed you." The dude moved his intense stare to me, but I remained expressionless. Kenzie's neck turned red. I *had* to know who this kid was to her.

"I've been pretty good. Living with Aaron and his friends has been interesting. I'm picking my classes for fall now. This guy has been entertaining me all summer."

The dude had a forced expression of kindness on his face as he reached over to shake my hand. "H-hey, man."

I squeezed my grip harder than normal. I didn't respond. Instead I just jutted my chin at him. He let go and directed all his attention back to Kenzie, and I had every urge to smack this kid.

"Look, Kenz, I wanted to tell you in person, not text, but I'm coming to school here in the fall. I know we talked and I said I was going out of state…but it makes sense paying in-state tuition. Isn't that awesome?" The guy smiled with a hint of hope, but Kenzie did not have the reaction I expected. She laughed.

"Sweet. Good for you, man. It's a nice school."

"You're...I thought you'd... you know. Look, who *is* this guy? Can I talk to you alone?"

That set off my alarm.

Kenzie raised her voice, a bit more dominance escaping her, and said, "This is Tanner Johnson, a friend of my brother and me. He plays on the baseball team. TJ, this is Sean. My *ex-boyfriend*."

Sean. The fucker who'd slept with her and left her. I gave him a tight smile.

Sean looked a little flustered and blinked a lot. He then stared at Kenzie a little too long and I wanted to say something, but my girl did it just fine herself.

"Well, this has been awkward. I'm not sure what you were expecting here, but it isn't some reconciliation. I'll be friendly if I see you around, but that's about it."

"I thought...I don't know. Maybe you'd be happy to see me again?"

"Sean. You dumped me. I'm not real upset about it, but don't make this weird," she fired back. "I'm being honest. We won't have any friendship, so please don't try."

"Okay. Uh, sure. Well, bye." Sean spun around so fast I felt air hit my face, and Kenzie turned to me with the widest eyes.

"Holy shit."

"Yeah, that was entertaining," I replied, holding back from asking a thousand questions. Like, did she text him back? Did she miss him? Was she glad he was going here? Instead, I acted real mature. "He seemed...fun."

"Ha. Ha." She made a bemused face and blinked back the uncertainty that had been there moments ago. "God, that threw me for a loop. I never expected to see him again."

"Do you miss him?" *Shit.*

"Uh, no. Not at all." She laughed and slid me a coy look. "The sex is comical, comparing what I had with him to you. Astronomically comical."

"I like where this is going. Please, continue."

She giggled and leaned into me a bit. It was simple, just her shoulder touching mine, but it felt like more. She didn't let a lot of people get inside her circle, and I was in. I felt special — a totally cheesy thing to feel — but I liked being in her world. "It was something to do — no pun intended — to have a boyfriend. My life was crazy with my dad being sick and me working all the time to avoid feeling things, taking care of the house and finishing classes. A boyfriend was a distraction from it all. I didn't really *like* the guy all that much. But we got dinner, we went to prom, we went to movies. We did things. It got me out of the house."

"As all good boyfriends do, doing things."

"Shut up," she goaded, resting her head on my shoulder for two seconds. It made my heart skip a beat and I wasn't sure why. "It's important to be friends with the person you're with — meaning, there is a foundation to completely be yourself without judgment. Zade and Callie, Aaron and Greta — they have that. That's tough to find and why I probably won't have a boyfriend for a good long while."

"Don't believe in love?" *Wait — do I even believe in it? Why did I ask that?*

"No, I do. It's a lot of effort to find that with someone, isn't it?" she asked, her green eyes hinting at something I couldn't figure out. They were the brightest shade, almost like outfield grass, and I loved the color.

"Yeah. It is. We're a lot alike, you know. For different reasons, relationships just aren't in the works for us. At least not for a good while." *Good, she won't be with anyone soon.*

"That's why this fling is perfect." She gave me a toothy grin, making me laugh, and I wished for the first time that our fling could maybe be something more. But the illusion burst when she asked about my one true love — baseball. "You going to try and head to the field next week?"

I swallowed the uncomfortable ball in my throat. *Baseball.* That was my life. My dad had tried calling, again, and the itch to get my mom and brothers safe brought my focus to the front. *Money, draft, baseball.* "I'm gunna try and just have a presence there, but not dress for practice, or Coach and our trainer will kill me dead."

"Don't take this the wrong way, TJ, but I'm not going to be upset if you have to wait another three weeks before you can play. I've really enjoyed hanging out with you and we still have…let me see…twelve more things to knock off my list."

"Yeah?" I reached around her and flipped her book to our list. "Damn. Twelve more times between your legs, naked, screaming—"

"Tanner! Shh!" she laughed, putting her fingers to my lips to get me to shut up. "We are in public, Mr. Johnson. Behave."

"I like it when you're bossy."

"If that's your kink, I can boss you around all night." She pursed her lips with all her confidence, looking adorable as hell, and I didn't think. I leaned forward, kissing her softly, tentatively, and hummed in pleasure when she parted her mouth for our tongues to connect.

It didn't last long, but that kiss felt different. Real different. She looked up at me with hooded eyes and it felt like a sucker punch in the gut seeing all that warmth directed at me. *Say something. Do something to make it not weird.* Clearing my throat, I said, "Do you need help picking classes? I am a wise senior who's survived up to this point."

"Yeah, that'd be great."

Thank god. Normal. We are back to normal. "What do you have so far?"

She tilted her screen at me, but in order to see it, I had to scoot closer to her. This put our torsos together, her body heat combining with mine, and it took a copious amount of effort to not react. *Focus on her classes.*

"Since I have no idea what I want to major in, like, seriously, no clue, I'm going for all gen-eds. English 101, American Politics, Psychology 101, but this is where it gets tricky. I'm at nine credit hours. I need fifteen. Do I pick a language since I skipped over them in high school? Or do I pick a math class that I know will be super hard? Both? Help meeee."

Her dramatization of asking for help made me laugh and she joined in. "See what time they're offered. You're a morning person, but you might work late nights. Psych is tough. Your grade is the midterm and final. That's it, so you'll need to make time to study a hella amount of hours."

"Ugh, studying is not my thing. I'm a worker. I like tasks I can cross off my list, but studying…that's a hard concept for me to tackle. Okay. Times available. Let's see." She scrolled on the screen, her *focused* face involved her teeth coming down on her lip and her forehead wrinkling in the middle. "Hm, this one is eight a.m. Monday, Wednesday, Friday. No thank you."

"Try to load up your classes on two days. I know that's not conventional, but it helps me a lot during season. Sports management has a lot of hands-on, project-based classes that take up a lot of time so I try to only go to classes Tuesdays and Thursdays."

"Is that what your major is?" she asked, bringing her gaze to my face with a slight tilt of her head. "Sports management?"

"Yeah. It was beaten into my brain that baseball is just an injury away from not having a future. My mom made it pretty clear I had to have a back-up plan if baseball doesn't work out. I love sports and coaching, teaching, working with a college team...I'd be happy doing any of those."

She gave me the toothiest grin. "Tanner, I don't think there's much in the world you *wouldn't* be good at, but I can see you liking any of those options."

"Thanks, Kenny." I nudged her shoulder, wishing I could show her how much I enjoyed hearing her say those things. "It's a constant worry — one injury could derail every dream I've ever had. It's not an excuse for my behavior last week, because you didn't deserve the brunt of it, but it terrified me. If I was out for two months, someone else could earn a starting spot in the lineup. It's that simple."

"Hm, I'd like to give your coach credit. You wouldn't be replaced that fast."

"It's a business, so yeah, I could. I accept the rules and am willing to play, but the line of what could be or what could've been is real thin for me. That's what I need to be focused all the time."

"No, I get that for sure." She snorted and gave me another look I couldn't decipher. "Man, all these fans and cleat chasers, they have no idea the emotional and physical toll the sport has on you. They see fame and fortune, the pretty face with the big paycheck, but it's so much more than that. I'm glad you all have a circle of people you trust."

"I am, too. You're in that circle, you know. At least for me." *And her brother's, but I'm not bringing him up.*

"Yeah, I worked myself into yours pretty quickly."

"That you did, Kenzie."

Another moment passed between us. The things I wanted to say but didn't know how clogged themselves in my throat. I couldn't do it. It wouldn't be fair to either one of us. I chose silence and Kenzie opted to stare at her screen. I would take what I could get. *Ten more days of her being with me.*

Chapter Twenty-Five

Kenzie

It was hard to miss someone I wasn't not allowed to have. It was even harder to keep my spiraling emotions inside, locked up, because I had no one to talk to it about. My brother? I'd rather die. Greta and Callie? They'd tell their boyfriends, meaning I'd also rather die. That left *no one* because the one person who'd wiggled their way into close-friend status was the guy I needed to talk about. Tanner Johnson. Dreamboat. Sex god. *Off-limits.*

My crush had morphed into something more, a totally new territory for me, and I was not handling the unknown well. Jeff's room had been cleaned four times, the bathroom scrubbed, the kitchen reorganized and the floors mopped for what I assumed was the first time ever. That was just after the first day Tanner reported back to practice—not to play, but to be there.

Five more days.

He'd been walking better, not wincing going downstairs or when he'd gotten real creative in the shower with me that morning. My body heated up just thinking about his mouth on me, but I stopped it. Not only would he go back to baseball in five days, but we only had six more times allotted to do it.

Yeah, we were sex-crazed but the short timeline of our fling almost made it hotter, more frantic, more desperate. Fuck, it was going to be hard to say goodbye to that. The guys were at the field until seven on a Tuesday night, and that left me alone for another couple of hours. *Great*. Not what I needed. But by the luck of god, my phone went off from my future roommates and I got butterflies again.

Lorelei: Ladies! If you're on campus, my brother and I are heading to Fritz Frenzy for dinner and games in an hour. I'd love to see you if you can make it!

Rachel: I'll try and stop by!

Kenzie: See you there!

Thank god. I showered, spent some extra time on my hair, blow-drying it and straightening out the curls, and added some extra eyeliner and lip gloss. No glasses today for me. Throwing on my favorite ripped jeans and turquoise crop top, I texted Aaron to let him know I'd be out with my future roommates.

I *actually* communicated what I was doing with my life, unlike him. Well, besides the whole Tanner thing. *That's my secret to the grave.*

The walk to Fritz wasn't long and I recognized a couple of people on the way. *How cool!* I knew them from working the Lion and it made the huge campus seem a little less big. It comforted me in a way I hadn't realized I needed and I had a huge smile.

"Kenzie! Over here!" Lorelei hollered at me and I found her and a stupidly handsome guy sitting across from her. He had her same coloring of olive skin, light gray eyes and black hair, but other than that, they had no similarities. She was beautiful, he was strikingly handsome. *Woah, baby.*

"Hey, Lorelei, this must be your twin brother?" I sat next to him, across from her, and held out my hand. "Kenzie Hill."

"Logan Romano."

Ugh, he spoke like he knew how hot he was, adding a little wink after he said his name. I chuckled, giving Lorelei a knowing glance. "Is your brother always this charming?"

"Yes, I hate it. Don't like him." Her eyes pleaded with me, and while she said it like a joke, I felt the vulnerability in her words. I got it. I really fucking did.

"He's too pretty for me. Not my type. No offense, Logan."

"What is your type then?"

Tanner Johnson.

I did not say that name—hell no—but I pursed my lips, thinking of what my type was. Huh. I had no idea. Just not guys who knew how good they looked. "Tall. I like a tall man with sexy eyes."

"Girl, me too. You need to come see practice with me sometime then. The football team is stacked with tall dudes. You'll get your pick with your cute face and blonde hair." We shared a laugh and it felt like I'd known her months, not just a couple weeks, and there was even a sense of comfort with Logan.

"Logan, I gotta say, you remind me of my brother a lot. The charm, the athleticism, the looks—I take it you have no issues with the ladies."

He had a real smug smile on his face when he said, "Zero issues."

I pretended to gag, earning a laugh from his sister. Then Lorelei leaned over the table. "Kenzie, your brother plays on the baseball team, right?"

"Yup. He plays shortstop and he's team captain. So trust me, Lorelei, I know what it's like having someone like this"—I pointed to her brother—"as a sibling. We gotta watch out for cleat chasing friends, people who try to use us to get closer to *them*. It's tough but I'm so glad we got roomed together."

Her face softened.

"Heyo!" Rachel said, joining us at our table, and the excitement about living with them almost burst through me. It was convenient how they were both from the area so we could meet like this before the year started. It was the best vibe, knowing we would have fun and adventures together. Rachel declared she hated most sports besides golf—a concept I didn't get because it was so boring—and didn't give Logan one look the entire conversation. That amused him and pleased Lorelei. At one point, she asked him what type of game he played.

We ordered pizza and sodas, already forming plans on how we would decorate our trio dorm—where we each had a small room for just a bed and would share a kitchen, living area, and bathroom. Logan had been placed in the same dorm, just three floors above us. We were halfway done eating when *someone* thought it would be a good idea to drop by. And by someone, I meant fucking Aaron, Tanner and Zade.

My weird massive bodyguards. Fuck.

Lorelei missed her mouth with her pizza, Rachel froze and stared and Logan sat up straighter at their approach. "Aaron, why are you here?"

"You texted me you'd be out. We felt like going out."

"You *felt* like going out? To the exact place where I told you I would be?"

"Fine. I wanted to meet your roommates to see if they were batshit crazy or not."

Oh my god. I cringed and made the awkward introduction. "Lorelei, Rachel, this is my obnoxious brother Aaron. I apologize in advance for his attitude. This is Zade Willows and Tanner Johnson. They are overbearing baseball idiots."

"Kenzie, that is no way to speak about us. We're more than idiots."

"Shut up, Zade."

He winked at me before shaking their hands. When he got to Logan, he said, "Who are you?"

"Her twin brother."

"Interesting." Zade put a hand on Aaron's shoulder. "Why does he look familiar?"

I answered. "He's on the football team."

"Oh, that's it. Nice to meet you, dude." Zade didn't wait before sitting on the other side of the table, right next to Rachel. The poor girl turned beet red when Zade helped himself to some fries and it was weird to see my two worlds colliding. Aaron sat next to me and Tanner — who hadn't said a word yet — sat across from me.

"You all excited to move in? I remember how fun it was freshmen year." Zade pointed to Tanner. "Dude, do you remember all the dumb shit we did?"

"Yeah, but not as dumb as Hilly, here."

"We don't need to rehash the past." Aaron flagged down a waitress and ordered a beer — prompting TJ and Zade to do so as well. Apparently, they were staying.

"Um, guys, I love that you assumed you can stay, but can we see if it's all right with *my* roommates?"

"I don't mind," Lorelei said way too quickly, her gaze lingering on each one of them. Even Rachel squeaked that she was okay with it. I sighed, accepting defeat.

"Fine. Stay and embarrass me, you hooligans."

"Tell us your best Kenzie story, Aaron," Lorelei said, the traitorous bitch, and I elbowed my brother in the side, prompting everyone to laugh.

"Don't you dare."

"This one time, she was like three or so, she didn't know how to go to the bathroom by herself and — "

"No! No, fucking shut your whore mouth!"

They all cackled, but Aaron didn't care. He continued, trying to embarrass me to death. "She was upstairs alone at our aunt's house and couldn't wipe her own ass. Instead of yelling for help, she slid down the stairs, butt-naked, leaving evidence all down the carpet. We still talk about it today."

"Oh, my god. Kill me."

Logan really liked the story, laughing hard and hitting his fist against the table. I dared to look through my fingers covering my face and found Tanner smiling at me with a little too much heat in his eyes. I sucked in a breath at his warm expression and forced myself to remember Aaron was right there. "Fuck you, Aaron. How about the time you stuck your hand in the toilet and — "

"Now, now, Kenny, shh. I have a reputation to uphold. You don't. So, Lorelei, tell me about yourself…"

The evening went on, my brother embarrassing the shit out of me and my new roommates eating up every word. It was incredible to experience it — new friends and my brother's friends and Tanner all together laughing and joking around.

We all said goodbyes, hugging one another and making plans to hang out again, and even Logan gave me a hug. Tanner stiffened, but I refused to think about it. *Five days* flashed in my mind on the walk back and my momentary high from dinner turned to an anguished knowledge of my running timeline with Tanner.

"I approve of them. Your roommates, I mean," Aaron announced on our trek to the house. He led with Zade, leaving Tanner and me to walk arm to arm. It was hard not touching him — something I really wanted to do — but I managed to contain myself.

"Thanks, Aaron. I mean, what would you do if you didn't?"

"I don't know. Scare them. Logan worries me, though. Why's a dude hanging out with all chicks?"

"Because he's a good brother and hangs with his sister? Don't be a dick."

"Don't get involved with him."

"Here we go again. *Jesus*," I scoffed, hoping to find Tanner smiling with me. But he wasn't. His face was tight, almost pained, and my stomach dropped. *Oh no.*

"Just doing my brotherly duty. I'll leave it alone for a week."

"Feel free to go longer than that. I won't stop you."

He flipped me off and babbled about practice the rest of the way back. Tanner remained silent, each step causing a wave of anxiety to build in my chest. *Is he cleared for baseball early? Oh my god. Are we done?*

I sure as hell wasn't prepared to be done. The worry grew the closer we got, and by the time we reached the house, I was a nervous bundle. "I'm going upstairs. I'll see you guys tomorrow."

"Bye, Kenny! Don't wipe your ass on our stairs," Zade said, so I punched him in the gut. "Damn, that hurt."

"Good. I meant it too."

He laughed and I took the stairs two at a time, figuring out the best plan of attack. I paced my room for two minutes before Tanner snuck in with those goddamn bedroom eyes that had me weak. "Can I stay with you tonight?"

Wait, what?

"Huh?" I said, sounding stupid.

"Can I sleep with you tonight?" he repeated, moving closer to me and pulling me against him. "Please?"

"Yes. Of course," I mumbled into his chest. "I thought something was wrong."

"Nothing is wrong. I just—I want to cherish every second with you. Let me take care of you in every way tonight, Kenzie. Please."

How can a girl say no to that?

He kissed me, deeply and with all the passion I dreamed about when I thought about *love*. There was no rush when he removed my clothing and spent an hour kissing every inch of my skin—licking and teasing my most sensitive areas, reading my body so well that I lost control. Three times he brought me to orgasm with just his mouth. I arched my back as the pleasure spread to every limb, the need to have him so strong it startled me.

"Tanner, please, I want you."

"You have me, Kenzie."

We fumbled with the condom. He dropped it twice before he unwrapped it and put it on. He gave me one more soul-crushing kiss—one to officially ruin any other kiss I'd ever experience—before laying me on the bed with such gentleness my throat dried.

"You are so beautiful, Kenzie," he whispered before pushing into me in a slow, incredibly controlled thrust. He did it again, rolling his hips at the perfect pace, kissing my eyes, my cheek, my neck and mouth. I clawed at his back, trying to hold him tighter. He gripped my back with one hand, my ass with the other and increased his pace, hitting me at the right angle to have lust getting me wet and ready for him to stretch me wider. "Your body is amazing. I love how you feel against me. Your soft skin, your sounds. You could destroy me, Kenzie."

"So could you me," I whispered, hating how heavy our words felt. He arched my hips with his hand, allowing him to go deeper, and I moaned as the slow burn formed again at the base of my spine. "Yes, Tanner," I breathed.

"You. Are. Perfect." He spoke choppily. His back muscles worked overtime as he increased our rhythm — my orgasm was close and he tilted me up higher so I took him entirely, sending the right stimulants to my clit for my orgasm to rock me. I shuddered against him, my eyes stinging at the tender way he watched me. There was no other moment in my life where I'd felt like this — cherished, appreciated, *cared for*. He let me ride out waves of pleasure, kissing away my loud moans, and in the process, got closer to release. "Ah, baby. You're so — fuck. Yes!"

He held on to me, pumping into me three more times before he stilled. Our heartbeats matched in rhythm, our sweaty chests rubbing together, and I felt whole. Complete. "I'll be right back, Ken."

He got up, went into the bathroom, and slide back into bed completely naked. "God, I wish I could take a picture of you right now so I can remember it forever."

"Why's that?" I grinned like a love-struck fool.

"Because you're beautiful. Your cheeks are a little pink, your eyes wild and sated, your nipples perky and your body is just…my weakness." He ran his hand from my neck, down my collarbone to my hips, down my thighs and ending on my feet. "I mean this sincerely."

Shit, his voice had changed and I sat up.

"I've never wanted to break my rules more than I do with you." He grabbed my hand and kissed my wrist, never breaking eye contact. "I know we're almost done with your list, and me returning to baseball, but, Kenzie, this is special."

"It is." I took his hand and stared at it, trying to memorize the way his tattoo moved when his hand did. "Why did you really get a tattoo of a triangle?"

"I view each leg as my mom, and two brothers. They hold me together when I get lost."

Oh lord. My eyes stung at his answer. It was so sweet, and true. He lived his life for them and damn — it hit me, like slamming into a brick wall. The reason my chest felt heavy all the time, the reason I'd been so upset thinking about our time ending and the reason my heart raced every time he walked into the room. *I'm in love with him.* I cleared my throat, the daunting realization sending my task-oriented brain into a frenzy. There wasn't a to-do list for this. No steps to take that were right.

"It's stupid, isn't it?" he asked after I was quiet too long.

I laughed and pulled him against me so we faced each other in my bed. "You're an incredible guy, Tanner Johnson. One of the best."

He grinned and pressed one more kiss on my lips. "This has been my favorite summer of my entire life. All because of you. Think we'll get caught if I sleep in here?"

"Let's chance it. What could he do, anyway? Kill you? He'd look awful in orange."

Tanner laughed and pulled me against his chest. It'd be easy to get used to this, to feel safe and protected with him, but I knew it couldn't happen. And that was the hardest part—I understood his reasons why.

Chapter Twenty-Six

Tanner

One more day. I reported back to practice tomorrow — Nicole had checked me out the day before and even complimented me on my discipline. But that meant I'd be playing in games and practices, focusing all my energy on the sport that would secure everything in my family's future. *Baseball, draft, MLB, helping my mom.* My chest hurt, thinking about being with Kenzie one final time. Technically, we had two more times on her list, but we'd agreed that once I returned to play, we'd end our fling.

I took a deep breath, trying to calm my pulse, when she smiled at her phone from her position on the couch. It was a lazy Sunday morning and Aaron had chosen to stay at the house last night. It annoyed me, but he hadn't noticed me sneaking into my room early this morning. *God, I love sleeping next to her.*

She mumbled in her sleep and never moved once she was out. Yeah, I was a fucking creeper and had watched her sleep a couple of times. She was cute. She could talk baseball with me, give me attitude when I deserved it, make me laugh and we had the best sex I'd ever experienced. Why couldn't we prolong it?

"TJ, you pumped to get back on the field tomorrow?" Aaron asked, reminding me why today would be the last day with her. He plopped down on the seat next to me. "Nice, watching *Step Brothers*?"

"It's a classic," Kenzie said, looking up from her phone with her glasses perched on her nose. "It's one of those movies you can't skip. You know? Like *Wedding Crashers* or *Superbad*."

"*The Godfather* is a movie you don't mess with. Not those."

"Incorrect, you weirdo."

"Anyway." Aaron directed his attention back to me. "I was thinking—I know you report back to the field tomorrow, but we should celebrate you feeling better."

"Celebrate?"

"Yeah. Let's go out tonight. Get a couple beers, enjoy the summer before our senior year. Zade's already in. Carter and Felix said a couple of the other guys want you back. We could call it team bonding or something if Coach gets pissed."

I glanced at Kenzie. She had her bottom lip sucked into her mouth and her eyes were wide—we hadn't explicitly made plans, but it was unspoken. *Our last night.* "I don't know, man, I don't want to overdo it."

"TJ. Dude. You're going. This is to celebrate you, fucker, so you can't back out. What would you do anyway? Watch a dumb movie with my sister for your class? Do that another night."

I gulped, trying to think of anything that would make sense for me to get out of it. But the longer the silence went on, the more I sweated. *Shit. Shit!* Nothing came, and Aaron gave me a confused look just as Kenzie chimed in. "Are you guys getting together here? I might hang out with my new roommates tonight and can crash there if you want to have it here."

"Sweet, we might just do that. Then precious TJ over here can't worry about overdoing it." Aaron hit my shoulder and I did my best version of a smile. "Dude, you need to get laid. You're cranky. I can't recall the last time I saw a chick sneaking out of here. You still hooking up with that girl...Mickey something?"

I froze, but Aaron didn't notice. He kept talking, asking, "Kenz, have you seen any of his hook-ups recently?"

She slid me a coy look before responding. "You know...there was one redhead girl a couple weeks ago, right around the Fourth of July. Saw her sneak out after that night of beer and blowing shit up. She seemed really nice."

"A redhead? Nice work, dude." Aaron reached out his knuckles and bumped mine, and it took all my self-control not to react.

Kenzie snorted, the traitor, and I narrowed my eyes at her, but she did a great job of ignoring me. She moved her dainty fingers over her phone, chuckling at whatever was on there, and I was struck with something like jealousy. I wanted to make her laugh, make her smile like that and I had no idea who it was. "Those your roommates?"

"Yup. They're a fucking hoot. Lorelei has a dare with one of her friends of who can get the most dates from Tinder this month, but only using pick-up lines that reference America. Like, *baby are you a national treasure, because you look like the constitution.* My favorite though— *baby, I'll make you see stars and stripes.* Rachel and I are contemplating joining the competition. Winner gets an American-themed basket and while that doesn't sound great, I like winning things."

I tried smiling, but all I could focus on was her going on dates, letting other guys touch her, kiss her, hear her sounds and make her happy. *Shit, did we forget to turn on the air?* "Is it hot in here?"

"Nope. I'm cold," Aaron replied, scrutinizing his sister. "You're not going to do that dumb shit, right? That's…I mean, it's funny, but not for my sister."

"Aaron. You did all the drugs, did *all* the girls and you're trying to tell me what to do? Nah. No thank you."

"But it's different."

"Why? Because I'm a girl? I can like sex, bro. Don't be sexist. It's a double-standard."

Oh my god, I hated this conversation so fucking much. Sweat pooled on my forehead and I got up to get a glass of water. What was happening? I should be pumped, ready to return to the field and get back on the grind of reaching my goal. I should not be fucking thinking about Kenzie and especially not about her having sex with other dudes.

The cup fell from my hand and spilled water on the floor. "Shit."

I used a washcloth to pick up the moisture and leaned against the counter as though it would help me find my bearings and tell me how to stop acting like this. Just because we were having a party, it didn't mean I couldn't sneak into her room after it was over. *Yes! That's it.* We could still be together one, maybe two final times before I reported back. It fit the timeline and would complete her list. I knew how she felt about that list.

Relaxed and content with my decision, I walked back out and Aaron was gone. "Where's your bro?"

"IHOP. He's meeting Greta there for their bimonthly pancake obsession. You know how they are." She set her phone down and gave me a funny smile. "You okay?"

"Yeah. I think so." I joined her on the couch, immediately putting my arm around her so she could rest her head on my shoulder. "I don't want to do that shit your brother was harping on me about. I'd rather spend my night with you."

She relaxed against me and lifted her face up to mine. She kissed the spot right where my cheek met my lips. "Aaron won't let you get out of it."

"I fucking know." I sighed, hating the pinching feeling around my heart. "We didn't talk about it, but tonight is…"

"Our last night. I know." She sat up, a seductive smile forming on her lips. "They'll be gone at least an hour. We could make sure to knock off one from my list. You up for it?"

"God, if I ever say no to that question, know something's wrong."

She took my hand and the two of us ran up the stairs, laughing. She pulled me into her room, shoving my back against the door and giving me the sexiest look I had ever seen on her. "Just when I think I can't get enough of you. You're the handsomest guy I've ever had the pleasure of being with. Let me show you how much…"

She showed me all right. Holy shit.

We knocked off one more time for her list and all that remained was one final time—the last chance I had to explore her. So when she kicked me out of her room, I tried not to panic. We still hadn't talked about it. Not one word about what would happen when I woke up the next day. I wasn't sure I could…that was what I told myself when she popped in to say goodbye, declaring she'd be out for the night.

* * * *

Zade passed me my second beer, his fourth, while a handful of our teammates howled with laughter at something Aaron said later that night. It was great — nine of us chilling together somewhere other than the field, and I should have been relishing the entire thing. My teammates had bought me beer and wanted to hang out to celebrate me getting to go back on the field. *How cool is that?*

I needed to stop acting like a dick. "Thanks, Z."

"Dude, you seem down. Why aren't you bouncing off the walls with excitement? You get to be back at it tomorrow. Is everything good?"

"Yeah, for sure. Just enjoying the moment." I scanned the living room and made sure to smile. It probably looked like a wince, but Zade seemed pacified and I sighed in relief. "How do you balance baseball and Callie?"

He snapped his head in my direction, his intelligent eyes alarmed, and he moved closer to me. "Uh, why?"

"Curious."

"Okay, uh, well, she knows it'll have to come first. It's that simple. It also helps she fucking knows the sport and can talk to me about it. Her family are huge baseball groupies — it's in their blood. I used to worry about her getting in my head, but, shit, it never happened. Honestly, she's the first person I call when something good or bad happens."

Kenzie can be that. She can. "Cool."

"You're not...seeing anyone, are you?"

"No."

"Why ask then?" Zade leaned onto his knees, his lips twisting into a scowl. I couldn't think of a reason why I would want to know without mentioning Kenzie. The silence grew, just like his glare, and he barked, "Answer the question, Johnson."

Shit. His tone had changed and my entire body tensed with anxiety. I wasn't sure how he figured it out, but the way he flared his nostrils and moved his gaze back from Aaron and me had me worried. "Come to the kitchen with me. Now."

I got up and followed him, close to a full-blown panic. *If he tells Aaron...* "Zade, listen."

"Shut the fuck up. Wait." He pushed open the patio door, shoved me outside and slammed it shut with a menacing glare. He crossed his massive arms and looked nothing like my friend from the past three years. He was pissed. *"His fucking sister.* I thought I was crazy, even thinking it could be a possibility. *Fuck.* How? When? God, why?"

"How did you know?"

"I didn't piece it together officially until Felix mentioned Kenzie and you snapped at him. That put me on guard, had me thinking about other times you two were together. Can't believe I didn't catch on sooner."

"It's been over a month."

He groaned and hoisted himself up to sit on the edge of the porch. "Why would you do that to her, or Aaron?"

"It's not what you think, man. I'm not fucking with her. She's...the best."

"Yeah, no one's going to believe that. You've never had a relationship longer than three days. *Jesus,* we can't afford this on the team. Not this year. Aaron will lose it and he just got everything settled down the past year.

You asshole." Zade pinched the bridge of his nose and each one of his exhalations felt worse than a punch to the gut. He was right. "Tanner. I'm more than average in the brain department. I cannot rationalize why the hell you think this is a good idea, at all."

"I didn't mean for it to happen, okay? It just did. We both wanted it and agreed it was just a fling. For fuck's sake, she's starting school and I'm planning to get drafted. There couldn't be a future there."

"No shit, there couldn't. Aaron would murder you. Rightfully so. She's been through enough. God, you're going to break her heart and I'm going to have to pick sides when Hilly comes after you. Fuck!" He got up and kicked the railing. "Why? Tell me why."

"She gets me." *I think I'm falling for her, hard.* "I like her."

"Doesn't matter, man. Don't you see it?" he asked, desperation on his face. "Aaron has seen you do way too much shit to ever give you his blessing. If you ask for it, he'll blow up. If he finds out there was even a chance of you two, he'll blow up. I'm protective of my sister and I'd never let her date any of you. But Aaron? He's worse."

"Doesn't Kenzie get a say in this? Aaron doesn't get to make this decision for me."

"Well, yeah, but, Tanner, why would you chance fucking anything up on our team? This is our year, the one we either get our dreams or don't." He stood and shook his head. "I'm not going to tell your secret. But you need to think long and hard about this. I love you like a brother, so take or leave my advice. Relationships are hard. You give and take, make sacrifices. You need to be willing to do that. You cannot hurt her. Ever. Would you cause a rift between and her brother, the only family she has nearby?"

He left me out the porch, alone, at my own low-key party, feeling like shit. I wasn't ready to say goodbye to her, but I'd be risking too much to try for more. *I have to be willing to make sacrifices — and I can't do that.* My shoulders felt as if a million pounds rested on them and when Kenzie's text came through, I had never hated myself more.

Kenzie: Let me know when it's safe to come over. If tonight is our last night together, I want to be with you as long as I can.

Tanner: I'll kick them out at midnight, but come whenever you want.

Kenzie: Great. Also, no pressure, but I have a creative solution I want to run by you.

Tanner: Solution?

Kenzie: Yeah, I think I found a way for tonight not to be the final night for us. Trust me. It's an amazing idea and I bet you'll go for it.

Fuck. This is what I want. More time with her, laughing and being with her. But Zade's words buried themselves in my chest and I swallowed down the hurt and regret.

Tanner: Sure, I'll hear it.

Kenzie: See you soon, TJ.

Our fling was supposed to end on good terms, like a fun memory we'd never forget. But I knew, without a doubt, she would hate me after we talked. And I deserved it.

Chapter Twenty-Seven

Kenzie

We spent hours picking out decorations online for our dorm and making fun of our siblings. Lorelei and Logan were locals, only living twenty minutes off campus, and their parents were absolute sweethearts. Their mom and dad made us a homemade Italian meal and reminded me so much of my own parents I almost hugged them. Rachel was cool too.

It was refreshing to feel so excited about moving in with my roommates and experiencing college with new friends. But the joy conflicted with an internal battle that seemed to get worse each day. I wanted to move into dorms, but dreaded the fact that I wouldn't share a wall with Tanner anymore because, at some point, Tanner had worked his way up to being one of my favorite people.

My heart raced in anticipation on the drive back to the house. My creative idea had hit me in the middle of eating pepperoni pizza. *Continue our fling, but never on days where he has a game the next day.* It'd leave one or two days a week when we could enjoy each other and fool around, while not committing to anything more than we could handle. There was no way he'd not be up for that — I saw it in the way he stared at me, and was so gentle. *God, I'm into him so much.*

Giddy. I was giddy.

I'd been so worried about experiencing college I hadn't thought about how easily Tanner could fit into my life. He'd changed from being my brother's friend to one of my best friends. *The base of all relationships is friendship.* Sure, I didn't think either of us was ready for a relationship, but we shouldn't have to end something that worked. It didn't make sense, the way he'd snuck into my life and made himself comfortable, but I wanted him to remain there. And I think he did too.

The Uber driver stopped the car just outside the driveway and I got out. Laughter rang from the porch, and I smiled at Carter, Felix and Aaron all sitting there with a couple of beers.

"Hey, gentlemen. Having a good night?" I chuckled at the sight of them, looking a little tipsy and real content with themselves. It also pleased me to see Aaron relaxing with people outside his tight-knit circle.

"Hell, yeah, pretty Hilly." Carter slurred his words and I gave Aaron a look. He snorted, shrugged and belched.

"Okaaaay, I'm heading inside. No puking out here." I pointed to all of them, one by one, and waited for someone to respond. Carter did with a fervent nod.

"Yes, ma'am."

I laughed, darting up the stairs and into my bedroom. No one was in the living room, or upstairs, from what I could tell, and I locked the door. I gave myself one glance in the mirror to make sure I didn't have anything in my teeth or on my face — that had happened to me before and it wasn't a good look. After ensuring I looked presentable, I went into Tanner's room with my adrenaline pumping. The room smelled like him, leather, sweat and his subtle cologne. *I love the way he smells.*

He sat on his bed, his shoulders slumped and head down looking at something on his lap—a phone perhaps—but he heard me, and my heart skipped a beat when his face lit up. Every one of his features morphed into joy and he stood, moving to pull me against him. "Kenzie, hey."

"Goddamn, a girl could get used to a greeting like this," I said into his neck.

He squeezed me, the hug lingering on and on, and each breath he took tightened his muscles. I slid down his body, but he stopped me before my feet hit the ground. He hoisted me up, rested my back against the door and brought his lips to mine. *Oh shit.* He tasted like beer, but it didn't bother me. No. Not at all. He slid his tongue inside my mouth, sucking my bottom lip hard and kissing me with so much passion I whimpered.

This kiss was different. It was aggressive and hard, desperate and hot. It was as though all the air in the world would disappear if we broke our kiss, and I relished it. Each stroke of his tongue sent shivers to my toes, sending ripples of lust throughout my body. "Tanner, god. You're...delicious."

He stilled at my words, dragging his hands to my hips and setting me on the ground. His warm chocolate eyes looked anguished, not at all like the joy I'd seen when I first walked in. "What is it, TJ?" I asked, my voice shaking just enough for him to notice.

"You said you wanted to talk." His tone was off. It wasn't gentle or kind like I'd grown used to. *Fuck. What's happening?*

My brain was fuzzy with that insane kiss and I took a second to remember it. He made no moves for us to go to bed, just remained standing. "Want to sit?"

"Let's stand." His expression hardened the longer I started at him. There were only a couple of inches between our chests, but it felt more—way more—as though I didn't know this version of him with his hard expression, unkind tone and stiff shoulders.

"Okay?" I hesitated at the intensity of his face. Nerves exploded in my stomach when his rigid jawline seemed more intimidating than sexy, and I took a breath. "I was thinking about us."

"We were *just* a fling, Kenzie," he said through gritted teeth. "There wasn't an *us* beyond the bedroom and our time is up."

What the hell? "Right. I know. I misspoke."

"What's your idea?"

"Uh, well, to *not* end our fling."

He groaned, his warm breath tickling my nose, and something like anger flashed in his eyes. "I told you baseball will always come first. Nothing will change that fact and I report back tomorrow. I won't have time for you, so please don't ask for it. You agreed to this." He moved one hand to his hair, pulling the end of it.

"Right, that's what we discussed." I gulped and wished I could rewind time and stop it where his hands had been around me and my heart had felt full. But I couldn't, so I carried on in a weak voice. "I just thought, maybe, if we agreed to only hang out when you didn't have games the next day. It wouldn't be a relationship. I don't think you or I envision having one for a good while, but, Tanner, I like spending time with you. You've kinda become my best friend and I understand your Dedication to the team and would never get in the way of it. I thought you knew that."

He had a look of revulsion on his face, the lines around his mouth tightening into unhappy wrinkles. My gut turned to lead and I almost felt as though I could throw up. I'd put myself out there, telling him my idea, and I hadn't expected this reaction at all. Not even a little bit. He pushed away from the wall, moved to the other side of the room and hardly looked like the guy I spent my time with. He swallowed hard, choosing to look at the ground. "No. No, I can't spend any more time with you."

"Because you don't want to?"

He didn't respond. He shrugged and held up his phone, showing the large numbers. Twelve-thirty. Officially, our last day. "Kenz, I have enjoyed every second we spent together, but it ran its course. We're done. Simple as that."

"Simple as that? I'm going to need more than a *simple as that*."

"Don't make it harder than it needs to be." He narrowed his gaze at me, glancing at his door for a second before returning to me. "Baseball will always fucking come first — plus, you're starting college. You need to explore all life's possibilities, not be trying to hang with someone who will never want to give you one hundred percent. You said no boyfriends, and prolonging this would eventually lead to that, right?"

"Not necessarily," I mumbled, hating the way my lips shook and my fingers trembled. "Somewhere along the way, I got feelings for you and I'm not ready to say goodbye. That doesn't mean a relationship. It just means more time. That's all."

He blinked real fast, his nostrils flaring, but he gave a firm shake of his head. "I'll always care for you, Kenzie, but just as friends. As Aaron's little sister. Agreeing to more of...*this*...is not something I'll ever do."

"Okay. Sure, yeah." *I will not cry. Nope. Hide it.* "We promised to be honest. I guess...this is it. I'll j-just head back to my r-room. Good luck, Tanner. You're going to kill it tomorrow."

He started to say something, but I was already through the bathroom door and into my bed before tears fell. It made sense now, that kiss. It was a goodbye. I didn't try to rationalize my feelings, or hide them until later. They took over my body and I cried myself to sleep—at the loss of something amazing, at the fact that our friendship was probably over, but also at the way he'd gotten me to love him unintentionally. It was all-consuming and when it wasn't reciprocated, it slashed my heart. I let myself feel every emotion—something I didn't do often—and I fell asleep with tears drying on my face. Tomorrow would be a new day and I would face it then.

* * * *

My eyes were a little red and that was the only indication of my miserable night of sleep. I was a master at hiding my inner thoughts. I'd had to be, all those years at home, and this was no different. *Deep breath in, then out, think of something safe. Work. I work tonight.* I thought of Clyde and bussing tables. *Yes, that works.* With that on my mind, I walked downstairs around lunchtime in jeans and one of the Zwillows Pillows shirts they'd gotten me for my birthday. *God, that was weeks ago.*

So much had changed since then.

I had roommates I wanted to be friends with, I had a job I loved and kept me busy and I'd gone from having low expectations of love to falling head first into it with someone off-limits. It was a wild fucking ride I hadn't signed up for and my poor heart couldn't handle any more pain.

The guys were at the field until noon and I used the free time to come up with a plan to get out of the house — only problem was, all the places I wanted to go were ones Tanner had shown me. Great. Maybe moping and watching TV without love would be the best idea. I did it all the time and they could ignore me when they got back. *Wouldn't be the first time.*

After a bowl of cereal, three cups of coffee and a banana, I lounged on the couch, binge watching *Criminal Minds* and forgot to vacate the area. To be fair, the episodes were getting intense and I couldn't stop watching. That was what I told myself, at least. It had nothing to do with waiting to see Tanner and wanting to know how he'd done on the field.

"Hey, Kenz." Aaron dumped his duffel to the right of the entryway and plopped down on the loveseat. He smelled like sweat and sunscreen, clearly not having showered before heading home. "What season of the show are we on?"

"Fifth."

"Sweet. Love this one." He got himself real comfortable and I waved at Zade when he came in. His reaction — a grimace. *Weird.*

"Like my shirt, Z?" I asked, trying to smile to break the tension that clogged the air when Tanner followed him in. "Thought you'd appreciate it."

"Jesus," he scoffed, moving his gaze from me to Tanner a little too quickly. But he looked back at me. "I can't believe you have that shit. I'll burn it if you leave it out."

"Can you sign it? It'll help me get *really* popular when I move into the dorms."

He rolled his eyes and lingered at the base of the stairs, watching Tanner move from the living room to the kitchen. "I was all for trading Jeff for you, but not anymore. You're outta here soon, Ken. And not a day longer."

"You'll miss me, Zade. You all will."

"Eh, maybe," Aaron said, prompting me to smack him with a pillow. He laughed and looked up at Tanner. "You'll miss having a friend here, won't you, TJ? She was actually nice to you."

The air stilled. Tanner's face looked like a statue, with his jaw tensing and his eyes going wide. Zade, too, stood taller. Aaron had no idea how heavy those words were and I waited for Tanner's response. He refused to look at me. Instead, he shrugged and unscrewed his bottle of water. "I guess, yeah."

"You'll be back over here though, right? You'll come visit?" Aaron asked, giving me a worried smile. "I kinda liked having you here."

"First off, I'm not leaving for another two weeks. Also, I'm not dying so you'll all see me again. Secondly, I'm going to miss living with you too, brother." I moved to give him a noogie, only to have him smack my hand away. "Are you all hanging out here tonight?"

"Probably. We leave for a tournament tomorrow — only going two days this time, so don't carry around a bat trying to attack criminals."

"You should've texted me, asshole. I was only protecting myself and I would've done a great job, thank you very much." I pointed my finger at Aaron's chest and Tanner's gaze hit my bare legs. It wasn't fair. He shouldn't be able to give me those type of looks if he didn't want to try. My chest felt heavy again and I needed a distraction. "I'm going to head to a café before my shift starts. If I don't see you guys later, good luck at your games."

"Thanks, Ken. We might stop by the bar tonight — Greta's working and she's experimenting with some new open mic shit."

"Cool. See you then."

I walked past Tanner with my head held high, not giving him a clue how messed up my heart was around him. My plan was in place — lose myself in homework and pick up every extra table at the bar so I couldn't think.

* * * *

"This duo ain't cutting it for me. What do ya think, Kenz?" Greta asked, leaning on the bar and giving me a curious look later that night. "You're frowning, so I take it they're bad?"

"Uh, no. They're fine." I took another deep breath and focused on wiping the same spot with a rag. The two guys on stage sang off-pitch and it was almost comical — but I couldn't find it in me to laugh just yet. Tanner, Aaron, Zade and some other teammates were at the bar and every time I wasn't busy, I snuck a glance at him and felt slapped when he never looked my way. In fact, he hadn't acknowledged me once.

He has to still feel something, right? Why does he have to be here?

"Girl, you're great at hiding your emotions, but you have this haunted look in your eyes. Are you okay?" She put her hand on my back and patted me. It was a kind gesture, but I would not be talking to her about what happened. Hell, I wouldn't tell anyone.

I couldn't.

"Yeah. Cramps."

"Fuck. Sorry. Those are the worst. Need some meds?"

"Took some, thanks." I gave her a tight-lipped smile and set the rag back in the bucket of sanitizing water. A new group of people walked into my section and I gladly left Greta behind the bar to take their order. It was three booths away from the back section with the guys, but it faced the other way so I didn't have to see *him*. I took the new group's orders and moved back toward the kitchen but something slippery was on the clean tile, causing my foot to slide out from under me.

Air left my lungs and I defied gravity, flailing in the air as gracelessly as possible and hit the ground with my wrist bending the wrong way. "Shit! Ow!"

"Kenzie!" Tanner yelled my name, jumping from his chair to the spot on the ground where I sat with my legs in weird directions and my arm clutched to my middle. "Are you hurt?"

"Yes." I winced and hated how every person now stared at me. It was mortifying. Tanner reached out to my forearm and pulled it back, tracing his fingers over the tendons. "Ah!"

"I never took you for clumsy. You had a bad fall there." He was no more than three inches from my face, a smile playing on his lips and those deep brown eyes looking at me with so much warmth, I had to blink back tears. "Let's get you some ice."

I didn't think about how it looked to my brother, Tanner helping me up and walking me to the kitchen. Clyde freaked out, as per usual, and helped sit me on a chair to get me ice. Tanner stayed there until Clyde left, and when it was just the two of us, the embarrassment hit. "Th-thank you for helping. I'm fine."

"You fell hard." He crouched so we were face to face, his breath hitting my skin and teasing me. I wanted him to kiss me, tell me everything was fine between us, but he didn't. He frowned, a dark look crossing his features. "Rest in here for a bit. I need to head back out there."

He stood, turning to leave the room, but gave me one more tender look. "Thank you, Kenzie. For everything. I needed a friend like you this summer...and, well, I'll never forget it."

If I hadn't been certain before, those words solidified our end.

Chapter Twenty-Eight

Tanner

Seven days without kissing her, talking about the future, laughing at something stupid or sleeping next to her. We didn't talk more than a casual greeting. She joked with Zade and talked shit to her brother, but never me. I even texted her when we were away on a trip, asking how her shifts at work had gone. She always responded the same, that it had gone well and she hoped I'd played great.

No more inside jokes, flirting, teasing or acknowledging what we had. Just...existing alongside each other without our paths crossing.

Nothing in my life had felt like this before — empty. It was longing and a craving, but not just for sex. It was...more. Every night before I fell asleep, I thought about her, and when I woke up in the morning, I wished it was two weeks ago where I could sneak into her room and kiss her.

I'm a fucking sap from the movies.

I can't cause drama for our final season. This is for the best. She deserves more.

I worked the machine at a furious pace, pumping iron faster and longer than I tended to — something Aaron and Zade noticed. Coach said something too, but I disregarded it. It wasn't the drive to get better that fueled me. It was her, the need to work out hard enough so I could sleep easier when I got back to the house and not think about her being a wall away. She was silent in her room. She could be out, or not, and I had no right to know about it.

What happens when she moves out?

No. I won't think about it.

Sweat dripped into my mouth and I tasted the salty combination. Two more sets of repetitions and I would call it a day. Before Kenzie, a workout like this would have lit the fire to head to a party, hook up with someone or stay out all night. But now, that sounded unfulfilling. Awful. An act, when the person I wanted to be with wasn't an option.

She wanted to prolong it. I'm the reason it's over. The way her eyes dulled, looking at me. Fuck, that hurts.

"Yo, Johnson! You played fucking good last weekend. Why are you going so hard?" Aaron asked, whistling as he approached the workout bench. "You look like a maniac."

"Bigger, better, stronger," I mumbled. He didn't realize how close he'd come to finding out about me and his sister last week after she'd fallen. Zade had helped me out by stating he would've rushed to help her too, that we'd all grown to care for her. Aaron had bought it and I'd almost confessed, I felt so fucking bad. It was a shit-storm and I wanted it all to go away, but that meant forgetting about my time with Kenzie and that wasn't something I was ready to do. *I lied to her...about everything.*

"You're a beast. Whatever's got you fucked up is working, my friend."

"Thanks." I wasn't sure what he wanted me to say, and I hated to admit it even to myself, but I was glad when Carter and Felix walked over to us. They would direct Aaron's attention and I could sneak off. But, before I could, they said a name that caught all my attention. *Kenzie.*

"What the fuck did you say, Felix?" Aaron snapped. "My sister?"

"Aaron, I'm being honest with you. I respect you as a captain on our team, but I'm not asking for permission. I'm informing you. It's just one date."

Aaron pinched the bridge of his nose, exhaling real loudly, and I swore I saw red. I had to have misunderstood him. No fucking way he'd said *date* and *Kenzie* in the same sentence. It wasn't—*no.*

"*Why. Her,*" Aaron fumed.

"We get along, like the same TV shows, we're both new here. Dude, I don't know. I asked, she said yes and I'm really excited about it." Felix didn't wait for Aaron's reaction. He walked away with a small shrug, and while I would've admired his confidence at any other moment, I didn't when it involved Kenzie. The girl I loved.

What the fuck? Love.

Aaron slammed his fist against the metal bar of my machine and turned his lethal gaze to me. "Who the fuck does he think he is?"

I couldn't answer. My thoughts wouldn't come out. He stared harder, letting out a slew of curse words before he rubbed his palms over his eyes. "I'm acting wild, aren't I?"

Still no words. He took my silence — one filled with spiraling thoughts of regret — and nodded to himself. "I hate this idea, but that took balls telling me. Kenzie's got a good head on her shoulders and if he hurts her, he dies. Yeah. One date. I can handle one date. Thanks for the talk, TJ."

He didn't acknowledge the fact that I hadn't said a word. It was for the best — I wasn't in the right mind to talk to him and I rushed through the rest of my workout, followed by my scalding hot shower and grabbing a bag of ice from Nicole for my leg. It didn't pull or hurt, but I needed to rest it and take care of it so it didn't happen again. Something like the panic I felt when I missed a fly ball and had to rush after it went through me. Without thinking, I sent her a text to see if she was home.

Tanner: Are you at the house? Can we talk?

Kenzie: I'm here and sure.

I hitched a ride with Zade and hated the silence between us. He glared at me when I entered the car, and I did nothing to ease the tension. If anything, I got angrier with him. He'd demanded I ended this, saying that this could never happen. Now Felix was asking her out...instead of me. *Fuck.*

"I noticed you haven't been hanging out with Kenzie anymore. Things finally end between you two?"

"Yup."

"You don't seem real happy about it."

"Great observation. Gold fucking star for you."

"Don't be a dick. It's not my fault — "

"Yeah, it is! You fucking went off on me about how it's a terrible idea and that it'll cause tension on the team.

Well guess what, Felix asked her out and Aaron accepted it."

Zade gripped the steering wheel tighter and gave me a menacing glare at the stop sign. "Our team doesn't need fucking lies. If this shit is for real for you, then tell him. It's that simple."

I didn't respond as we got closer to the house. My chest felt like a million pounds, my heart racing at the thought of telling Aaron. What would I say? I wanted to date his sister for real? That I loved her? That we'd make it work despite him? My breathing came in pants and all thoughts of baseball left.

I don't have to give up baseball and her.

Zade's expression softened and he spoke with a calming tone. "Dude, this is more than just a fling, huh?"

"Yes. I don't know when it happened, but it did and my life's been pretty fucking sad since we ended it. No, *I* ended it. She wanted to keep it going but after our convo... I stopped it."

"And hearing Felix asked her out kicked you into gear?"

"Yeah."

Zade groaned, a reaction I didn't appreciate, and turned onto our street. "Don't tell her that. Trust me, chicks don't want to hear about some jealous thing."

I snorted, my nerves bubbling up my chest and into my throat. *I'm going to try to get her back.* Relief. Happiness. Hope. So many positive emotions ran through me at the thought of kissing her again. "Thanks, Z."

"I hope I didn't make the wrong call. You gotta do what's right for you, man, but you owe it to Aaron to come clean."

I nodded just as he parked in the driveway, and I didn't wait before jumping out of the front seat and heading inside. The screen door squeaked like it normally did, the TV left on like Kenzie preferred, for background noise, and my breath caught in my throat when I saw her sitting on the couch with her glasses. She set down the cup of coffee she had and gave me a worried look.

"You look like an insane person. Are you okay?" she asked, moving her legs from the couch to the floor.

"Can we talk?" I pointed upstairs.

"Sure?" She hesitated, her lips curving down into a frown and darting her gaze from me to the front door. Zade strolled in, whistling, and went right into the basement. *Good man.*

"Come on." It took a lot of effort not to pick her up and carry her up there, but I managed. I let her lead and I admired the way her black shorts hugged her every curve, her gorgeous skin teasing me. I knew how it felt, how it warmed when I touched it, and, fuck, I needed her.

She went into her room and ushered me in, shutting the door behind us. "Okay. Tell me what's going on."

I didn't wait before I cupped her face in my hands and kissed the hell out of her. *Coffee.* She tasted like coffee and perfection. Her plump lips softened against me and she moaned. *God, yes.* I couldn't get enough of her or kiss her long enough. Our tongues collided, her sucking mine into her mouth, and I wanted to spend hours with her, just like this.

Like we used to.

"God, I fucking missed you," I breathed into her, moving to kiss her neck and earlobe. She bucked beneath me, and I licked one of her favorite spots. "This has been hell."

"Wait." She stopped and put one hand on my chest, pushing me away a couple of inches. She adjusted her glasses and looked at me with swollen lips. "Why? Why *now*?"

"What do you mean?" I tried to hug her, pull her against me, but she shook her head. "I'm sick of pretending I don't want you every minute."

She closed her eyes, her face softening for a second, before she opened those green eyes and glared at me. "We've said no more than ten words to each other since that night—the one you said you couldn't prolong this. That was almost two weeks ago. Why now?"

"I just realized I didn't want to pretend anymore." The nerves came back at her expression, the flutters in my gut that had words coming out real choppy. "It's just—with baseball—and your brother—I heard him today with Felix and—"

"*What?*" she seethed, giving me a look I wished I never had to see. She moved from the door to the other side of her room, her cute little ass swaying as she paced. "You know Felix asked me out."

"Why did you say yes?"

"Because I'm sick of being sad and it is something to do," she responded, her eyes turning darker the longer she stared at me.

"Don't go with him. It'd kill me to know you were with him...no, just, please." *God, I'm begging. I sound pathetic and I don't care.*

She sucked one of her cheeks into her mouth and stared me down. I had never felt so small in my life. "When did you find out, exactly?"

"A couple hours ago at the gym. He approached Aaron and told him he'd asked you, and your brother yelled at him, but didn't kick his ass. It got me thinking, if he could do it, then maybe I could talk to him or something and I wouldn't feel bad about what Zade said, causing problems on the team." *Oh god, she's not smiling.* No, her face lost all traces of happiness, even though my lips had been on hers less than two minutes ago. I didn't understand. "Kenzie, I want us to go back to how we were, more than anything."

"Have you felt this way since we stopped?" She crossed her arms and tapped her foot on her hardwood floor. The sound echoed, and each tap felt like I was losing hope.

"Yes, no, kinda. I've missed you, our talks, everything, but—"

"The catalyst was hearing that Felix asked me out," she said, all emotion gone from her voice.

"And your brother didn't kick his ass."

"Tanner, you don't get to come back into my life after leaving it for your own reasons. This is fueled by jealousy, not...whatever you're spinning this into. I can't—I won't settle for this. I gave you a chance to continue and you said you couldn't because of *baseball*. Your Dedication to the team hasn't changed, so, really, there is nothing telling me you won't disappear again. No. You hurt me."

"Kenzie..." My voice broke a little at the end. "I think I love you."

"Don't you dare," she seethed, giving me a scathing look. "We could've worked out, Tanner. It would've been incredible but...we would've gone on pretending this summer didn't happen if you hadn't heard Felix asked me out. I'm going to ask you to leave my room. Maybe we can be friends in a couple months."

"Is this… it?"

"It has to be."

Her expression remained unmoved, and I did what she asked. I left her room, shutting the door and hating every emotion in my body. Sadness, regret, heartbreak. *She's going out with another guy and it's my fault.*

Chapter Twenty-Nine

Kenzie

Felix had a heart of gold, the smile of an angel, and yet I couldn't get into the date, four days after the talk in my bedroom with Tanner. Felix and I walked back from a wonderful dinner at a Thai restaurant and shared stories from our childhoods. He had two sisters and missed his family like crazy.

A great guy. Handsome, polite and never talked about himself too much. *He* would be the right person to give my heart to. I just hadn't gotten it back yet. We touched fingers accidentally as we walked, and I giggled, not feeling the rush of butterflies or tingles like I did with Tanner. Felix took my hand in his and intertwined our fingers, swaying our hands back and forth as we approached the house. "I can't remember the last time I held hands with a girl."

"Me, neither," I deadpanned, hating how guilty I felt. He deserved to have all my attention, not bits and pieces.

I sighed and debated how to tell him. He stopped us in the driveway and put his hands on my shoulders.

"I'm going to be honest with you."

"Oh?" My body tensed with whatever he was going to say. He smiled and brushed my hair out of my face.

"You're incredible and I had an amazing time. I've had a crush on you since the first time I met you, but I know when someone isn't into me."

I closed my eyes, ashamed at how easy he could read me, but he lifted my chin with his fingers. His face held nothing but patience and I would've given anything to feel a spark with him. *Just to get over Tanner.* "Felix…"

"Look, don't feel bad. I see your anguish and it's okay. I had a great time with you and would love to spend more time with you, when you're ready."

"I feel awful about this. You're…the best." I winced, totally putting him into the *nice guy* category. "I'm not in the best head space right now and I was excited you asked me for dinner. It isn't fair to you, I'm sorry."

"Don't apologize. We're the new kids here. We can be friends, if you want?" He looked so hopeful that I nodded a little too hard and threw my arms around him.

"I really need a friend. I can be a good one for you, too," I said into his neck. He ran his hands up and down my back, not going too far low, and squeezed. Then he released me.

"Friends it is." His dark brown eyes — not the same color as Tanner's but similar — sparkled at me, and he jutted his chin to the porch. "I'll still walk you to the door."

"Such a fucking gentleman," I mumbled, earning a loud cackle from him. We rounded the sidewalk and approached the stairs. A large, dark figure sat on the porch chair in the dark. *Tanner.* Jesus.

"I do what I can. Oh, hey, TJ." Felix waved and brought his hand to my face. "Until next time."

"Thank you," I said, hating how easy it was with him. He cupped my chin and gave it a quick squeeze before he walked back onto the street. Thinking about the conversation that was to come made my heart hurt, and I gave myself a pep talk.

He hasn't changed.

He's jealous, not committed.

He'll break me even more.

I exhaled and put on my bravest face, spinning around and crossing my arms. "I'm assuming you ordered food because there would be no reason for you to be out here."

"Did he kiss you?" His voice sounded scratchy, as if he hadn't had a drink of water for days. I stared at his blue shirt, rather than his eyes, because seeing any pain in them would weaken my resolve.

"Not sure how it's your business, but no. He did not."

He sighed, relief evident on his face. "Did you have a good time on your date?"

"Why are you doing this?" I threw my hands into the air. "We don't have a future, Tanner. This is just prolonging the inevitable. I might've said I didn't want a boyfriend, but I *do* want someone I can go on dates with, introduce to my brother—hell, someone I can see more than two times a week if there isn't a baseball game."

"Kenzie..." He got up from the chair and moved closer to me. He looked messed up, hair disheveled, dark eyes, stubble on his jaw he hadn't shaved in a while. It would be easy to fall into that trap, so I opened the door. "Please."

"Please, what, Tanner?" I snapped. My poor heart couldn't handle any more sadness or angst. It was already filled with thoughts of my dad, starting college and my idiot brother.

"Tell me what I have to do."

"There is nothing *to* do, okay? We want different things and the fling ran its course." I hated how my eyes stung, and how the words felt like huge lies, clogging my throat with their falsehoods. But it was better that way. The door shut and with it my control. I ran up to my temporary room and counted down the hours until I could be at the dorm.

* * * *

Two days later, I got my wish. Our housing coordinator emailed us that the dorms were ready for early move-in for those who'd signed up for it. In a series of super-excited texts, Lorelei, Rachel and I decided I'd move in first since they were out of town. I'd set up shop for them, get my bed ready and scope out our neighbors on each side. I couldn't wait to get out of the house. Seeing Tanner walk around shirtless was enough to break the strongest woman. It was as if he was trying to lure me back to him…and it almost worked, twice.

"Kenz, this summer went quicker than I thought." Aaron plopped onto Jeff's bed and gave me a long look. "You excited to move into the dorm with your new friends?"

"Yeah, I am." I smiled and finished putting my belongings into my suitcases. I'd begun preparing for the move days ago and almost everything was ready. Jeff's room held no traces of my short time there and while it was a bit sad, it was like closing a good book. "The next Chapter. I've been waiting a long time for this."

"You've seemed sad the past couple weeks. I know we don't talk about feelings and shit, but...is everything okay?" He had a worried expression on his face and looked so thoughtful my heart warmed at his concern. I nodded.

"I will be. It's just life."

Liar. I haven't slept well in weeks and my chest hurts whenever Tanner looks at me.

"I think we should have weekly lunch dates. We can catch up and talk and stuff."

"God, it's amazing you got Greta to fall for you with how well you are with words..."

"Fuck off," he replied, laughing at my stupid expression. "I tried to tell them it wasn't necessary, but...come downstairs."

"Why?"

"Trust me."

Shit. What is it? My anxiety got the best of me with worst-case scenarios going through my head. But I followed him down the stairs and was met with a banner, balloons, and the whole gang. Zade, Callie, Greta and Tanner. They each smiled at me, waving pompoms in the air, and my breath caught in my throat. "What...what did you guys do?"

"It's your official moving into college crew. Hilly told us your parents couldn't make it out here, so we'll be your family." Zade held his arms open. "We all agreed we'd trade Jeff for you, but his name is on the lease and he might be pissed."

"God, you guys are great." I hugged Zade, moving to Callie, then to Greta, who squeezed me too hard. "Jesus, G."

"Sorry, it's a character flaw."

That left me facing Tanner, who still looked so goddamn handsome my pulse went haywire. I felt everyone's stares on us, and I opened my arms for a hug. "Thanks for the help."

He crushed me to his chest, his familiar scent and sounds bombarding me. *Fuck. Fuck I miss this. I miss him.* "It's been nice having you here, Kenzie."

"Yeah," I said, pushing away from him and staring at everyone. "You don't have to help me move in, you know."

"We want to," Tanner said. He kept his gaze on me the entire time and when Aaron mentioned loading up his car with my stuff, a wave of strong emotion hit me. My eyes watered and an overwhelming worry halted me.

College is starting.

No more Tanner.

New people, new life style.

New classes.

No more Tanner.

"Hey, hey, come here," Tanner said when he saw my face, and I went to him. He patted my back, rubbing his hands up and down my arms, and kept speaking in a calm, deep voice. "I know it's overwhelming, but think about how exciting it will be? All the stuff you can add to your list? The dorm food, the adventures with Lorelei and Rachel, the parties and memories. You're always welcome to sneak off to our house if you need to, but I think you're going to have an amazing year. You deserve it, Kenz."

I sniffed, pressing my face farther into his shirt, and it never crossed my mind that some of the crew could see him like this. It didn't matter. "Thanks, TJ."

"That's what best friends are for, helping each other out."

I froze at his words, glancing up at him and sucking in a breath at his warm expression. "What did —"

"You're helping with this shit, too, TJ. Get your ass in gear," Zade hollered after dropping off one load, and I jumped away from him. We weren't doing anything wrong, but it still worried me.

"Chill out, man." Tanner gave me one more glance, worry etched around his eyes, before he helped load the car. We got all my bags into the trunk and Aaron, Zade and Tanner got into the car with me, the girls following with the other load, and we headed toward the dorm. It was six blocks from their house and the drive was too short. There was so much left to say, to Tanner, to my brother — hell, even Zade. They didn't have to take me in all summer and make me feel welcome, but they had.

Hills didn't express emotions and it got worse when we dropped off each bag. Zade and Aaron made inappropriate jokes the entire time as Tanner and I danced around each other in silence. Every time we ran into each other, I jumped, and hoped no one saw. It was awful and, when we dropped the last box, I hugged them goodbye. "Fuck, I'm gunna miss all of you assholes."

"I know. I feel weird. Like, my chest feels funny," Aaron said, pulling me in for another hug. "Text me any time, seriously."

"Will do."

"Yeah, I didn't think I'd become friends with another fucking Hill, but here we are and I'm already planning our next beer pong tournament," Zade said, getting a huge grin from me. We all turned to Tanner, waiting for him to say something similar as a goodbye, but he remained silent, staring at me.

Nerves got the best of me and I stuttered, "W-well, thanks for the help. See you around."

"I'll see you soon, Kenzie. I promise." He smiled, the playful grin I'd fallen in love with, and winked. "Bye."

They left, leaving me alone in my dorm meant for three people, and I *hated* it. I wished I'd waited for Rachel or Lorelei to get there first, or that I could've stayed at the house longer, or even talked to Tanner to try and be friends again.

That's what best friends do for each other.

Does that mean he wants to be friends again…just friends?

Fuck. Was being friends with him worse than pretending that nothing had happened between us? Because I sure as hell couldn't forget, and the sadness was enough to have me make the bed and plop down onto it. Maybe I'd text Clyde for a shift that night so I didn't have to sit alone, but when I checked my phone, I already had a text.

Tanner: Check your to-do list.

Okay, weird request. I frowned, scanning my bags to remember where I'd stored my ongoing list — probably my backpack. I checked in the pocket and came up empty. Shit. Maybe I'd left it at the house. I unloaded my two bags and my clothes were a mess all over the bed My pulse raced. Why was my list important? Had he added something?

Please, yes.

My purse! Yes! That was where I'd left it. I dumped all the contents onto the tiled floor, yanked the notepad from the pile, jumped onto the clothes and got comfortable. It looked like someone had added to my list and my smile was so large it hurt my cheeks. He'd started a new page and, in his choppy, bold handwriting, written —

Kenzie's to do list:
-listen to Tallen's apologies, multiple times
-realize he was a total dumbass afraid to fight for you
-accept the fact Tallen is an idiot and has learned from this
-get meals with him every day when he's in town
-go on first, real date with Tallen (all planned by him)
-go on second date with Tallen
-go on third date with Tallen
-wear Tallen's jersey to fall ball games
-come visit Tallen three nights a week (he'll come to you as much as you want)
-watch shitty movies with him
-be his girlfriend? (if you want – he doesn't need labels)
-let him cook a romantic dinner for you
-accept the fact he loves you, all of you
-MOST IMPORTANLY – make sure he's still alive. He's telling your brother everything. Right now.

I gasped. "Oh shit."

Chapter Thirty

Tanner

This is a fucking stupid idea. The worst. Could ruin the team.

But I was going to do it anyway.

Aaron tapped his fingers on the wheel of the car, unaware of the bomb I was about to drop on him, and I gulped, putting on my game face. How to start? How did I go about telling one of my best friends I was in love with his sister?

There wasn't a fucking handbook for this.

Zade rambled on about his plans for the day — the girls were going shopping for something before coming back to the house — and my palms sweated the closer we got to our shitty driveway. My phone buzzed in my hand and I knew it was Kenzie. I ignored it. I had to keep my word before I read what she texted. *Because even if she won't take me back, I'm coming clean.*

I would tell her brother. Now.

"Aaron, you got a minute to talk when we get back?" I asked, my voice scratchy.

"Sure, man." He moved his gaze from the road to the rearview mirror, concern in there. "This about your family?"

"No, not exactly."

"What are you talking about, TJ?" Zade asked, his voice growing stronger. He turned around from the front seat and widened his eyes at me, trying to convey some message, but I ignored it.

"Let's wait until we get back."

"Sure," Aaron said, unaware of Zade's odd behavior. I flipped Zade off, took a deep breath and tried to figure out the best thing to say. I loved her. I wanted to be with her and I wouldn't hurt her. She was perfect for me, and I thought I could be right for her. The biggest hurdle was not telling Aaron...fucking up our relationship on the field, and it was a risk I had to take. It was stupid to assume I didn't have room for her and baseball. Zade made it work. Aaron, too.

He pulled into the driveway and took his sweet-ass time getting out of the car. Zade lingered, and stood right in front on the porch with his arms crossed. "Talk outside, boys. It'll be better for all of us."

"Dude, why?" Aaron asked, but Zade pointed to me and when Hilly finally picked up my stress, he narrowed his eyes. "What the fuck's going on?"

"I'm fucking in love with your sister."

Silence. The only sound came from birds chirping, cars driving by from the busy street blocks away and my heartbeat pounding in my ears.

I continued, slurring my words together to ease the severity. "I want to be with her, just her, and I'm pretty sure she wants to be with me, too." There. I'd said it. My chest heaved in anticipation of what he would say. Or he could punch me, fight me, hate me. I waited. Zade waited, but Aaron remained silent for a good minute before he smiled.

"You're joking, right?"

"No." I remained five feet away from him and kept my distance. "We didn't mean for it to happen, trust me. But it did and the reason we aren't together is because I'm a dumbass. But I'm going to earn another chance with her."

Aaron ran his hand under his jaw, the smile no longer on his face, and his razor-sharp gaze darkened. "What if I say absolutely fucking not?"

"One punch."

"Wait, what?" he asked, clenching his teeth.

"You get one punch, anywhere on my body." I moved toward him. "I should've told you when I realized it was real. Zade convinced me it was a terrible idea—"

"*Zade* knew?" he fired back, glaring at our third roommate, who looked unamused at our conversation. "You knew he was fooling around with my sister and didn't say a goddamn word?"

"Don't bring me into this. I'm here to make sure you fucking idiots don't injure yourself before our games next week. That's it." He held up his hands and scowled. "If I can say anything...it's that I didn't know it was more than a hook-up. *That's* what I thought was a terrible idea."

"You were hooking up with my sister? In our fucking house? With me there?" Aaron asked, his words getting louder each second, like a dam was about to break. "I'll kill you."

"I told you, one punch. But it doesn't matter. I love her. I'll treat her right. And I think she loves me too. We get each other. She fills that missing piece and I don't care if you don't like it." The more I spoke, the more I felt it. The truth. Her being the piece.

"Fine."

"Great."

He moved fast, reared back his right arm into a fist and collided it with my face. I froze, forcing myself not to duck out of the way when his flesh hit mine. It felt like a fucking bomb went off on my right cheek, my skull pounding as the wave of his punch ricocheted through my skull. I stumbled, holding my head in my hands as I fell to the ground. This was worse than a hangover.

So much worse.

Like eighteen semi-trucks had rolled over my face.

"Dude, you good?" Aaron asked. I wasn't sure how much time had gone by, because my brain was swimming. It could've been a minute, or thirty, but I blinked a couple of times before finding my bearings.

"That hurt worse than I imagined."

"No shit. I didn't mean to get you right in the face. I was just aiming for something and fuck… Let's get you some ice." He pulled me up from the ground and clapped me on the back. "One punch was a good idea. I feel better."

"Glad *you* fucking do."

"I'm not the most approachable person. I've been working on that. I wish you would've told me earlier, but now that I hit you and got some aggression out, it kinda makes sense."

"What makes sense?" I groaned when we went up the two steps and into the living room. Zade had a half-smile, half-scowl on his stupid face and I flipped him off. "Thanks for the backup, dumbass."

"You earned this all on your own."

Aaron shoved me onto the couch. "You and she spent a lot of time together. You have dumb senses of humor. You're both quiet. Just...if you hurt her, I won't be able to forgive you."

"I understand. Your friendship means a lot to me, Hilly, but I'd regret it forever if I didn't try with her. She's...she's what I need. She makes me happy and I think I make her happy too."

"You *can* make me happy," a female voice said. I knew that voice. *Oh my god!*

I jerked my head toward the door, regretting it immediately. Kenzie stood there, in our doorway, looking so fucking cute in black shorts and a faded jersey that my heart lurched in my throat. "You're here."

"Yeah. You said you were going to tell Aaron everything and I wanted to make sure you're alive." She sucked her bottom lip into her mouth, eyeing her brother and me in the process. "You're going to bruise. Let me get some ice for you."

She brushed past us and rustled around in the kitchen, coming back out holding a zip lock bag. She sat on the coffee table and leaned forward to press the ice against my face. "So." She glanced between me and her brother. "I take it you know."

"Yeah. I know," Aaron responded, but not in the angry tone I expected. "I got to punch him."

"Thanks for letting me know. I couldn't pick that up on my own," she fired back. When her warm gaze landed on me, she smiled and my stomach fluttered again. *She'll forgive me. I know it.*

"Kenzie."

She stilled, looking at me through her glasses, her long lashes fanning her cheeks, and fuck, I felt stupid all over again for thinking I'd be fine without her. I reached out, taking her hand in mine and trying not to wince when I adjusted my position to get closer to her. She blinked and her mouth parted when I set the ice on the table and cupped her face. "I'm sorry for how I handled everything. This is new for me...I have no idea what I'm doing but all I know is I want to be with just you as long as you want me. If that means boyfriend, girlfriend, exclusive, whatever. I don't care."

"Labels don't matter to me," she said, her voice shaking a little bit. "And you're sure...you really want this?"

"God, yes. I let your brother punch me. And I didn't block it." I moved to pick her up on my lap — forgetting Aaron was sitting next to me. He jumped up.

"Hell no, none of this shit when I'm in the room." He covered his eyes with his hands and backed into the TV console. "No, no, no. I barely gave you permission two minutes ago."

"Permission?" Kenzie snapped, wiggling her cute body on my lap. "We don't need your permission to do anything we want, Aaron. So nice fucking try."

"I'm going to — uh, go somewhere — not here."

"Let's visit Callie and Greta. I'm sure we can give these two a couple hours," Zade said, returning from upstairs. Aaron gagged and strode out of the room. But he turned back and pointed at us.

"I will take Kenzie's side every fucking time. We're brothers on the field, Tanner. This is a one-chance-is-all-you-fucking-get type of situation."

"I don't plan on messing up again."

"Good. Good. Cool. Well, uh, I need some time to *not* fucking think about this." He opened the door and let it slam shut.

"Glad you pulled your head out of your ass, TJ. Not the best way to do it, but it worked. Happy for you both. I'll make sure he doesn't do anything crazy."

"Thanks, Z," I said, waiting for him to leave. The second he did, I moved my hands to Kenzie's ass and pulled her against me. My face pounded, my head hurt, but she was with me and the coil that had wrapped itself around my chest sprang free, and my life didn't seem so empty. "It's going to be messy."

"Yup." She rested her forehead on mine. "I didn't want to fall in love with you. I had all these plans."

She loves me. Fuck yes. "I had mine, too."

"We really going to do this thing? Whatever it is?" I asked, moving my lips from her forehead to her jaw, giving her a line of kisses until I reached her mouth. I stopped and waited for her to make the next move.

"I want to. Let's start slow, yeah?" She breathed a little more heavily and ground against my erection.

"I'll go whatever pace you want. I just want to be with you."

That did it. She brought her mouth to mine, kissing me with all her energy and passion, sloppily bringing her tongue into it. Her kiss felt like a claim, as if she was making me hers, and, fuck, I loved it. "You're kissing the hell out of me right now."

"Well, I want to make sure you think about that kiss for a long time." She ran her fingers over my shoulders, looking at me with so much heat in her eyes that my breath caught in my throat.

"Job well done, then."

She giggled and I brought her back down to me. I could spend hours kissing her, telling her how incredible she was and how excited I was to be in her life...but I could only say three words. "I love you."

She let out the littlest sigh before smiling so large it took up her entire face. "I love you, too."

"Let's say we move this upstairs and you can play nurse and take care of me?"

"I think we can add that to my to-do list."

And we did, completing a bunch of other tasks I had on *my* list, too.

Epilogue

Three months later
Kenzie

First big college friends'giving. Ten of us, all cooking and bringing food to pass around while we watched football, played games and ate our faces off. My heart had been so full thinking about it and when it had come to fruition, it felt damn good. I ran over my list of things to do before guests arrived at the house — Aaron had insisted on having it at their place since it was the biggest — and despite not living there, Greta, Callie and I did most of the decorations and set up.

Stupid boys were not helpful.

My coffee was perfect, not too hot or cold, and I took a sip just as Tanner stirred in bed next to me. Those beautiful dark brown eyes stared at me, evidence of sleep still on his face, and he smiled. "Morning, babe, why are you up already? It's barely seven."

"Going over everything for today. You know...cleaning and making sure the cooking gets done. I read a lot about how to prepare—"

"You worry too much." He carefully took the mug of coffee out of my hands, the notepad from my lap, and set them both on the table. "I think I know what I can do to make you relax..."

"There isn't time. I need to shower..." I trailed off when he played with the hem of my shirt. It was one of his, his name on the back, and I wore it to bed as often as I could. He tickled my sides and touched just under my breast, knowing damn well it would make me jump. "*Tanner.*"

"My girlfriend is hot. I want to appreciate her body. I *am* thankful for you. Let me show you." His voice was sleepy and hoarse, all sorts of sexy, and it got me panting. "Mm. Let me take this shirt off you so I can see those perfect nipples of yours."

I panted. He positioned himself over me, removing the shirt and staring at my hardened nipples. He had a fixation with my tits—I wasn't complaining at all—and I squirmed at his attention.

"Goddamn, these never get old." He held eye contact, tracing the outline of one with his pointer finger, teasing the end enough for me to arch my back underneath him. "I love your reactions when I touch them. Every fucking time."

He used his other hand, kneading and caressing each breast until he lowered his head. "Watch when I do this." He flicked his tongue against my pebbled nipple, making me hold tighter onto the sheet. "You make this sound in the back of your throat that I love."

He teased me for another minute before taking one into his warm mouth. His beard rubbed against my skin, causing the perfect amount of friction, and the low burn of an orgasm kindled. "I love your mouth on me," I moaned.

He liked that. He hummed against my skin, pressing kisses along the center of my body. My chest, my belly button and lower...biting the hem of the black boy shorts I'd bought to wear for him and dragging them down my legs. "I know what my appetizer could be."

"Jesus." I snorted at his stupid line. "No, just...*oh*." He brought his tongue to my folds, probing me wide open so he had full access to every part of me. I gripped his crazy curly hair, pulling on it when he sucked every part of me. Hard, fast, slow, gentle, and I gasped his name when he brought me to a powerful orgasm. "Wow."

"So fucking beautiful." He pressed another kiss just above my clit, before reaching for a condom from his drawer. I helped him put it on, and he flipped me over so I lay on my stomach. He spread my legs wide and slipped inside me, covering me with his large body.

I loved it.

"God, you feel so fucking good," he groaned, rocking his hips against me in a steady rhythm. He bit down on my earlobe, increasing his pace, just as he brought his hand to my clit. He swirled in a perfect pattern, matching his thrusts, and I gripped the bedsheets to prevent myself from crying out.

"Yes, Tanner. *Please*."

"Nothing makes me happier than hearing my name on your lips."

He kissed me on my spine, just below my neck, and helped me reach another orgasm before he continued his practiced movements into me. Rocking at the right angle, adjusting my hips so he went deeper, filling all of me. We remained like that, sweat pooling between our bodies, and he tensed, holding down harder on me. "Yes, Kenzie, *Jesus!*"

He spilled into me, giving four final thrusts before he stilled. He didn't make any hurried moves to get up, though—just pushed my hair from my neck and nuzzled his nose there. "I love you, so fucking much."

My face heated. Despite our insane sex life, his words and actions that showed me how much he loved me made me blush. They were intense feelings to have, ones I hadn't thought I was ready for, but it worked for us. Give and take, going slow, making sacrifices for each other. I smiled into the pillow even though he couldn't see it. "I love you, too."

"So fucking much?"

"Yes, Tanner." I wiggled my ass against him so he would move. I turned around, faced my handsome boyfriend and ran my fingers through his hair. "So fucking much."

His eyes lit up, but his smile fell just a little. "You didn't want to increase our three-night rule to four, though."

Oh man. That face. He had full lips that had me drooling every time he pouted. Plus, I knew how they felt against me. Anything he did with his mouth got me hot. But I remained strong. "Coming from the guy who didn't think he had time for me because of baseball. Ironic, huh?"

"You're avoiding the question."

"You didn't ask one," I fired back, loving our constant banter. He sighed, discarded the condom into his trash and rejoined me on the bed. He remained in his naked glory, picking me up so I sat on his lap as he leaned against the headboard.

"Such a cute pain in the ass. My unasked question was why? What do I gotta do to try and get four sleepovers with you? I hate waking up alone…and poor Jeff, I hate sharing a wall with him now."

"Poor baby," I cooed and patted both his cheeks with my hands. "I need time to myself. I have no doubt we'll live together again someday in the future, where we can do it in every room you want any time, but, TJ, I need this sliver of independence for myself. It has nothing to do with you. Trust me."

"I'm a selfish bastard, I know." He rested his forehead against my shoulder. "It makes me happy to see you doing well. Your friends are awesome and you smile all the time. I feel lucky I get to be a part of it."

My eyes stung just enough for a sniffle, but I relaxed into him. "You realize the dorms close for four weeks during the holiday break, right?"

"Are you…can you…four weeks?" he asked, looking wide awake now. "With me? In my bed?"

"I'm hoping you'll let me stay." I gave him my cheesiest smile and it worked. He crushed me against him in a huge hug, and I felt overwhelmed by how much I loved him. "I take it as a yes?"

"Fuck, yeah. I can't wait." He kissed me again, moaning into my mouth. "Let's convince your brother to stay with Greta so we can get the place to ourselves."

The mention of my brother was like ice water in my veins. "Good call. I hate to leave this naked hug, but speaking of Aaron… I need to shower and get ready for our parents to stop by. My list is a mile long and your sexy body distracted me too much already."

"I'm the best at distractions," he said with too much pride. I flicked his pec and hopped off the bed, getting more and more used to the happy feeling that glowed inside me. He slid off, too, dressing in old shorts and a rugby shirt.

"What are you putting on clothes for?" I slid into old sweats, a sports bra and a fitted shirt.

"I'll help you."

"Why?"

"Because I want to spend more time with you, but also I love how excited you get when you cross something off your list." He said it like it was no big deal, but it was to me.

"God, you're the best person, Tanner Johnson."

He slid me *that* look, the one that made my toes curl and my stomach swoop. "I'll never stop trying to be that, either."

Falling in love? Check.

Finding my own tribe of friends? Check.

Becoming my own person? Check.

Figuring out what I wanted to do in life? No check — but that's okay.

Life was about the adventure and I couldn't wait to see what happened next.

Want to see more from this author?
Here's a taster for you to enjoy!

Cleat Chasers: No Easy Catch
Jaqueline Snowe

Excerpt

Convincing the hostess to let me into the second semester sports fundraiser was easier than it should've been. With one little promise of featuring her on my blog and *bam*, the young girl ushered me into the ballroom where the school's biggest and best athletes mingled with coaches, alumni and the press.

Ah, the things people do for attention.

I tapped my pen against my lip while I took in the surroundings. It wasn't black tie, but it was fancier than a casual get-together and I sent a prayer of thanks to my roommate who'd convinced me to wear a sleek black dress. It was a little tight and I kept running my hand down to the side to make sure my love-handles weren't bulging out. My coordination was abysmal and I tripped over my own two feet sometimes, but at least I didn't stand out — which was the goal.

I needed a new story to boost views on my blog or I would be shit outta luck. No views meant no affiliates, which equaled less money, and with my less-than-stellar first two years at school, I had no internships or job opportunities waiting for me at the end of the semester. The real world was knocking with graduation looming and I hadn't a clue what I wanted to or could actually do.

But, I did have a clue about what the student body loved to gossip about more than any other topic – the latest on the hot jocks. Girls, guys, scholarships and walk-ons. Readers loved hearing about the latest flings or scandals and this fundraiser was hot-jock central.

"Ambar Henderson?" A familiar voice caught my attention and I glanced at my left to see Peyton Gentry smiling at me. "What are you here for? Sneak in for the free booze?"

"Ha ha." I plastered on a fake smile despite the flash of hurt. Peyton and I had become friends freshman year – right in the smack of my party days – and he always brought it up no matter how much I had changed since then. "I'm here for a story, not the booze."

"Right." He smirked and lowered his voice. "Is it a juicy one?" He slung an arm over my shoulder in a quick hug and, while I didn't dislike Peyton, I was glad when he removed his arm. "Heard there's something weird going on with the volleyball team with one of their new freshmen."

"Yeah?" I waited for him to respond, but his attention drifted elsewhere and he gave me a weak wave before heading off. "Great to see you too, Peyton," I mumbled to myself. He was an average player on the soccer team but always managed to make himself seem bigger, better, more handsome. I snorted to myself at the headlines I would love to write someday.

Athletes and their egos – size does really matter
The bigger and not better – egos exposed

I took a deep breath, gathered as much courage as I could and walked about the event searching for anything that could be of interest. There were a couple of girls I recognized from the volleyball team, but they seemed normal, laid-back even. Each table had a large tented sign with the sport listed and it amazed me to see how much attention was given to athletes at our Division I school. Were there events like this for scholars? For those who made the Dean's List year after year? *Doubtful.*

Schools spend money on sports, not smarts

Yeah, that headline wouldn't sell shit. I derailed those thoughts and tried to ignore the tinge of jealousy weaving its way through my body. All these athletes had futures after college. They had tutors, scholarships, teams that supported them and, as someone who came from the opposite end of the spectrum, it was easy to envy them.

A loud cackle exploded near the front where the baseball players sat talking to what I assumed to be the coaches. They wore polos with the school logo, were significantly older than them and had the whole coaching vibe with the hard face and knowing eyes. Zade Willows, Tanner Johnson and Aaron Hill all wore suits and smiles and a part of my stomach fluttered. They were so handsome and such decent human beings I wished I could've written a million stories on them. Their faces alone would get readers. But I'd already done a story on Aaron and his girlfriend, so that well was dry. Plus, they were my friends and I refused to cross that boundary.

Moving on to another sport, I weaved through tables, trying to listen to conversations for something to spark motivation. Fifteen minutes passed without any luck and the familiar sensation of failure washed over me. *How can I pass my senior classes when I can't even write a stupid blog post without getting writer's block?*

God, I wish I could drink.

It wouldn't hurt anyone if I snuck one bottled water and I blended in with the crowd as I approached the refreshment table. That was the good thing about being average-looking. No one really noticed me like they did my beautiful and tall roommates. I undid the cap and took a huge gulp when I felt someone staring at me.

Water spilled down my mouth and onto my dress when I found cold, unamused gray eyes narrowing at me. *Jeff Maddow.* He defined my perfect male specimen with his honey-brown hair styled just enough to be cool, his massive broad shoulders that went well with his defined pecs — perfectly showcased in the dark-gray dress shirt plastered across his chest. *Good lord.*

Shit, did he say something?

Did I?

His light gray eyes were framed by perfectly dark eyelashes and, God damn, those cheekbones were enough to make me forget my own name. He blinked and tilted his head to the side with impatience as he approached me. "Ambar Henderson, how the hell did you get into this event? You are neither an athlete nor a sponsor."

"I have my ways." I jutted out my chin and ignored the sweat pooling down my back.

"Did you sneak in? No, wait, let me guess. You bribed someone." He smiled like it was a joke, but his tone made it clear he was not happy. "I should call security."

"Really, Jeff? Come on." I hated how my fingers shook when I ran them through my hair, trying to act nonchalant. "I didn't bribe anyone."

"I wouldn't put it past you." He brought up a glass of champagne to his mouth and held my gaze as he took a sip. It was annoying to be attracted to someone who thought so little of me, but, alas, that was life.

"What do you care if I'm here? I'm not bothering you or anyone for that matter."

"False." He finished the glass and took a step closer to me. For one stupid second, I wondered what it would be like to feel his full lips against mine, but the look on his face sobered that thought. "You are a known campus blogger who finds out information about people to get views. You're no better than a tabloid magazine for a college. Athletes have enough to worry about with how hard *we* have to work. They should feel safe here, celebrating and networking, not worrying about being featured on a girl's pathetic blog to get attention."

"You know that's not what I do, Jeff," I defended myself but my voice lost its gusto. "I'm here for ideas...more like motivation. Nothing more."

"Right." He shook his head and tensed his jaw as he scanned the room. "Motivation to find out who's sleeping with who? Who has a better batting average when they're in a relationship versus being single?"

I gritted my teeth and willed my skin to not turn red. My cheeks burned when I attempted to defend my reasoning for writing those blogs. "It was for entertainment, Jeff. Plus, the stats didn't lie."

He gave me a look like many of my professors had. *Disappointment.* "Do you ever think about writing something credible or for a good cause?"

"The story about Hilly and Greta was—"

"Fine, sure." He waved a hand in dismissal and gave me a look that made me feel even smaller than my just-over-five-feet frame. "But you could *actually* spend time writing stories that matter. Not dumbass pieces that exploit athletes and encourage cleat chasers to come after us." He pressed his lips together and let out an aggravated sigh. "Stay away from my team, Ambar."

Then he stalked away to the front of the room, his stiff shoulders telling me everything I needed to know. He wasn't a fan of what I did or who I was. It wasn't news, but his words hit one of my deepest insecurities. *What am I even doing with my blog? My life?*

God damn it. Find a story! I finished the water and tossed the bottle into a trash can when a familiar deep, masculine laugh caught my attention. *That's my Uncle Martin.* My mood lifted instantly and I headed toward him. He was dressed in a three-piece suit and had his hand on a shoulder of a middle-aged man I didn't recognize. He finished telling a joke — a specialty of my favorite family member — before he noticed me and ushered me over. "Ambar Henderson."

"Martin Rhett," I replied, mirroring his hugging stance and smiling into his chest when he wrapped me in a bear hug like he had since I was a child. "I don't even know why you're here, but I'm so glad."

"Business partners in the community. We love supporting athletes!" He kept his arm around me and introduced me to the gentlemen around us. "This is my favorite niece, fellas. She's a senior this year and is a hell of a writer."

Various hellos and greetings echoed around me and I relished my uncle's words. *A hell of a writer.* He never made me feel stupid or unremarkable. He'd encouraged me my entire life and seeing him at the event gave me the necessary boost of confidence.

"Nice to meet you all," I said, looking all five of them in the eye and shaking their hands. There was a brief moment where I faced the direction of the baseball table and met Jeff's gaze, but I forced myself to not stare or think about why he was watching me. "Anyone have a good story for me? I'm looking for a topic on my senior project and could use some ideas."

"Ah, my girl is always working." Uncle Martin laughed and led me away from the group with a smile that had taken years to practice. Once we were out of earshot, he changed his expression. "How did you get into the event, Ambar? I thought this was for athletes only."

"See, the thing is… I was on my way out." I gave him a cheesy smile. "Lunch next time you're in town?"

"Of course." He pulled me into another hug. "Stay out of trouble, okay? You have four more months of college and I don't want anything *more* to happen. You know?"

Like my little drug and drinking binge freshman year?
Or my academic probation?

"I know, I know." I frowned and felt every ounce of shame in my bones. "I'll head out. I really did come for ideas. Nothing more."

"I believe you. Now go through the side door. I'll cover for you." He indicated the large black double-doors and winked. "While I can't condone you sneaking into an event, it does bring me joy to know you do have a little Rhett in your blood."

"See you later, Uncle." I smiled and snuck one more glance around the ballroom before leaving. It didn't mean anything when Jeff continued to stare at me with an unreadable expression on his face. If anything, he should've been happy I was leaving his precious party. *Ugh.*

New headline.

Jeff Maddow should pull the stick out of his own ass to get a better batting average.

About the Author

Jaqueline Snowe lives in Arizona where the 'dry heat' really isn't that bad. She enjoys making lists with colorful Post-it notes and sipping coffee all day. She has been a custodian, a waitress, a landscaper, a coach and a teacher. Her life revolves around binge-watching Netflix, her two dogs who don't realize they aren't humans and her wonderful baseball-loving husband.

Jaqueline loves to hear from readers. You can find her contact information, website details and author profile page at https://www.totallybound.com